The prisoner had his head bent. He was not listening to the words the clerk was reading. He was not even in the courtroom. He was in a very different place, in a cave on the summit of a mountain, thinking not of the man whom he was accused of murdering but of another who had fallen fifty years ago with a bullethole in his forehead . . .

The clerk resumed his seat and, after a word from the bench, the uniformed man beside Jonathan tapped his shoulder and pulled up a chair and directed him to sit. The court settled, a short, rather red-faced man rose from his place on the counsel's bench, and the trial began of Jonathan Wentworth Playfair, Knight, sometime Judge of the High Court, accused of murder.

Peter Rawlinson was an MP for twenty-three years and became Solicitor General, Attorney General and later a Peer. For many years he was a barrister at the top of his profession.

By the same author

PETER RAWLINSON

Indictment for Murder

ORION

To Peter and Avril,
with much affection

An Orion paperback
First published in Great Britain by Chapmans in 1994
This paperback edition published in 1995 by Orion Books Ltd,
Orion House, 5 Upper St Martin's Lane, London WC2H 9EA

A CIP catalogue record for this book is available
from the British Library.

ISBN: 0 75280 296 8

Printed and bound in Great Britain by
Clays Ltd, St Ives plc

1

THEY brought him up a narrow, winding stair to the box surrounded by a rail which was the dock. He was an old man using a cane, a tall, stooped figure with a lined, narrow face and a sharp, aquiline nose beneath a full head of white hair. He stood with his hands gripping the ledge in front of him, as in this place he had seen so many do so many times before. He looked straight ahead of him to where the clerk of the court stood, wigged and robed in black like the barristers seated in two rows immediately below the dock.

Above the clerk sat the judge, in short, bobbed wig and scarlet robe trimmed with ermine, flanked on one side by the judge's clerk in morning dress and on the other by the High Sheriff of the county in dark blue military uniform. To his left were the steps leading to the witness-box; to his right, the jury-box, as yet empty; below this, the press bench, already full. In banked tiers behind and to either side of the dock were the seats for the public, filled on this afternoon not by the regulars – those elderly men in shabby raincoats and women in smocks and turbans who came whenever the court was in session – but by a smarter, more lively congregation, many of whom had never before been in a court of law. Long before the appearance of the prisoner the ushers had locked the doors, and even those with official business were forced to push their way through spectators in order to get to the clerk or to the benches of counsel.

The court itself had been built in Victorian times within a great flint and stone hall, all that remained of the mediaeval castle destroyed by Oliver Cromwell in the seventeenth century. The furnishings of the courtroom – the benches, the seats and the boxes – were painted battleship grey, relieved only by the bright colours of the royal coat of arms above the judge's seat. It was a scene the prisoner knew well, for he had often been in this place. But he had never seen it as he saw it now. In the past he had been seated on the judge's bench looking towards the dock in which he now stood. Then it had been his clerk on one side of him and the High Sheriff attending him on the other. Now he stood, a warder at his elbow, facing the judge who was sitting where he had so often sat. On the flint wall of the ancient castle, high above the coat of arms over the judge's bench, hung the great, wooden, painted wheel that depicted the table and places of the Knights of the Round Table. It had hung in this hall for hundreds of years, but it had been made not in the time of the legendary King Arthur but in the sixteenth century, when King Henry the Eighth had it borne to the Field of the Cloth of Gold. The wheel or circle was divided into wedges or segments, marked on the outer rim with the name, and thus the seat, of each of King Arthur's knights. At the top was the seat and name of the king; on his left, Galahad. Next to Galahad, Lancelot, the adulterer, the lover of the queen. On the king's right was the place of Mordred. Who was Mordred? the prisoner wondered. What part had Mordred played in the legend of Camelot? When he was back home he would check the role of Mordred. Then he corrected himself. If they let him go home.

'Prisoner at the bar,' the clerk called out, and the prisoner lowered his gaze to the black-robed figure below the judge's bench. 'Is your name Jonathan Wentworth Playfair?'

'Yes,' he replied. 'I am Jonathan Playfair.'

Then, from the paper he was holding the clerk began to read the formal indictment of the crime of which Jonathan Wentworth Playfair was accused. While the clerk read, the prisoner bent his head, looking down at his hands, which were gripping the rail at the front of the dock.

Looking up at him among the reporters crowded into the press box was Leslie Bramley, the chief crime reporter of the *Globe* newspaper. It had been the campaign by the *Globe* – starting with a few paragraphs introducing the accused's name, then swelling into columns of description and comment – that, Bramley and his editor claimed, had forced the hand of the Director of Public Prosecutions and obliged him to launch a prosecution. Which was why Bramley studied the figure in the dock with such satisfaction, noting how he now stood with his head bowed, looking down at his hands on the rail. Bowing his head in shame, Bramley thought. That was how he would write it – after the man had been convicted.

But the prisoner had bent his head because he was not listening to the words the clerk was reading. He was not even in the courtroom. He was in a very different place, in a cave on the summit of a mountain, thinking not of the man whom he was accused of murdering but of another who had fallen fifty years ago with a bullet-hole in his forehead.

The clerk paused in his reading and raised his head. He looked towards the prisoner in the dock, spoke and waited. When there was no reply, he spoke again, louder. Still the prisoner was silent, and a murmur arose throughout the court as people turned to each other, whispering, muttering, as the clerk repeated the words for a third time even more loudly. 'How say you? Are you Guilty or Not Guilty?'

Jonathan raised his hand and rested it for a second on his forehead, in the place where the bullet had entered the head of the man of whom he had been thinking. The noise in the court increased – and he became conscious of the sounds of the place where he was. He looked up and saw the clerk, waiting, expectant. Then he heard another voice, speaking from the side of the dock. A head and shoulders had appeared, leaning over the rail towards him – a sharp, dark face with eyes the colour of raisins under the grey wig, the face of the counsel whom his solicitor, Harold Benson, had briefed to defend him.

'Sir Jonathan. You must reply to the clerk. You must plead to the charge.'

Jonathan looked at him gravely. Then he nodded. 'Of course,' he said. 'Of course. I was not paying attention.'

He turned and faced the clerk, who asked a fourth time: 'How say you? Are you Guilty or Not Guilty?

'Not Guilty,' Jonathan said, with a slight bow. 'Not Guilty.'

Again a sound like wind stirring the leaves in the branches of a tree filled the courtroom. The barrister slipped back into his seat, turning as he did so to his junior counsel beside him, shrugging his shoulders and shaking his head. 'What can you expect?' his gesture implied. 'What can you expect of the old man?'

The clerk began the business of calling the jury to be sworn, but the prisoner did not even cast a glance in the direction of the men and women who, one by one, filed into their places. When they were assembled, they stood, holding the book in their right hands – save for two unbelievers who affirmed. None were challenged by the defence. Five women and seven men. Three of the women were middle-aged, one with blue-rinsed hair; two with grey. They were dressed in sober black or dark blue. The other two women were younger, one in brown and the other, incongruously, in pink. Of the men, three looked as if they were in their mid-forties and two seemed younger, perhaps in their thirties; all were in open shirts. The other two were older, one in a smart blue blazer with brass buttons; the other in a suit. When the ten were sworn and the two had affirmed, the clerk read to them the charge on which they were to try the accused – that he, in this city, on June 21st of last year, had murdered David Spencer Trelawney.

The clerk resumed his seat and, after a word from the bench, the uniformed man beside Jonathan tapped his shoulder and pulled up a chair and directed him to sit. The court settled, a short, rather red-faced man rose from his place on counsel's bench, and the trial began of Jonathan Wentworth Playfair, Knight, sometime Judge of the High Court, accused of murder.

As he sat on the hard, straight-backed chair which the warder had pulled up for him, Jonathan's eyes were again on his hands, now clasped in his lap while prosecuting counsel, in an agreeable, gravelly voice with a slight West Country burr, began to tell the jury about the circumstances that had led the prisoner to stand his trial. Jonathan shut his eyes and closed his ears to the words, on every one of which everyone else in that place was hanging. He was no longer now in the cave on the mountain where a man had fallen with a bullet-hole in his forehead. He was in a quiet room in a silent house not far from this court, standing by a bedside while the June sunshine flooded into the room.

*

It was Midsummer Day, the windows were closed and the room very warm, but Jonathan, in his light jacket over dark trousers, had felt no discomfort as he stood looking down at the dead man lying on the bed. He was used to death and the sight of the dead. He had been broken to it early. In his youth he had been surrounded by it – on the streets and houses of home, when the bombs fell from the enemy aircraft high up in the night sky, and, later, in the mountains where he had fought in battle. But the death which had then been so constant a companion had never been silent like the death he had just witnessed in that quiet room. Then it had been accompanied by the noise of bombs or battle: the scream of the shells through the air and the crash as they threw up rock and dust, blanketing out the sun; or the crack of calibre-88's mounted in the Tiger tanks, and the whine of the bombs from the six-barrel mortars as they came in flights, like, he had thought at that time, the arrows at Agincourt. And above those sounds, the cries of the wounded and the dying.

Those had been the sounds of death in the time of his youth. But in this room there had only been the sound of breathing, heavy at first, then growing lighter and lighter, ceasing without even the rattle of death, while the sunshine fell on the white bedclothes and the pattern of flowers on the walls.

He had stood for a long time looking down at the white hair on the pillow, the white of the moustache and the white stubble on the chin and at the features he had seen pass from childhood to old age; and he had thought of the other companion of their youth who had died in the same battle as the man with the bullet-hole in his forehead. Rory had not died in silence, although at that moment a quiet had fallen over the battlefield as the men of the two armies waited in their holes in the ground a hundred yards apart in the cold night air of an April in northern Africa. He had died to the sound of his own voice as he lay on a hillside, both legs broken by the bullets from the German machine-guns. For suddenly, eerily, the dying man had begun to sing – Irish songs about love and desertion, betrayal and exile and, finally, the song with which, at home, he always ended his singing as he stood, often very drunk, balanced precariously on the edge of the fender around the fireplace before he fell from his perch into the arms of his friends.

'The King he said to the Queen,' Rory sang, his voice ringing out over the mountainside, 'Was ever such wonder seen. Take the crown off my head, And give me instead, Flanagan's Flying Machine.'

Twenty yards away in his slit-trench on the summit of the hill, Jonathan had listened, his head bowed on his arms. When the dying man finished the song, he had said the Paternoster in Latin – and died. And the flares went up and the firing began again.

Rory Connor had been the first of the three of them to die. Now, half a century later, in this neat, comfortable room, Jonathan watched over the death of the second. But although the room was quiet and the scene peaceful, in the eyes of David Trelawney when he looked up at Jonathan before he closed them for ever, there had not been the look of one friend to another.

After a minute or so, Jonathan had walked from the bedside to the window and flung it open, to let in the summer air, to let out the man's spirit. He stood at the open window, looking across the road to the garden of the cathedral close where children were playing. He could hear their laughter, and the cry of one of them. He saw a woman in yellow dart across the grass and pick up the child, and the noise of the wailing ceased. Beyond was the cathedral and its tower. Abruptly he drew the curtains and, taking his stick, left the room. He went down the stairs, wanting to hurry but forced to move slowly because of his knees, which as always on stairs, made his steps unsteady. In the hall he had stood for a moment, listening. There was no sound now in the whole of the empty house.

He knew he should not leave. He knew he should summon someone or wait for the nurse to return. But he needed to go – to run, if only his knees would have let him. So he opened the front door and went out into the street and around the gardens where the children were playing, walking as fast as he was able. The woman in the yellow dress with the child in her arms turned and looked at him as he went. She would, he knew, recognise him again.

In his seat in the dock, Jonathan heard the sound of the scrape of a heavy chair on the wooden floor – and he was back in the present.

He looked up towards the figure in the red robe on the bench above the clerk, and heard the young voice of the judge saying, 'If that is a convenient moment, Mr Bracton, I will rise now.'

'Certainly, my lord,' the prosecutor answered.

The man in uniform tapped Jonathan lightly on the shoulder.

'I know,' Jonathan thought, 'I know,' and he rose to his feet. Then came the voice of his own counsel, the man with the dark face and dark eyes who had reminded him that he must answer the clerk and plead to the charge. What was to happen now was important, and he listened attentively.

'My lord,' he heard his counsel say, 'because of the particular nature of this case and the facts surrounding the death of David Trelawney, and because of the accused's frailty and advanced age – he is seventy-seven – and the utter improbability that he would fail to attend at his trial, the accused soon after his arrest in July last year was granted bail by Mr Justice Templar, the Presiding Judge of this circuit. Mr Justice Templar made a detailed examination of all the circumstances concerning the alleged crime and the accused, and heard that the police had no objection to bail. As a result, and even though this was a murder charge, Mr Justice Templar granted the application. The accused has, therefore, been on bail awaiting trial until he surrendered this afternoon. I now ask that bail be continued throughout the course of the trial on the same recognisances.'

'Where is he living?'

'He has an apartment in Pembroke House, Tildsley, the home of his cousin, Mr James Playfair, a Deputy Lieutenant of this county. Mr Playfair is a surety and lives at Pembroke House with his wife. And,' counsel emphasised, for the judge he was addressing was young and new and the judge who had first granted bail senior and experienced, 'Mr Justice Templar was satisfied that in this case bail was permissible.'

'That was in July?'

'It was.'

The young judge paused. 'Have the prosecution or the police, Mr Bracton, any objection to bail being extended during the trial?'

'None, my lord,' said Richard Bracton.

Another pause. 'Very well. Bail will be continued throughout the trial on the same terms and conditions.'

So I shall get home, Jonathan thought, as the figure in red rose and left the court. How many times, he thought, had not he himself gone through that same door, walked up the same steps to the judge's room and then, still robed and preceded by his clerk and High Sheriff, gone to the Great Door to be driven away to the Judges' Lodgings on the outskirts of the city.

'The court is adjourned until ten-thirty on Monday morning,' the clerk called out above the hubbub that had broken out as soon as the judge had disappeared.

Monday, Jonathan thought. Why Monday? But of course. Today was Friday. The trial had been fixed to start on the Thursday, but the previous case had lasted a day longer than expected. The judge trying that case had gone and the new, young judge, a judge who did not know Sir Jonathan Playfair, had only arrived on Friday morning. Other business had delayed the start until the afternoon.

'We'll wait until the court has cleared a little before letting you out, sir,' said the warder beside him, 'if you don't mind.'

The warder had been doing this job for many years, indeed from before Jonathan had retired. 'It gave me a funny feeling having him beside me, I can tell you,' the warder said that night to his wife. 'Before I'd only seen him sitting up there on the bench.'

Jonathan resumed his seat. He saw Hugo Shelbourne, his QC, the man with the dark face, and the junior counsel, Andrew Benjamin, both in their wigs and robes, approaching the dock, followed by his solicitor, Harold Benson. Shelbourne, a tall, thin man of about fifty; Benjamin, younger, short and slight; Benson, awkward, angular, with a pronounced Adam's apple and a shock of grey hair which fell over his ears and his collar. In his shabby tweed suit and black tie, he looked more like a don than a lawyer.

'We now have some idea how the Crown are putting their case, Sir Jonathan,' said Hugo Shelbourne briskly. 'So I suggest we have a talk this evening.' He was leaning over the side of the dock.

'Do you think it necessary?' Jonathan asked.

It had been Benson who had briefed Shelbourne – without consulting Jonathan.

Shelbourne looked at Benson. 'Well, there are certain points

Bracton has already made which I think we ought to discuss,' he replied, with a note of irritation in his voice. 'When the evidence begins on Monday I shall have to cross-examine the nurse and the doctor and—'

Jonathan interrupted him. 'They will be speaking the truth. If they don't, I will tell you.'

Harold Benson said, 'There are the details about the time when you arrived at the house, Sir Jonathan, and what was said by you to the nurse and—'

'Very well,' Jonathan said, 'if you both consider it will be useful, we can talk. But not this evening. I'm tired. Come to my home at noon tomorrow, Saturday, and we can discuss whatever you wish over a glass of sherry.' He spoke as though he were conferring a favour.

Shelbourne looked again at Harold Benson and cursed under his breath. His home was thirty miles away. If they were to meet tomorrow it meant his driving thirty miles home this evening; thirty miles back tomorrow, Saturday; and then thirty miles home again before returning on Sunday evening to be ready for court on Monday. And, this weekend, he was expecting a visitor.

'Tomorrow—' he began. Jonathan interrupted him. 'Yes, I'm too tired this evening. I'm sure you understand. So tomorrow, if you please.'

By now the ushers were clearing the court. Some of the public before they left stood on their seats to get a better look at the prisoner – until they were shouted at by the clerk and driven out of the courtroom. James and Mary Playfair joined Shelbourne and Benson beside the dock. James, Jonathan's cousin, was a bald, tubby man, eight years younger than Jonathan, dressed in a formal dark suit, a black tie under his stiff white collar. When they had driven to court that morning Jonathan had thought that James looked as if he was attending a family funeral, which, in a way, perhaps he was. Mary, James' wife, with her grey hair tucked under a dark crimson hat and with her faded good looks, was in a sensible coat over a sensible suit. She looked as if she were going to a fête at the Women's Institute.

'The car's waiting, whenever you're ready,' said James. 'It's bloody cold outside. Looks like snow.' He handed Jonathan his overcoat over the side of the dock. 'Thank God they've let you come home.'

'That was to be expected after I'd got bail from Templar in the summer,' said Shelbourne stiffly.

'Is that so?' said James. 'Good. Good. Anyway, you're coming home.'

They got away eventually, James in the front next to the chauffeur; Jonathan impassive and erect in the back with Mary; the photographers running beside the car. There were more waiting at the gates to the drive, but James had telephoned from the car and the lodge was ready; the gates swung open and the chauffeur accelerated up the drive.

Pembroke House was a large, square house of Portland stone, built by a Playfair in the first years of the nineteenth century. Jonathan had known it since the time of his and James's grandfather. After their children had grown and gone, James and Mary had lived there alone until Jonathan had moved in, occupying an apartment they made for him out of three rooms on the ground floor entered through a large door on the left of the hall – a drawing-room lined by bookshelves, with a high ceiling and french windows opening on to the park; a bedroom furnished with mahogany wardrobes and a tall four-poster bed; and, leading from the bedroom, a bathroom made out of what had once been a sitting-room. A lobby on the other side of the drawing-room had been converted into a small kitchen and pantry with an electric stove, a refrigerator and a sink. Normally Jonathan ate with his cousins in the main dining-room.

'I told Mason to keep up the fire,' said Mary as Jonathan opened his door from the hall. 'And they'll bring you some tea. I'll look in later.'

By now it was dark and the curtains had already been drawn. Jonathan hung his overcoat in the wardrobe in his bedroom and then went and sat by the fire. The butler, Mason, brought him tea on a tray.

'It is good to have you back, Sir Jonathan,' he said gravely.

'Thank you, Mason. I'm glad to be home.'

After he had gone, Jonathan poured himself a cup of tea and

sipped; the toast and cherry jam he left untasted. He stared into the fire where the apple-wood logs crackled and blazed cheerfully.

This, then, was the final chapter. He had thought the story was over when he had stood by Trelawney's bedside, but he should have known that it would not, could not, end there. He knew he should have stayed. When he had reached home, he knew what must happen. And it had, two days later when the police had come – the aggressive inspector and his nervous detective-sergeant. That had been six months ago.

Jonathan stared into the fire, and began to think of the story's beginning – when, even as a child, he had run when he should have stayed.

'Jonathan, Jonathan.'

He remembered her voice calling him, heard it now as clearly as if she had been with him in this room – the voice of the woman, her fair hair mistily framing her face, whose photograph, fading and sepia-coloured, stood in a silver, oval frame on the desk by the window. It had been taken when his mother, Julia, was twenty-nine and he eight, almost seventy years ago.

When she had called, she was in the field across which he had just run to reach the river bank by the pool. There he had hidden in the shelter he had made in the reeds, his head on his arms, hugging his bare knees.

'Jonathan, Jonathan.'

The voice was louder now, coming from the edge of the field by the river bank. She would have guessed he would have gone to this place, his secret place – except that it wasn't very secret, for she knew about it. So did Beau, his father. So did David, to whom he had shown it on the day before. But if the place wasn't really secret, it was still his private place. She had no right to come there.

It was not a proper river, just a stream a few feet broad which flowed out of the lake where his father, Beau used to fish for pike from an old flat-bottomed boat, and it meandered away between high banks, through the woods and meadows along which the otter hounds hunted, until it joined the true river, which flowed out to the sea on the coast many miles to the south. When the water of the lake was high, it poured in a torrent through a rusted iron sluice-gate, and the stream became swollen. But that did not happen often. Usually it was a quiet, narrow stream, and where he had built his hideaway it broadened into a shallow pool surrounded by tall reeds. Here, many years ago, a tree, long dead, had fallen across the stream. Not right across, for it only stretched two thirds of the way and there was a gap of about three feet between the opposite bank and the end of the trunk. To cross, he had to jump from the end of the tree. Sometimes he fell, but he had never fallen when the stream was in flood and he had always been able to stand with the water up to his waist. In any event, since his eighth birthday he could swim.

The one person he allowed to come there unasked was Nicola. She was younger than he, with a snub nose and freckles, and she lived a mile up the lane, in the Manor. He had no secrets from Nicola.

'Jonathan, Jonathan', his mother called, now louder still. She must be standing at the top of the steep bank behind him, but she would not be able to see him in his shelter in the reeds.

David and he had been in the lane when the accident had occurred. They had been on the way home after he had shown David the woods and the lake. Nicola had come when he was showing David his secret place, and she had stood watching them. He didn't think David had seen her, but when he called her to join them she had turned and run off. So the two boys had gone on alone. From the crumbling boat-house by the lake they had taken Beau's old boat. The oars were locked away, so they had to paddle with their hands and a branch David found, and the voyage had taken them some time. Afterwards they walked back home between the high banks of the lane, and they could hear Jim Williams, the farmer's eighteen-year-old son, working in the field above them on the tractor. It was a shiny 1924 model, which had been delivered new only that morning on the back of an open Ford lorry. Jonathan had taken David to the farm to see it in the afternoon, and Jim had given the boys a ride, sitting them on his lap one after the other, circling the farmyard before he took it off to work the field. He had not been very good at driving, reversing when he was meant to go forward and steering clumsily even in the empty yard. He was more used to horses.

After their ride the boys had gone to the woods and the lake and Jim took the tractor to the field. He was still at it when they passed in the lane and he must have been turning by the hedge on the steep bank when he either failed to turn the wheel sufficiently or accelerated when he should have braked. Whichever it was, the tractor broke through the low hedge and fell, turning on its side, crashing and sliding halfway down the bank until it came to rest just above where the boys were walking in the lane, pinning Jim in the seat. They heard him cry out and when the motor cut they heard him groaning. They scrambled up the bank to where he lay, blood on his face from the scratches from the thorns in the hedge. When he saw them looking down at him he cried out, 'Get help. I can't move.'

'Where?' said David. 'Help from where?'

'From the farm. My God, my leg. I can't move.'

'Come on,' said David, and he began to slide back into the road.

'Go to your house,' Jim shouted. 'It's nearer.'

Jonathan had stayed, looking at Jim trapped in the tractor and the blood on his face.

'Come on,' David shouted. By now he was in the lane and running in the direction of the house. It was when David was almost out of sight at the bend that Jonathan had climbed up the bank away from the lane, scrambled through the hedge and ran, not with David to get help, but across the fields to his hiding place by the dead tree across the stream.

Later the boys had been climbing an old, tall apple tree at the end of the orchard.

'You should have seen the horses,' David was saying. He was sitting astride a branch above Jonathan. 'They got a rope around the tractor, and the horses pulled it off him. He wasn't badly hurt, but his father, the old farmer, was furious.'

Jonathan could see his own father, Beau, coming from the house – a tall, handsome man, then in his early thirties, very bronzed, with dark hair brushed back from his forehead and a thin black moustache which he had grown in France after he had first gone out as a young man just before the battle of Loos, nine years earlier. He was dressed in an open flannel shirt and his old, white, rather yellowed trousers with a Free Forester tie wrapped around the waist through the belt loops. He had been playing cricket on the village green when they had all been sent for and run to where Jim lay trapped under the tractor, the match abandoned. 'Your mother said he was only scratched and his leg badly bruised,' David went on. 'She said he was very lucky.' Jonathan didn't want to know about it. He wanted David to stop talking about it. But David Trelawney was his guest, as Beau had reminded him before David had come to stay – and when the accident had happened, David had run for help while he had run away.

'Hullo, boys.'

Jonathan looked down and saw his father standing at the foot of the tree, knocking out his pipe on his heel. 'Are you all right up there?'

'We're fine, sir,' David shouted down. 'It's a great tree to climb.'

'Well, you'd better come down now. Tea's ready.'

On the ground, Beau slipped his hand into Jonathan's and held it. David had run on ahead. 'Did you show David the lake?'

'Yes.' Jonathan didn't say they had taken out the boat. They weren't meant to do that.

'I like him, don't you?' said Beau. 'Jim's all right, you know. No broken bones, only a broken tractor.'

'I'm glad,' said Jonathan.

'But he must have looked pretty awful, lying there.'

'He had blood on his face,' Jonathan said.

'I suppose he had. Lucky the tractor didn't roll on him. Then he would have been in trouble. You all right, old chap?'

Beau stopped and looked down at his small son. Jonathan nodded. Beau still had him by the hand. 'It never does, you know, to run away.' Jonathan nodded again. 'You have to face things, even nasty things. It doesn't do to run away.'

And the two walked together to the house.

David was already at the school where Jonathan was going for the first time at the end of the summer. 'Jonathan's too young to go to boarding-school,' he had heard his mother, Julia, say to Beau in the spring.

'Everyone goes away at eight,' his father had replied. 'It brings them on.'

David's father, Richard Trelawney, was a friend of Beau's from the war. They had served together in France, until Richard Trelawney had lost an arm at the Somme and spent the rest of the war as adjutant at the Regiment's training camp in Yeovil. Beau had come through unscathed, from his first battle in 1915 to the end in 1918 along the Hindenburg Line, where he had won the Military Cross. Few of their contemporaries had survived. Now David was spending a week with the Playfairs in Sussex while his parents were in France. David's mother, Annette, came from Auvillar, in Périgord.

'While you're away, let David come and stay with us. The boys can get to know each other,' Beau had said. 'It'll help Jonathan when he goes to the school.'

At the tea-table, Beau tossed a rock cake across the table to David, who caught it deftly. 'Well caught,' said Beau. 'You did very well today, David.'

'Thank you, sir.' David grinned. 'The farmer was very angry.'

'Can't blame him,' said Beau. 'I hope the tractor was insured, but knowing old Williams I don't expect it was.'

No more was said about the accident during the week David spent with them, but Jonathan watched as David basked in Beau's approval. When the time came for David to be driven home to Canterbury, Jonathan stood in the lane as the Playfairs' open bull-nosed Morris disappeared up the lane, with Beau at the wheel and David turning and waving madly.

'I'll look after you when you come next term,' David had said before he left. And David had been as good as his word, showing him the ropes, protecting him, introducing him to Rory, the third of what became in their schooldays a triumvirate.

When the car had disappeared around the bend of the lane Jonathan took the boat his father had made for him, a simple, flat piece of wood with a stick for a mast to which Jonathan had tied a lead soldier. He ran back to the stream and launched it. Behind him he heard Nicola sliding down the bank, but he did not turn; he waded out into the water to rescue the boat, which had become stuck against a branch.

'Has your friend gone?' she called. But he only grunted, and waded back to where she was sitting on the bank.

'I didn't like him,' she said.

'You didn't talk to him so you can't tell.'

But he was pleased. 'He's older than us,' he said. Then they wandered down the stream to find a better place to launch the soldier on his voyage.

That was how it had begun. Nearly seventy years ago. Now he was standing trial for the murder of the man who had been the boy who had come to visit.

There was a knock on the door, and Mary came into the room. Jonathan stood up.

'Is there anything I can get you, Jonathan?' She looked at the tray. 'You've eaten nothing.'

She knelt and put another log on the fire. 'Are you going to dine with us?'

'Not tonight, Mary. I'm not hungry,' he said, sitting again in his chair. 'Tomorrow, perhaps.'

'You ought to eat,' she said. 'You must keep up your strength.'

'I shall,' he said. 'I shall.' She looked up at him as she worked at the fire. He smiled at her and added, 'There's a long way to go yet. They've only just begun, and the prosecutor, Bracton, is long-winded, like they all are nowadays. I'll have some biscuits with my whisky before I go to bed'.

She stood and looked down at him. That he of all people, she thought, has to endure this.

'I'll bring you some soup later,' she said and left.

2

HALF an hour after Jonathan had been driven away from the court, Hugo Shelbourne appeared from counsel's robing-room to be met by the photographers and television cameramen whom he knew would be waiting for him. Whenever there was an important libel case in the High Court, or a sensational defence at the Old Bailey, the newspapers and television news invariably carried pictures of Mr Hugo Shelbourne QC walking in his black court coat and long white bands, either across the Strand with the Gothic façade of the Law Courts in the background, or down Old Bailey away from the Central Criminal Court. This evening he guessed they'd want to photograph him against the wall of the castle, and he was only too ready to oblige.

Hugo Shelbourne was not a great lawyer; but in court he was immensely effective – pugnacious, sarcastic, often very funny, some-times wickedly funny at the expense of the witness he was cross-examining or, which was much resented, opposing counsel. Juries liked that, even if judges and his fellow barristers did not. But what mattered was that he won cases – and that, as he used to say, was what it was all about. Solicitors, who queued to brief him, agreed.

He was a tall, handsome man, in his early fifties, with a dark, narrow face and black hair only slightly flecked with grey. He knew he would be photographed and, because snow was forecast, he had put on a Russian-style winter cap of white lamb's-wool and a thick black cloak, pleated and gathered beneath his chin by a heavy gold chain and clasp. Altogether he presented a suitably impressive and flamboyant figure.

The photographers, as he had anticipated, asked him to walk from the Great Door set in its arch in the flint wall and he did as they wished. Suddenly he felt a tug on his arm and found he had been joined by an almost scarecrow figure in a shabby duffel coat with a long scarf in the colours of Merton College, Oxford, wound around the throat. It was Harold Benson. He plucked at Shelbourne's arm and said earnestly, 'I'm glad I caught you. I thought we should have a chat before we see Sir Jonathan tomorrow.'

Shelbourne, struggling to retain the serious look that on such occasions he assumed for the cameras, hissed under his breath, 'We're being photographed.'

Harold dropped his hand and looked about him wildly.

'Good heavens!' he said. 'I had no idea.'

When the cameramen had what they wanted they gave a cheery wave to Shelbourne, packed their gear into their cars and, amid much shouting and laughter, drove away.

'They're enjoying themselves,' Harold said.

Shelbourne grunted. So was he, until Benson had butted in. He looked at his watch. 'You can walk with me to the hotel, if you like. But I want to get away as soon as I can.'

They set off down the private path, reserved for lawyers and officials, which led from the court in the castle to the city.

Six months ago Shelbourne's clerk, Isles, had announced that a Mr Harold Benson, a Hampshire solicitor of whom Isles had never heard, was on the telephone wanting to speak urgently about the former judge Sir Jonathan Playfair. At the time Hugo Shelbourne had some recollection of reading something in the newspapers about Jonathan Playfair and the death of a friend, but when he picked up the telephone he had certainly not expected what he then heard. For Harold Benson told him that the local chief superintendent of police had asked that Sir Jonathan be brought to the police station tomorrow morning at ten o'clock when he would be charged with murder.

'Murder!' Shelbourne exclaimed. 'Playfair to be charged with murder! Of whom?'

'A man called Colonel David Trelawney. Can you come immediately?'

He did not hesitate. As it happened he had never appeared in court before Playfair when Playfair was a judge and he did not know Playfair personally for, even when younger, Playfair had never been a man for drinking champagne in the bar at the Savoy; nor for parading on the lawns at Epsom or Ascot – all regular haunts of Hugo Shelbourne. So Playfair as a person meant little to him. But Playfair as a client meant much. The trial of a former High Court judge on a charge of murder was the kind of case in which Hugo Shelbourne revelled. It would be, he knew, a spectacular.

If Shelbourne had been elated, Harold Benson was not. He had been uprooted from his quiet country practice, drafting his neighbours' wills and conveying their land and houses, into an unnerving and to him unfamiliar world of policemen and police stations. When Jonathan Playfair had asked Harold to act for him and said it was a matter that involved the police, Harold had protested. 'You don't want me, Sir Jonathan. You need someone who knows about criminal law. I've never been in a court. I know nothing about trials.'

'But I do,' Jonathan had replied.

'But why me?'

Jonathan had smiled and said he had his reasons.

They had met the year before at a charity function in the grounds of Pembroke House, and discovered they both had an interest in old books. Jonathan had taken Harold to his rooms to show him his library and thereafter Harold had often come to visit. He was a lonely man, living alone, mourning his wife, Margaret, who had been killed six months earlier in an accident on the motorway. On his visits he and Jonathan would sit under the great cedar tree on the lawn at Pembroke House or stroll through the rose garden, talking about books. Quite often Harold spoke about Margaret. Although remaining on formal terms they had become very friendly, so when Jonathan Playfair insisted that he wanted him for his solicitor, Harold could not refuse. But when he heard that the police intended to arrest Sir Jonathan Playfair and charge him with murder, he knew he needed help. He would not be able to handle this on his own. But it was only when Shelbourne was already on the road that he had told his client what he had done.

After a lengthy pause, Jonathan said, 'Well, Mr Benson, if that's what you want, so be it.'

'It's not what I want,' Harold had cried. 'It's what you need.'

When Shelbourne saw Harold Benson for the first time, in the hotel where they had arranged to meet, he was astonished. In his tweed coat with leather patches on the elbows, crumpled shirt and frayed tie, Harold Benson was unlike any solicitor Shelbourne had ever worked with in any trial anywhere. He looked, Shelbourne thought, more the kind to go brass-rubbing with than defending in a sensational murder case. Some weeks later, after Shelbourne had insisted that an experienced junior be included in the defence team, he had suggested that they really needed a solicitor with greater experience of criminal law.

'I'm quite satisfied with Mr Benson,' Jonathan had replied. 'You and your junior, Mr Benjamin, can supply the expertise.'

At the hotel on their first meeting, after Shelbourne had regis-tered, Harold led the way into the lounge. Shelbourne called for a large whisky-and-soda, while Harold Benson began to tell him about the behaviour of their client. 'He's not being at all easy. I can't get him to say what happened. He'll hardly tell me anything.' 'He will me,' Hugo Shelbourne had said confidently. But Jonathan hadn't, and as the weeks passed all Shelbourne himself could get from their client was that he could remember very little of what had been said or had happened when he'd been with Colonel Trelawney when he died. If Colonel Trelawney had died from a massive overdose of diamorphine, Jonathan Playfair said, it was not he who had administered it.

As Shelbourne drank his whisky Harold Benson confirmed that he was to bring Sir Jonathan to the police station at ten o'clock on the following morning.

'It'll be intriguing for them, charging a former High Court judge with murder,' Shelbourne said. 'The next best thing to a Home Secretary.'

When he saw Harold's expression of indignation, he smiled. 'Haven't you noticed, Mr Benson, that recently the police have been on the receiving end of a great deal of judicial criticism, for falsifying confessions, bullying during questioning, and so on? Moreover I understand that Playfair was never a favourite of theirs when he was on the bench. They thought him far too soft on the villains they'd caught. So you see, they'll be intrigued to have him in the dock.'

'But that's most improper,' Harold replied. 'Why didn't the Director of Public Prosecutions stop it?'

'The DPP? Stop the police? You don't seem to be very aware of what goes on in the world of the criminal courts, Mr Benson. The DPP is new, and he'd never have the balls to turn down the police if they'd made up their minds to prosecute. He'd be too scared they'd run off to the press – as they very often do – and he'd be pilloried for showing favour to one of his friends.'

About this Hugo Shelbourne had not been far wrong.

Colonel Trelawney's death had not at first been reported even in the local paper. Then Leslie Bramley, the chief crime reporter of a tabloid, the *Globe*, heard that the local police had brought in a car salesman for questioning over the deaths of a number of prostitutes in the Southampton area. He sought out an old acquaintance, Detective-Inspector Johnson. 'He's probably the right man,' Johnson said, 'but there isn't sufficient evidence for us to hold him – so far.' Then he'd added. 'Not as much as we have in that case of the old colonel who died recently, although I'm still looking into that.'

Bramley had pricked up his ears. The policeman had told him more and Bramley began to make enquiries.

A few days later a paragraph appeared in the *Globe* referring to the death of ex-Commando Colonel David Trelawney DSO, at the very time when an ex-judge, Sir Jonathan Playfair, had been visiting him.

'It is believed,' the paragraph went on, 'that a police investigation has been commenced and a report sent to the DPP, who, many years ago, was a pupil of Sir Jonathan at the Bar. They are said to be close friends.'

Over the next few days more references appeared about Colonel Trelawney's death, now described as 'mysterious', and it was again reported that Sir Jonathan was the last person to have seen Colonel Trelawney alive.

'What intrigues some enquirers is that Sir Jonathan, even though present when the Colonel died, did not at the time report the death and has given, so far, no explanation for his silence.'

Next day there followed a description of the ex-judge's career, commenting on what the *Globe* described as 'some of his strangely lenient sentences'. Alongside this article was a picture of James Tyson. The caption read:

Mr Tyson was recently appointed DPP by the present Attorney General, to the surprise of many who considered that others with better qualifications should have been preferred. The Attorney General, Mr Tyson and Sir Jonathan are all Benchers of the Inner Temple, and the Attorney General, like Mr Tyson, was also once a pupil of Sir Jonathan Playfair. All three are known to be good friends.

The next day the *Globe* published a report that the local police were satisfied that Colonel Trelawney's death was due to foul play. 'If that is true,' the *Globe* asked, 'who reported the death, and when? Is there any evidence as to who might be responsible? If so, why has there been no arrest? Is anyone being protected?'

Other newspapers then began to show interest.

In the evening of July 14th the Director of Public Prosecutions went to see the Attorney General. The DPP was a mild-looking man with red hair streaked with silver, a moderately successful silk on the Home Circuit who had accepted the surprising offer of the appointment as Director of Public Prosecutions with alacrity. When he entered the room, the Attorney General greeted him cheerfully. 'Good evening, James. What's brought you here?' the Attorney boomed. He was a large man, disliked by many but useful in the House, where he was a combative performer at the despatch box. 'Nothing too terrible, I hope, but Tom tells me' – he indicated the Legal Secretary, the Head of the Law Officers' Department, sitting beside him – 'you didn't want to talk about it on the phone. When that happens, I get nervous.' He looked genially at the DPP. 'I think of one of my predecessors who years ago was standing in front of the fire in his room when the DPP called unexpectedly. "Sit down, Attorney, sit down," the DPP said. "You'll need to – because we've arrested a spy who's a bugger – and is the private secretary of one of the Defence Ministers".'

The Attorney laughed happily. 'He sat down pretty sharp, I can tell you. So I hope what you've come about tonight is nothing like that. In any event, I'm already sitting.' And he laughed again.

'No, Attorney,' said the DPP. 'It's nothing like that. But it is sensitive, and that's why I've come to you.'

'Is it to do with a colleague, a minister?'

'No, and if there's a prosecution it doesn't need your permission. But there's a public-interest element, and you should be informed. It concerns Jonathan Playfair.'

'Old Jonathan? What about him?'

'Have you read any of the recent press references to him?'

'No. What have they been writing about him? Whatever interest can he be to the press?'

'It's mainly in the *Globe*.'

The Attorney laughed genially. 'I don't read that rag, James.'

'There have also been references to the story in some of the broadsheets, Attorney,' said the Legal Secretary gravely. 'It's becoming a matter of some public interest. The Lord Chancellor's private secretary spoke to me earlier today about it.'

The Attorney looked at him balefully. 'Well, make sure the Lord Chancellor keeps his judicial nose out of my business.'

'There have also been references in the press to you and me,' said the DPP.

'To you and me? What are you talking about?'

The Attorney's previous good spirits had by now evaporated. The interest of the Lord Chancellor and the DPP's reference to press comments about himself had seen to that.

'Perhaps you should read the police report.' The DPP handed it across the Attorney's desk. 'The press are asking why no action has been taken.'

When he had finished reading the Attorney laid the report on his table in front of him. 'There's not a great deal there, James. And what conceivable reason would there be for Jonathan to do what they suggest he did?'

'Money. Trelawney while alive kept Jonathan from family money, and he's recently been very badly hit by claims from Lloyd's. He has also refused to say anything about what happened when he was alone with Trelawney. He'd sent the nurse away and he knew she was due back but he didn't even wait for her to return. He informed no-one when Trelawney died. He just left.'

'Is the old fellow ill?'

'The doctors say not. The press are asking why nothing is being done. Some of the press always had it in for Jonathan when he was a judge, but now they're linking all three of us. The Old Pals Act, that's what they're hinting.'

The Attorney remained silent, thinking. He hadn't at all liked what the DPP had just said. The government was going through a nasty patch. Even its usual supporters in the press were hostile. Now there were hints that an old friend was being protected. At last he said, 'You consider there's enough here to prosecute?'

'The police, and the officer in the Crown Prosecution Service in charge of the case, Patrick Trent, think there is,' the DPP replied.

'And the police are obviously leaking stories to the press about the progress of the investigation,' the Legal Secretary added. 'We can't ignore the interpretation the media would put upon a rejection by the DPP and you of a recommendation to prosecute made by both Mr Trent and the police.'

Both the Attorney and the DPP looked at him. The DPP broke the silence. 'The advantage of a prosecution is that it would bring it all—'

The Attorney interrupted him. 'Bring it out into the open, eh?' He leaned back in his chair. 'Still, a former High Court judge in the dock on a charge of murder!'

'A press campaign against the law-enforcement officers for protecting a personal friend,' said the Legal Secretary quietly, 'would be very ugly.'

The Attorney got to his feet. He put his arm around the DPP's shoulders as he led him to the door. 'Poor old Jonathan,' he said. 'I'm desperately sorry for him, but we can't be seen to be showing any favouritism, can we, James?'

'So your advice is—'

The Attorney was not so easily trapped. 'It's your decision, James, but I see the sense of what you have in mind.'

Later that evening the DPP telephoned the local chief superintendent of police and authorised him to proceed. 'Get him to come to your office with his solicitor and charge him there. And see there are no leaks before he appears in front of the magistrates for committal for trial.'

It was then that the chief superintendent had arranged with

Harold Benson to bring Jonathan to the police station at ten o'clock next morning and Harold had summoned Hugo Shelbourne from London. But soon after dawn on the following morning two police cars swept up the drive of Pembroke House. The household was woken by the thundering on the front door. Mason came in his dressing-gown. The police, led by Detective-Inspector Johnson, shouldered their way past him into Jonathan's rooms. Jonathan was roused, ordered to get dressed and driven away to the police station. At the entrance to the drive the police car stopped. It remained stationary for quite a time before it turned very slowly into the lane, giving ample opportunity for the many photographers and television cameras to take their pictures. More were waiting at the entrance to the police station. Inside, the old man was placed in a cell.

Mary had at once telephoned Harold Benson, who had collected Shelbourne and they both arrived just in time to hear Jonathan being charged. Harold, stuttering with rage, leaned across the table and shouted at the detective-inspector, 'I arranged with the chief superintendent to bring Sir Jonathan here at ten o'clock. Why did you arrest Sir Jonathan at his home?'

Shelbourne pulled him away.

The chief superintendent arrived at nine o'clock, and took the detective-inspector into his office. Shelbourne again quietened Harold. 'What they've done may help us,' he whispered.

They waited in an interview room until ten o'clock, when the magistrates sat in the court next door. From the magistrates court Hugo Shelbourne drove at once to the city where the Presiding Judge of the circuit was sitting at the court in the castle. Shelbourne recounted the arrangements Benson had made with the chief superintendent and told of the dawn arrest in the presence of the media. The judge asked the police for an explanation, but received none. Shelbourne then applied for bail. Sir Jonathan, he said, was an old man under the constant supervision of his doctor; he possessed no valid passport as he had long since given up travelling abroad; and there was no conceivable likelihood of his avoiding any trial. He lived in the house of his cousin, Mr James Playfair, who had now arrived at the court and would stand surety for his cousin. There was no need to keep Sir Jonathan in custody pending the trial.

Harold had been impressed by the way Shelbourne argued the application. The judge was not impressed by the police behaviour. When asked, the police, now somewhat abashed, had not objected to bail. Finally, Mr Justice Templar, while he acknowledged that it was rare to allow bail where there was a charge of murder, accepted that the circumstances in this case were exceptional, especially having regard to the facts surrounding the alleged killing and the accused's record, age and frailty. He granted bail.

That had been six months ago, in the previous summer. Now, in the late afternoon of the Friday in February when the trial had begun Jonathan Playfair's lawyers – the one so elegant, the other so shabby – were walking to the hotel in the city where they had originally met in July. They went for some time in silence, Harold thinking about Jonathan; Shelbourne about the visitor whom he was expecting for the weekend.

'I wish he'd not been fit enough to stand trial,' Harold said suddenly.

'Then they'd have been forced to put him away,' Shelbourne replied coolly.

'That might have been better than what he's now going through.'

Again the two men walked in silence. Then Harold said, 'Here we are with the trial begun and he still won't give us any details of what happened that afternoon.'

Shelbourne made no reply. If Playfair chose not to explain, and if Playfair were convicted, it would be Playfair's fault, not his.

'Half the time in court this afternoon,' Harold went on, 'he wasn't even listening to what the prosecutor was telling the jury.'

'More fool he,' Shelbourne replied.

Harold glanced at him, pained by the other's bluntness. They were now at the entrance to the hotel. 'I don't think he's conscious of what's happening,' he went on stiffly. 'I used to see much of him before this began, and he always appeared to be perfectly sensible and clear in his mind, meeting people, managing his affairs, and so on.'

'It doesn't sound as if he's been managing them very successfully,' said Shelbourne, 'for I understand he's broke. So what about our fees?'

He shouldered his way through the swing doors. Harold halted for a moment, then followed. Shelbourne flung himself into a chair in a corner of the lounge and ordered tea. 'Tell them to bring down my case from my room. And hurry,' he shouted after the waiter. He turned to Harold. 'Tell me about our fees. They say he's been ruined at Lloyd's.'

'I've been put in funds,' Harold said stiffly. 'From Lady Mary, Mr James' wife.'

'Good,' said Shelbourne, drinking his tea. After a time Harold said, 'I'm glad that at least they've extended his bail for the duration of the trial.'

'Yes, I managed that for him. But old Jonathan's not likely to run away. No, the danger is that he may do himself in. Then bang go our refreshers.'

He laughed, then, sensing the other's disapproval, added, 'We can't afford to be sentimental, Mr Benson. Our job is to keep cool heads on our shoulders. Lawyers for the defence should never get emotionally involved.'

Harold Benson glanced at him over the edge of his teacup. This was just another job to him, Harold thought.

'He's very old,' was all he said.

'That,' Shelbourne replied, 'is no reason not to try someone who's apparently quite sane.'

'To me he's an old man at the end of a distinguished career. Which is what makes the spectacle so intolerable.' Harold put down his cup. 'Even this afternoon I think they were still hoping there'd be no trial, that he'd be unfit to plead. Did you see the look on the judge's face?'

'I did. What's the judge's name again? Harris?'

Harold nodded. 'Yes. Graham Harris.'

'I'd never heard of him,' Shelbourne said. 'He seems very young. But perhaps that means I'm growing old. Isn't it when the policemen begin to look young that you're really old?' He laughed his brisk laugh and finished his tea. 'Nowadays they are appointing judges hardly out of their nappies. But you're right. Harris did look at me as if to say, "Come on, Mr Shelbourne, get up and say the plea's Not Guilty by Reason of Insanity – and then we can put the old fellow away without any fuss." However our client, in the end, has pleaded Not Guilty, and he's going to say he knows nothing because he remembers nothing – although he insisted on visiting Trelawney, who didn't want to see him; he was the last person to see Trelawney alive; his fingerprints are on the apparatus that pumped into Trelawney the drug which led to his death; and Trelawney alive was keeping him out of his money. So altogether we've no easy task. Still, as he says he's not guilty, our job is to make it as difficult as possible for the Crown to prove that he is.'

'Will you call him to give evidence?'

'How can I? He remembers nothing.'

'He may insist you do,' said Harold.

'Then God help us. And God help him. Now I must be off. I'll see you at Playfair's house tomorrow, for that glass of sherry he has so graciously promised us. Perhaps it'll loosen his tongue. Pay for the tea, will you? Put it on client's account?' He chuckled and, gathering up his bag in the hall, left the hotel.

He's enjoying it, Harold Benson thought. Like the press and the public.

3

WELL before Jonathan and his lawyers had left the court the judge had been driven away in the ancient limousine which the local authority provided to transport the judges to and from the Judges' Lodgings and the court in the castle. The High Court Judges who came from London on circuit to try the most serious criminal cases were known as The Red Judges from the colour of their robes, which distinguished them from the lesser judges, the circuit judges, who wore black or purple. The Red Judges were obliged to live in 'Lodgings' provided by the local authority, which in this city was a large Victorian villa a few miles from the court; and it was to there that Mr Justice Harris was now being driven.

Because it was the first day of the sittings the policemen on duty at the castle were in their high-necked, formal uniform and white gloves. Others, unseen, in helmets and flak-jackets, were high up on the roof and in the top windows of the buildings overlooking the courtyard. While the police in the courtyard saluted at the arrival and departure of the judge, those above eased forward the safety catches of their automatic rifles. For in December two IRA gunmen had been convicted of causing explosions in Southampton docks and sentenced by Mr Justice Templar to twenty years imprisonment. Anonymous letters and telephone calls had been received at the Judges' Lodgings and at the court. But the High Sheriff, a retired soldier, had insisted that this was no reason why the ceremonial should be abandoned.

'I won't let the bastards disrupt it,' he had said. So the police in the forecourt had been put into their full dress and four trumpeters from the nearby depot of the High Sheriff's regiment played a fanfare as the judge, in his wig and red robe, emerged from the Great Door which was the entrance to the courts and climbed into the ancient Daimler. The step into the old-fashioned car was high, but the young judge sprang in nimbly and sank back against the worn beige covers of the back seat. His clerk, Priestly, top hat in hand, took his place in the jump-seat in front of him facing forward, and the Daimler, preceded and followed by police cars, rolled out of the castle yard through the gate under the archway.

Mr Justice Graham Harris pushed aside his robe to get at his handkerchief in the pocket of his grey trousers. The upholstery gave off a musty smell; the old car had no heating and it was cold, but the judge was sweating. He mopped his face, pushing his wig back from his forehead. Then, stuffing the handkerchief in his sleeve, he straightened his wig and looked self-consciously ahead as a small knot of onlookers standing at the corner on the pavement stared curiously at the red figure in a wig sitting in the back of the car. The judge – he was just past his forty-third birthday and, as Shelbourne had said, exceptionally young for a High Court judge – had only been a High Court judge for six months and it was his first time out of London on circuit. When he, the most junior and the youngest, had been told that he had been chosen to preside at the trial of Regina v. Jonathan Playfair, he had been appalled. Why me, he had thought? Then he realised that they had to find a judge who was not a friend of the accused and, if possible, had never appeared as counsel when the accused had been sitting on the bench. There weren't many on the bench who fulfilled those conditions. But he did.

As the old Daimler lumbered out of the town, Graham Harris for the hundredth time wished the choice had not fallen on him. He had only once in his life been in a criminal court, and that was when as a young barrister he had been briefed to defend in a complicated fraud trial. Since then his experience and practice had been in the Commercial Court and international arbitrations. He knew nothing about handling a jury. All he knew was, as the Lord Chief Justice had said when telling him he was to preside at the trial of Jonathan Playfair, 'Keep it simple, Harris. Don't come down either for the defence or the prosecution. Be seen to play it right down the middle. This, of all cases, is a case for the jury to decide. Leave it to them.'

Keep it simple! Play it down the middle! While every word and gesture would be watched and noted to see if he was leaning towards the defence because the accused had once been a judge or too far in favour of the prosecution to show that an English court was no respecter of persons! Throughout the afternoon he had studied Playfair, sitting so impassively, apparently so unconcerned to be in the dock in a courtroom where he had so often sat as a judge. Throughout the two hours during which Richard Bracton had been speaking the prisoner had looked to Graham as though he were somewhere else; as though what was happening was happening to someone else. When he had failed to answer the clerk's question – Are you Guilty or Not Guilty? – Graham had looked at Shelbourne. For one moment he had thought that, after all, there would be no trial; that the plea would be Not Guilty by Reason of Insanity, and he could send the old man to hospital. But Playfair had at last said 'Not Guilty' and the trial had begun, with all eyes on the old ex-judge in the dock and on the young new judge on the bench.

'It's going to snow, sir.'

Priestly turned and leaned back over the edge of the jump-seat. Graham looked out of the window and up at the lowering, leaden sky, but he said nothing.

'I understand you're staying in the Lodgings for the weekend. I have to drive all the way back to Mitcham.' Priestly, who had been with Graham since he had been appointed to the bench, was an ex-policeman and an experienced judge's clerk and Graham was very glad to have him.

'Yes,' he said. 'I've a reserved judgement to write, and I can get on with it better in the Lodgings than I can at home.'

It wasn't true. That wasn't the reason why he was not going home. The reason was that he couldn't face home. He didn't want to be at home with Anne, nor she with him, and she would be glad he wasn't coming. The tension in the house at Christmas had been unbearable.

They had been married eighteen years; she had been just nineteen and he twenty-five, starting his second year at the Bar, and they were both as poor as church mice when they had married in Chelsea Register Office. Neither family had been present nor been told of it. Graham had only an uncle, a local government officer in Birmingham who had given him some kind of home after his mother had died. He had never known his father, who had disappeared soon after he was born. Scholarships had taken him to grammar school and then to Durham University. Anne's family lived more grandly in Somerset. She had run away when she was seventeen to live first in a squat and then with slightly more respectable friends in a house in Battersea. She had met Graham at a party. He had been the only one wearing a tie, and she had fallen for him. So much so that she had got a job on a magazine in Brewer Street.

For a witness to the marriage, Anne had asked an older girl, a journalist, who had arrived rather tight. She said she always was when she went to weddings at Register Offices – they were so grotty. The best man was a young academic from Durham. He had not been tight, although he was by the time the four of them had finished lunch at an Italian restaurant off Fulham Broadway. When they emerged, at four o'clock in the afternoon, the last Graham and Anne had seen of them was the best man pushing the rump of the matron-of-honour into a taxi and falling in on top of her. The bride and groom had gone back to their shabby two rooms in Earls Court. They had not minded. Neither at that time could keep their hands off the other.

So the babies had come quickly – a boy and a girl, fifteen months between them. But, fortunately, so had the briefs. By the time Anne was twenty-one they had two children. From Earls Court they moved to Wandsworth Common; two years later to a larger house in Bayswater. Ten years after their marriage they had a house in Oxfordshire and a small flat in Pimlico. By then Anne was reconciled to her family, although neither of her parents were ever at ease with Graham. He, buried in work, only came home to the country at weekends, staying during the week in their flat in Pimlico, where in their early days Anne had joined him for one or two nights during the week. Even at weekends he had to work at his papers long into the night. Then there had been the travelling, to Hong Kong or Singapore, or to arbitrations in Geneva or Zurich.

He rarely now took her out in the evenings when she came to London, so she had stopped coming, while at weekends he spent hours in his study.

Quite recently Anne had announced that both children ought to go to boarding school. When he asked why, she said that a boarding school would give the children more of a life – there would be more for them to do in the evenings. So the children had been packed off to Bedales where they could be together.

At the age of thirty-seven Graham had taken silk, but the pressure of work had not slackened. Then, only six years later, he had, quite unexpectedly, been offered an appointment to the High Court bench. This, he knew, would put an end to the interminable pressure of night and weekend work; rarely now would there be mounds of papers to tackle on Saturdays and Sundays; no more travelling the world. He might even get home to the country some nights during the week. Now, he had thought when he had accepted the appointment, there would be more time with Anne and the family. That had been last summer. But it was too late; Anne was in love with someone else. Francis Keating was a neighbour, a heavily built, amusing man of about fifty, the local divorced 'spare man'. Anne had told Graham she'd met him out hunting the previous winter. By June, Graham now suspected, they must have become lovers. So, when he told Anne in July that he was to become a judge and that from now on their life would be much easier and they would be able to spend more time together, Anne had been cool and distant. By October, when he had begun his first term as a judge, he began to hear the local gossip, that Anne and Francis Keating were often seen disappearing early from the hunting field and on weekday evenings dining together in local hotels. Christmas had been a nightmare, the parents pretending before the children. By the time the holidays were over and the children had gone back to school, he knew it couldn't go on.

An about-to-be divorced judge, he thought, trying a former judge for murder! How that would have shocked their predecessors.

'Don't forget, sir, the High Sheriff's coming for a drink this evening.' Priestly was again turning over the back of the jump-seat. Graham saw through the window of the Daimler that they were approaching the Lodgings.

'What's his name again?'

'Colonel Basildon. When he heard you were staying down, he told me he was going to ask you if you'd care to hunt tomorrow. He said he'd let you have a horse.'

'No thanks,' Graham said.

Priestly turned to face his front and they drove on in silence. Then he leaned back again. 'Not a very happy afernoon in court,' he said quietly.

'No, it was not.'

Graham stared fixedly out of the window. They were turning into the drive of the Victorian villa.

It was very cold in the large house as Graham laid his wig on the hall table. Priestly helped him out of his robes. 'I'm going to have a bath,' he said. When he was on the stair his clerk called up to him: 'I'll be off now, sir. I want to get on to the motorway before the snow starts.'

'I hope you have a good run to London,' said Graham, his hand on the banister. 'See you Sunday evening. Before you go, remind the servants I'm staying here for the weekend. Tell them I'll dine at seven-thirty.'

'Don't forget the High Sheriff,' Priestly called out.

'Oh, God,' said Graham as he went on up the stairs.

The servants were not used to a judge staying on over the weekend, and Priestly knew that they wouldn't like it. And they hadn't.

'Selfish bastard,' said the butler to his wife when Priestly had gone. 'Now we'll have to work all weekend.'

'I haven't got any food, and it's going to snow,' she replied.

'He doesn't seem interested. Nor in the wine. He's brought hardly any with him. Last night he didn't take port. Not like the old days. They all used to drink port, all the proper judges did. Even Sir Jonathan Playfair liked a glass. The poor old bugger.'

Colonel Basildon, short and square with a trim figure and a greying military moustache, arrived at six o'clock. He had been uncertain whether the judge's invitation given to him that morning by Priestly had included his wife.

'As I'm not sure of the form, I'd better go on my own,' he told Susan.

'Not very friendly,' she replied.

'He's very young. His clerk said it's his first time on circuit.'

The butler showed the High Sheriff into the drawing-room, which, despite the fire, was almost as cold as the hall. Colonel Basildon, in his tweed suit and regimental tie, stood in front of it, warming himself. Graham appeared. He was in pale corduroy trousers with a sweater over an open blue shirt.

'I'm sorry I wasn't down to greet you. What'll you have to drink? Whisky-and-soda?'

'Thank you.' The High Sheriff straightened his tie. He wasn't used to being entertained by a judge dressed like this. 'Is it your first time down here?' he asked as Graham fixed him a drink.

'Yes, first time on any circuit,' Graham replied.

'You never came when you were at the Bar?'

'No.' Graham brought the whisky. He took nothing himself. 'I never did that kind of work. I'm very new, you know; and very ignorant of what goes on, so you'll have to show me the ropes, guide me through the protocol.'

'Of course. I suppose it depends how long you're here. There are a few locals whom the judges usually invite. I can give you the names. But I hear you're staying in the Lodgings for the weekend. Is Lady Harris joining you?'

'No,' Graham replied, shortly. 'She's not.'

He flung himself into a chair by the fire, putting his leg over the arm. The High Sheriff saw he was wearing slippers, and no socks.

'If it would amuse you to hunt tomorrow,' Colonel Basildon said as he took the chair opposite Graham, 'I could lend you a horse.'

'No, I don't ride – and I've a lot of work to do.'

There was silence for a moment. He's a prickly young fellow, thought the colonel. Then he said, 'Nasty case you've got, judge – especially if it's your first on circuit.'

My first criminal trial, Graham thought. 'It is,' he said. Again there was a silence.

'I knew them both, you know,' the High Sheriff added.

Graham looked at him.

'Both?' he enquired.

'Yes. Old Jonathan, and Trelawney, David Trelawney.'

'Tell me,' Graham said.

'I used to meet Playfair with my father. He used to come and dine and browse in our library.'

'And Trelawney?'

'I only met him once or twice. My elder brother used to bring him to the Turf for lunch. That was soon after the war. He had a wonderful war. Second World War, that is. A lieutenant-colonel at twenty-six. He got every decoration that was going.'

'Had you met him recently?'

'No, he seemed to have dropped out a bit. I think he was living in Paris for a time. Somewhere abroad. Then quite recently I heard he'd come to live here in the city, but I never saw him. Shortly after he came, he got ill.'

'Do you know why he came to live here?'

'No, I suppose he was getting on and wanted to settle some-where.' The colonel shook his head. 'It's a wretched business, wretched. But from what I've read about it, I can't think why they ever started to prosecute and—'

Graham cut him off. 'I think it's beginning to snow,' he said. He was looking across the room at the window behind the High Sheriff's head. The butler had not troubled to draw the curtains.

'Is it, by God?' The colonel drained his glass. 'Then I'm afraid I'd better be going. There's the devil of a hill just before the drive to my house. But it'll be good for the scent tomorrow – make for a good day, if it doesn't get too deep.'

He got up. Graham too rose. 'Well, goodnight, judge. Thank you for the whisky. Have a good weekend. I'll be back first thing Monday morning to escort you to court. I suppose they'll start the evidence on Monday?'

'They will.'

When Colonel Basildon got home he said to Susan, 'You missed nothing. Just him, in his open shirt and no socks. He's an odd fellow. Moody, highly strung. Funny them sending such a young fellow to try old Jonathan, but then I suppose they had to find someone who didn't know him.'

At the Lodgings, the butler explained they had no provisions but, snow permitting, they'd get more in tomorrow. He asked Graham if he would mind dining off ham and eggs.

'That will do very well,' Graham replied.

After his supper he again studied the witness statements in the case of Regina v. Playfair. Then he put them aside and sat staring into the fire, as at the same time, some twenty miles away, Jonathan was staring into his. Jonathan was thinking of the past; Graham Harris of the present.

The death of the old hero, thought Graham, and the trial of the old judge, each old enough to be my father. Why should Playfair want to do away with him? But then why had Playfair behaved so oddly, leaving the dead man and telling nobody. Hardly the behaviour of a man with nothing to hide. Then there were the fingerprints – and the letter. Was money the reason, the motive, as the prosecution alleged? What was behind it all?

Then he forgot Regina v. Playfair and thought about Anne. At this moment she would be with Keating. Probably in bed. Not, he hoped, in their bed. She wouldn't, surely, do that.

He rose from his chair, put the guard in front of the fire, turned off the light and walked through the icy hall to the stairs and up to his bedroom.

At Pembroke House, at about the time when Graham Harris in the Lodgings was being served his ham and eggs, Mary had brought Jonathan a bowl of soup. He made a show of eating it, but when she left he poured the remainder down the sink in the pantry. Then he walked slowly up and down his room. After a time he went to the french windows and drew back the curtains. The snow had come and the lawn was already dazzling white, lit by a floodlight which James had installed after some houses in the neighbourhood had been broken into. Jonathan watched the snowflakes floating like feathers, glistening as they were caught in the light. Suddenly it went out. Then it came on again, went out and came on. It had been doing this recently. James had said he'd have it seen to, but he hadn't. The light flashing off and on made Jonathan remember once again what he had been thinking of in court – the flares that had lit Rory Connor when he lay dying on the mountainside fifty years ago.

He drew the curtains and went back to his chair, staring now into the fire. Rory; his mother and father, Beau and Julia; Nicola – they were all dead now. David was the last. He himself could not survive long. Ever since David's death he had been thinking so much of their youth, when they had first come together as a triumvirate at their first school. Rory, with his fiery red hair, had been the devil-may-care one; he, Jonathan, the one for books and work; and David, the leader – Head of everything, captain of games, brilliant at cricket, even as a small boy at Beau's cricket matches. What a charade Beau's matches had been! Nicola had come one year, and David had spoken about her.

It had begun on Jonathan's first Prize Day, in 1925, when his father, with Jonathan's hand in his, had gone up to the headmaster and offered to bring a family team to play the school eleven. 'I've four brothers,' Beau had said, 'and Julia has a couple. With a few cousins and some odds-and-sods I could get up a side and take you on.'

The headmaster had looked doubtful, but his wife, a pert little woman with bobbed, auburn hair, had said eagerly, 'What a splendid idea, Captain Playfair. That sounds great fun. I'm sure the boys would love it.' From the day when he had first come to inspect the school she had been very taken by Captain Playfair. So, to Jonathan's dismay, it had been settled.

On the day of the first match, the Uncles had been late. Then, led by Beau in his bull-nosed Morris Oxford, with Julia beside him, her Pekinese on her lap, with much tooting of klaxons and pumping of 'serpentine' horns, a cavalcade of Humbers, Armstrong-Siddeleys, Wolseleys, Ford flivvers, an open Chrysler, even a Morgan three-wheeler, and, grandest of them all, an immense touring Hispano-Suiza, swept into the drive, with girls in very short skirts and very scarlet lips hanging over the sides waving giddily. The 'Uncles' came in all shapes and sizes, and in different styles of dress. One even carried a saxophone. As their captain led them up to the cricket field with the flappers clinging to their arms, he played a 'blues'.

'Aren't they delightful?' said the headmaster's wife to matron, as they brought up the rear of the procession. 'This really will be *most* amusing.'

When the Uncles took up their positions on the field one or two tripped and fell, and as the afternoon went on substitutes were hastily summoned by Beau to replace those who had wilted. Even the saxophonist was required to down his instrument, which he had been playing to an admiring circle of small boys.

At the tea interval the Uncles trooped off to eat strawberries and cream and be revived by iced coffee, generously laced (matron observed acidly) from the flasks which most of the Uncles had been carrying on their hip-pockets.

Beau, alone of his team, covered himself with glory, lashing out with his broomstick with which the grown-ups were made to bat, despatching the ball all over the field. But despite his efforts the school eleven, as was proper, won easily. All in all the school, led by the headmaster's wife, voted it the best match of the season. Everyone had enjoyed it, except the reluctant headmaster and Jonathan, who had sat disconsolately with his mother, trying not to watch his family making fools of themselves.

So the match had become an annual fixture, the great occasion in the small school's summer calendar. In Jonathan's last year he had been selected to play – but only because it was the last time the school would ever meet his father's exotic team. That was the year when Julia had brought Nicola, a solemn little ten-year-old, and it had been when Jonathan was taking her for a stroll during the tea interval that they had seen Beau kissing the headmaster's wife behind the pavilion.

Jonathan, the last to bat for the school, had been out first ball to one of Beau's faster and meaner deliveries, preventing the not-out batsman, David, who had scored forty-nine, from making his well-deserved fifty. For the first and only time the Uncles won.

After the match Beau produced champagne, accepted hesitantly by the headmaster and eagerly by his wife and the staff, and then the Uncles piled back into their cars. The Aston Martins and Armstrong-Siddeleys, to the accompaniment of the squeals of the flappers and the sounds of the saxophone, roared away down the gravel drive, and the Uncles team was no more.

In the day-room at the school Jonathan had gone up to David. 'Sorry about getting out, David,' he said.

'It was a pity,' said David. 'I'd've liked to have got a fifty against your father's side.'

'If you ask me, this year they were more weird than ever,' said Rory Connor. 'Some of them could hardly stand up. Fancy having a family like that. Poor old Playfair, no wonder you're bats.'

The three of them walked out into the garden. It was by now dusk and soon it would be time for bed. It was then that David had asked about Nicola.

'Who was the girl sitting with you and your mother?' he asked.

'Nicola.'

'Is she a cousin?'

'No, she lives in the Manor, up the lane from us.'

'The lane where we saw the tractor fall?'

'Yes,' Jonathan replied.

'She's jolly pretty. I want to meet her when next you ask me to stay.'

Jonathan put down his glass. Nicola and David. She had been at the pool when he had been showing David his secret place before the accident with the tractor. She had come to the last Uncles match when David had said he wanted to meet her again. She came into it so often. Then and later.

He got up from his chair and put the guard in front of the fire. The lawyers were coming in the morning and they would ask questions which he had no intention of answering. He would tell his own story in his own way in his own time.

As he got into bed he made himself forget about the court and the trial. He'd think instead about Rory Connor, who had said that the Uncles were weird, and fifteen years later had died on the mountainside, singing to himself. 'Whom the Gods love', Jonathan thought – and at last he slept.

4

FOR Hugo Shelbourne it was a thirty-mile drive to his house in the country, and, when the snow came, the going was not easy. The night before he had stayed at the hotel where he had booked a large bedroom and sitting-room for the duration of the trial, but he was expecting a guest from London for the weekend and had always planned to get home as soon as the court rose on Friday. Because Playfair had refused to see them that evening he had got away earlier than he'd expected, despite having to spend time with Harold Benson. Glad as he was now to be on his way he was still infuriated by Playfair's demand that they come to see him tomorrow. Tomorrow he'd have to waste hours away from his guest.

In all his experience of many trials over many years, he had never encountered so maddening a client nor so useless an instructing solicitor. They seemed to think that all Playfair had to do was deny that he was guilty, say he couldn't remember what had happened when a man had died in his presence, and he'd be acquitted! On Monday the evidence would begin, but Playfair had already said he did not require the appearance of two witnesses – Francis Lightwood, a friend to whom Trelawney had written on the morning of the day he died, expressing concern over Playfair's visit; and George Symes, the solicitor to whom Lightwood had handed the letter. Shelbourne had wanted both called to give evidence. Their evidence, he had warned, should be tested in cross-examination. But Playfair had refused. So neither would be coming to court; instead their statements would be read to the jury and the first witnesses actually to appear would be the nurse and the doctor who had attended David Trelawney before his death. Of them Playfair had merely said they would be telling the truth; and if they didn't, he would tell him.

The first flakes of snow began to fall and Shelbourne switched on the windscreen wipers. Now the going had become really difficult and he had to concentrate on his driving, made no easier by his exasperation over Playfair. How on earth, he fumed, cursing the dazzle of the headlamps from the oncoming traffic, how on earth could he be expected to conduct cross-examination on the basis of last-minute messages from the dock! So on Monday, when the evidence began, two witnesses who should be called to give their evidence in person would not appear and two witnesses who would appear were to be challenged only if Playfair disagreed with what they said while they were saying it!

But Hugo Shelbourne had made up his mind what he would do. Before he'd left the robing-room that evening he had told his junior, Andrew Benjamin, that whether Playfair liked it or not he was not going to sit there like a dummy while the prosecution built up their case brick by brick. He was going to cross-examine and probe the prosecution evidence whatever Playfair might say. He also comforted himself that he'd been putting it around the Temple and to his friends in the press that Playfair had saddled him with an incompetent solicitor; was proving obstructive and secretive and was giving no proper instructions as to what was his defence.

By now the snow had become almost a blizzard, forcing him to peer through the windscreen, across which the wipers thrashed wildly, as he approached the last stretch of his journey on to the secondary roads and the narrow winding lane which led to his house. It had been a derelict farmhouse when he had bought it three years ago, with two acres of paddock and an unkempt garden, now splendidly landscaped. With it had come twenty-five acres which he let out to a tenant farmer. He didn't come every weekend. If he had a heavy case in London he remained in Edwardes Square in Kensington. Some weekends he went to stay with friends; on others he made discreet trips to Paris or Le Touquet. When he did come down, Mrs Green, the wife of his gardener from the village, looked after him and prepared the meals. Often he was accompanied by a woman friend, whom Mrs Green would call 'the flavour of the month'.

He had been married briefly as a young man, but marriage had not suited Hugo Shelbourne and he had remained unattached – or rather semi-attached, for he was never long without a succession of women. He needed them, he told himself, because of the adrenalin aroused by a life of courtroom battle. However, recently there had been fewer 'flavours of the month' and the expeditions abroad had been less frequent. For he had met someone to whom he had been much attracted – and it was she who was coming to stay.

By now he could see the lights in the upper windows. That should mean she had made it from London and he hoped Mrs Green had turned up the heating. Otherwise, he thought, his reception might be as frosty as the road he was travelling, for his visitor did not enjoy, she had made very plain to him, the frigidity she had too often encountered in too many English country houses.

He had first met her, or rather had first seen her, at a dinner party in New York, where he had gone on legal business. One evening he had been invited to dine at the apartment on East 61st Street of one of the American lawyers, and Hugo had noticed her the moment she had come into the room. It would have been difficult not to, for she was very striking – tall, with jet-black hair brushed back tightly over her head, bound at the nape of her neck by a crimson, velvet ribbon, the colour of her dress. She had arrived late and the party had immediately gone into dine. He had not caught her name and she was seated on the opposite side and at the far end of the table. His dinner neighbour was a sour-looking, expensively dressed woman of about fifty, with fair hair and a greasy, shiny skin, especially at the corners of her nostrils. When she began to talk he disliked her conversation even more than he did her appearance. For some reason she passed around little cellophane packets containing plastic penises and decorative packets of condoms. After a time he had looked across the table and seen the woman in the crimson dress with the white flower in her hair looking at him quizzically but he had no chance of speaking with her. For once he had kept silence at a dinner table, and, bored, soon left.

The next time he had seen her was a few months later, in

London, at the house of a friend in Hyde Park Gate. Again she had made a late appearance, and again she looked very striking, this time in white.

'Virginia,' the hostess had called out, 'you're next to Hugo Shelbourne.'

When they were seated he said, 'We were guests at the same dinner party in New York last summer.'

She turned and faced him. Her eyes were green and abnormally large. 'I remember. You didn't seem to be enjoying yourself.'

'I wasn't,' he replied.

'I suppose you were shocked,' she said.

'I was bored.'

'In England you have that kind of talk among the men after dinner, when the women have been obliged to retire,' she said.

'Not even then,' he replied.

'We're as good as you now.'

'Do you mean as bad – or, rather, as coarse?'

'You'll catch on, or rather you'll catch up. You English usually do.'

'What's your name, apart from Virginia?' he asked.

'Katz. Do you think it suits?' He had looked into her strange green eyes. 'I'm from New York, and I'm no WASP, as you can probably guess.'

He had not known how to reply, so he asked, 'Do you live in London?'

'Yes, since six months,' she replied, not looking at him. 'I know all about you. Two weeks ago I watched you questioning a friend of mine in court. You made people laugh at her.'

'I'm sorry,' he said. 'I expect I was only doing my job.'

'You were, and you looked as if you were enjoying it. Now,' she said, 'amuse me.'

He had tried, but not very successfully. She let him go on for several minutes. Then she said, 'Apparently you only make people laugh at other people.' She looked at him, unsmiling, her eyes studying him. 'You look,' she said, 'very sure of yourself.'

Before he could reply she had switched to the companion on her other side. They had not talked again that evening. Later Hugo

48

learned that she was the London editor of an American women's journal.

The next time he had seen her was a week later when he had joined a group at a night-club. He arrived late and, as he sat, he saw her at the other end of the table sitting next to an elderly man with white hair. This time she was in gold. He had danced briefly with his hostess and then, finding himself alone, had looked down the table towards where Virginia had been sitting. Her place was empty, and he thought she must have left. Then he felt a hand on his shoulder.

'If you like,' she said, 'you can dance with me.'

When they were dancing, she began: 'What I didn't say last week was that you look interesting.'

'And so do you,' he replied.

'Do you treat the women in your private life as you treat them in court?'

'No.'

At the end of the evening he took her back to her home in Cadogan Square, and she led him up the stairs to her flat on the first floor, bolting and locking the door behind them.

'There're drinks on the side table,' she said, going to an inner door. 'I'll have fruit juice.'

When she came back into the room she was wearing a thin, almost transparent robe through which he could see most of her body. Her feet were bare. He handed her a glass of fruit juice.

'Are you bullying anyone at present in the law courts?'

'I'm not in court at the moment, if that's what you mean. I'm resting – as the actors say.'

'When's your next performance?'

'In a week.'

'What about?'

'A newspaper called a City company promoter a crook, or words to that effect. He's suing the paper for damages for libel, and the newspaper, my client, is defending because, it says, what it wrote was true.'

'And was it?'

'I haven't the slightest idea.'

'You don't know and don't care?'

49

'I'll care about the verdict of the jury. My job is to persuade the jury that the newspaper is right.'

'Even if it isn't?'

'Who's to say if it is or it isn't? Not me.'

'You're just the hired hand?'

'If you like. It's for the jury, not for you or for me, to say who's right.'

'And you're paid to persuade them, to seduce them. Like a whore.'

He stood up. 'I'd better be going.'

As he walked to the door she said, 'You can take me out to lunch tomorrow, if you wish.'

He collected her from her office off Pall Mall. He was kept waiting in the outer room by a beaten-looking, wispy-haired young woman, her secretary, but the door was open and he could hear her on the telephone next door.

'That's not in my budget,' he heard her say. 'It'd cost too much fucking money, and it's not coming out of mine. If you think it's such a hell of an idea, get off your ass and send someone over to cover it. I'm not getting involved.' Then, 'Shit! There's no story in that. I'm not sending Lucilla. Do as you fucking well please.' He heard the receiver being slammed down. 'Shi-it,' he heard her say.

The secretary knocked nervously on the open door. 'Mr Shelbourne's here, Virginia,' she said.

She was all smiles as she came from behind the large desk and, to his surprise, kissed his cheek. She looked very smart in her office clothes, a black suit with a white blouse.

'You overheard me on the telephone? They talk like that in New York,' she said.

'So I've learned,' he said.

She took his arm. 'Let's go. I'm ravenous.'

But at lunch at the restaurant she ate only salad and drank only mineral water. She told him she was leaving for the States for a conference in New Jersey and would be away for two weeks. At the end of lunch he asked, 'When you get back, will you come and stay a weekend with me in the country?'

She examined him coolly. 'Perhaps,' she said. She gathered up her bag. 'I have the feeling you and I are rather alike.'

'In what way?'

'We're both pro's, and we both get, and take, what we want.'

He had got her fax at his chambers about ten days later: 'I'm taking you up on your invite. I shall come the weekend Friday February 15 to Sunday 17. Tell my secretary where and how I get there.'

That would be the weekend after the Playfair trial was due to begin, but he was not going to refuse her. The secretary told him Miss Katz would come by hire car and arrive at about six in the evening of the 15th. He warned that he himself might get there a little later but said that Mrs Green would be at the house to let her in and look after her. Now, as he saw the lights in the upstairs windows, he guessed she had arrived.

The snow was drifting in the narrow lane, obliging him to drive very slowly down the steep hill which led to his house. If it kept up, he thought, it wouldn't be easy to get out in the morning. Then he decided. He'd be damned if he'd go. It would only be a waste of time; Playfair would tell him nothing more. He'd leave it to Benson. Benson had Playfair's ear more than he, and he'd talk to Benson on the telephone and explain that the snow had prevented him – as well it might. He knew, if the worst came to the worst, he could get his tenant farmer to haul him out with his tractor.

The gate of the yard was open and he turned into the barn that served as a garage. Taking his grip from the back of the car, he went across the yard and up the path to the front door, slipping and skidding in the snow in his rush to get to her.

Hugo woke in the small hours. He was thirsty and felt ill. He leaned across to the bedside table and turned on the reading-lamp, shifting it so that the light did not shine fully on her. She stirred and gave a slight snore, and he could see her face, the lines around her eyes etched deeply, the corners of her mouth turned down sharply. She's ugly, he thought. She turned away from him, still asleep.

He got out of bed, pulled on his dressing-gown and went to the bathroom and mixed salts in a glass of water. He came back into the bedroom, switched off the light on the side table and went downstairs. He had left the heating on low all night to make sure the pipes did not freeze, but it was still cold in the drawing-room and he stirred the dying embers of the fire, throwing on some twigs and using the bellows until he got a blaze. He spread his hands before the fire, undecided whether to go to the kitchen and make tea, hoping the salts would settle his stomach. The evening had not gone as he had expected. The love-making had started on the sofa almost as soon as they had come in from the dining-room after the dinner that Mrs Green had prepared and which Virginia had hardly eaten, pushing aside her plate with barely disguised distaste, refusing even a single glass of the burgundy he had so lovingly decanted. He could see their brandy glasses on the table beside him, his half empty, hers wholly. They hurly-burly of the chaise-longue! But later there hadn't been much peace in the double bed!

None of the evening had gone as he liked. He had a ritual. He would change into a smoking-jacket, which, on this evening, his guest had regarded with obvious amusement. Then, before dinner, he would pour the champagne. There would be the burgundy with the food and, after the leisurely, relaxed meal, the wander into the drawing-room for liqueurs, of which he kept a great variety, mostly sweet. Then music, a Mahler adagio perhaps, as they sat together in the firelight. Finally the ascent, arm in arm, to the bedroom. That was what he was used to; that was what he liked. On this evening that was not what he'd got. Vodka had replaced the champagne; iced water the burgundy; the food was left uneaten; a slug of brandy replaced the crème-de-menthe frappé. As soon as they were in the drawing-room, without any preliminaries, she had come to where he was sitting on the sofa, taking his glass from him, pulling his head to her, exploring his mouth with her tongue, fumbling at him, eventually pushing him back and lying on top of him. His neck was cricked at an angle, one leg hung awkwardly over the edge of the sofa – and the velvet of his smoking-jacket was badly crumpled. At one stage she had seen him grimace and twist as a spasm ricked his back, but she had grinned and not relented or pulled away until she was finished with him. What had seemed to him like only a moment later she had led him upstairs into the bedroom, marching up the stairs ahead of him, not looking round but holding him tight so that he was forced to follow her, feeling foolish as he stumbled up the stairs behind her.

In bed it had been much the same. She had found him clumsy and had sworn at him. At last she'd fallen asleep, while he lay sleepless beside her. She was very different from anyone before.

Now, sitting in the chair in the half-light, he thought of the person in crimson or gold whom he had so desired – and of the face on the pillow. He began to regret what he had let himself in for.

The first he knew she had come into the room was when a white figure slipped beside him and knelt by his chair, and he felt her hand on his thigh, exploring.

'I thought you were asleep!' he exclaimed.

'Did you think it was a ghost? Well, it's not. Feel.' And she took his hand and put it on her breast. Then, holding his hand where she had placed it, she began to question him about the trial of Jonathan Playfair. She had not mentioned it when he had arrived; she had not asked him what he had been doing or from where he had come. As she had just returned from the States, he thought she probably knew nothing about the case, and so fierce had been the activity on the sofa he had even forgotten to look at himself on television. Before and during the dinner she had not eaten she had talked only about herself and the magazine and the conference in New Jersey. In the drawing-room there had been no time for talk. But now, squatting beside his chair, she asked about the trial. There was interest in the States, she said, in the English judge charged with murdering an old war hero, and she wanted to know more. So, while she still held his hand on her breast, he told her. She listened in silence. Then she said, 'I have a surprise for you.'

'What surprise?'

'I'm coming with you.'

'Coming with me where?'

'To court.'

'But the trial—'

'I know. I'm coming to the trial. I'm covering it for the magazine. My bosses in New York are interested. The result, the verdict, will come long before we publish next month, but New York want a background piece. You know the kind – the person-

53

alities, the judge and his victim and everyone involved. Including you.'

For once the prospect of publicity didn't appeal.

'I told them I know you,' she went on. 'That's why they've specially asked me to do it. That's why I'm coming with you.'

'But I'll be staying in a hotel and—'

'I know, you're at the Grand. You'd left when I called them from the car. They said you have a suite. I told them I'm joining you.'

'At the hotel?'

'Sure. The Grand hadn't another room. I said I was with you. New York's fixed a press pass for the court, so by day I'll be watching you and by night I'll be beside you.'

He said lamely, 'I'll have time for nothing but the case. As for sharing my room, there are journalists everywhere.'

'Who cares.' She looked up at him and this time put her hand on him. 'So we go to the trial together. Until then, relax.'

To get her hand away, and to cover his confusion, he got up and threw a log on the fire. 'You'll get your death of cold,' he said.

'Then let's go back to bed. We don't have to get up in the morning. We're snowed in, remember?'

'I couldn't sleep. I shouldn't have had brandy.'

'I'll make you sleep,' she said, getting to her feet. 'Follow me.'

And, obediently, Hugo Shelbourne QC followed her up the stairs to the bedroom.

5

JONATHAN was dreaming. He was back in the courtroom in the castle. On the judge's bench was a line of figures in khaki uniform, their military caps on the desk in front of them; in the centre an older officer, with red tabs on the lapels of his tunic. In the well of the court stood another with his cap on his head. He was shouting up at Jonathan, and Jonathan began to shout back, leaning over the edge of the dock, thumping it with his hand. 'You don't understand,' he was answering. 'You don't understand.'

The man in the cap began to smile; then, sweeping off his cap, he threw back his head and laughed. Others in the court joined in, until the laughter grew louder and louder, echoing and re-echoing, filling the whole place from the floor to the rafters high above the silent, motionless judges. Jonathan looked up at the painted wheel of the Round Table. Instead of the names of the king and the knights – Arthur, Lancelot, Galahad, Mordred – there were now different names. Hartley was the name in the place of the king. Trelawney was on his left, Connor on his right. Then Playfair – and Willis.

Jonathan looked down at the soldier below him and whispered, 'But it wasn't like that. It wasn't like that.'

At this the laughter ceased and the noise faded away. Slowly the man in the cap raised his hand and stood with his arm outstretched, his finger pointing up at Jonathan, who stared back at the silent, unsmiling faces of the judges while the noise of the laughter began again. Jonathan turned his head and saw Nicola coming towards him wearing a white evening gown with a train. There were ostrich feathers in her hair. She plucked one of the feathers from her head and curtseyed and handed it to him over the side of the dock.

Jonathan woke. He sat up and switched on the light. He dabbed his forehead with a handkerchief, wiping away the sweat. Then he picked up his book and began to read. But the words danced before his eyes and he put it down and switched off the light. Pulling the bedclothes around him, he lay in the darkness.

Why had Nicola come to him in his dream? She had never before, although he thought of her so often – of her as a child by the tree over the stream; of her face when they had caught Beau kissing the headmaster's wife; of another summer day in another place, another cricket match. It was strange, he reflected, how his memories of her were punctuated by cricket matches, a game he couldn't play, a game he so disliked. Beau had longed for a son who would be captain of cricket, as he had been in his day. Did he, Jonathan, hate cricket because his father had so wanted him to be good at it?

One memory was of his last Fourth of June. By then he had won the scholarship to Cambridge and was idling away his last weeks, mainly in the Drawing Schools, until at the end of July school would be over for ever. Julia had promised she would bring Nicola, whom he hadn't seen since she had gone to school in Switzerland. But when Jonathan had telephoned home, he hadn't dared to ask if Nicola were coming because Beau had answered and had said they'd arrive at noon and go straight to the cricket. They were joining the Trelawneys, and they all wanted to see David play. So he still wasn't sure if Nicola was coming.

He had gone to Agar's Plough early. Rory was with him. None of Rory's people were coming. 'They're not such asses as to come all the way from Galway to watch a cricket match and a few fireworks,' Rory had said. 'If it'd been horses, they might have. Not for cricket.' So Rory was to spend the day with them.

At the field Richard Trelawney was parading around in a pearl-grey suit with the empty sleeve of his missing arm tucked into the pocket and on his head a white panama with a regimental ribbon. He looked very grand as befitted the father of the captain of the Eleven and President of Pop. But, beneath his jaunty hat, his face was drawn and pale and his ginger moustache now pepper and salt. It had been about then that the illness had started which was to kill him three years later. Annette was on his good arm, in a long, tight-fitting pale blue dress with a broad-rimmed hat decorated with flowers, flirting with everyone, exaggerating her French accent. When she flirted with Beau, Julia only smiled. Then.

It was about this time that Jonathan realised that his mother drank – not like Beau and their friends, but seriously and secretly. It was probably because of the drink that she looked at people so intently, and smiled at them, that slow, beautiful smile. They thought she was interested in them and was listening, but really it was because her mind was in a haze of gin. She had not known then about Beau and Annette, but she'd always known what her son felt about Nicola.

Annette Trelawney asked Jonathan when his parents would be arriving. 'Soon, very soon,' he replied, hoping that soon, very soon, he would be seeing Nicola. Annette said they'd kept a place for the Playfairs' car next to theirs, a cream and black Wolseley saloon. Jonathan knew that car. In the spring, walking in Hyde Park, he had seen it parked by the Serpentine, with Beau sitting beside Annette, his arm around her shoulders.

It was not until just before lunch that the Playfairs arrived, not now in a bull-nosed Morris but in a bottle-green Bentley tourer. Jonathan's grandmother had died two years before and Beau, with his brothers, had inherited. Jonathan directed the Bentley into the place the Trelawneys had kept for them. He had already seen her sitting in the back, hatless, her dark hair cut short, waving a thin, brown arm. He leaned over the side of the car and kissed his mother. Beau jumped out, slapped him on the back and went straight to the Trelawneys. 'Sorry we're late,' he said. 'Julia kept us, as usual.'

Jonathan took Nicola's hand in his and looked into her brown eyes.

'Remember me?' she said, smiling.

'Of course,' he said, shyly. 'I'm so glad you could come.' He dropped her hand. 'This is my best friend, Rory Connor.'

'I've seen you before, at the Uncles match at Plimpton's,' Rory said. 'You had pigtails then.'

Nicola laughed, and ran her hand through her short hair. 'They went a long time ago.'

The four grown-ups were now sitting on the rug. Beau was opening a bottle of champagne.

'Would you like to stroll around?' Jonathan asked. 'You've missed the speeches in Upper School – anyway they're all in Latin and Greek.'

He wanted to walk with her, to be seen with her, and he didn't mind that he had Rory in tow.

'Yes, of course,' she said.

As they strolled off, she said, 'You look very smart in your tails. And I love your buttonhole.'

'We only wear buttonholes today,' Jonathan replied.

'David wears them all the time,' said Rory.

'Why?' she asked.

'Because he's President of Pop.'

'What's Pop?' Nicola asked. 'On the drive down your father kept talking about Pop. He seemed to think David Trelawney was a great swell.'

'He is,' Jonathan replied. 'Pop is what the Eton Society is called. They run the school.'

'A bunch of self-elected snobs,' added Rory.

Nicola laughed. 'Then why aren't you both in Pop?' she asked.

'We're not grand enough,' Jonathan said. 'And David's captain of the Eleven. He's playing now, back there.'

'Cricket's boring,' Nicola said.

When they came back to the cars Beau was half-asleep. 'Where've you been?' he said.

'Showing Nicola around,' Jonathan replied.

The Trelawneys had vanished – to find David, Julia said, as she gave them their picnic. David had not appeared until after the match was over, when they went to the Boat Club at Maidenhead to dine before the Procession of Boats and the fireworks. Before dinner they sat on the lawn by the river. David, prompted by Beau, was describing the match, especially his part in it. Nicola got up and wandered into the club-house. After a few minutes Jonathan followed her. She was standing in the dining-room, looking at the old, sepia-coloured photographs on the walls of groups of young men, all with long, curly moustaches, wearing blazers and little striped caps or pill-box hats.

'He'll look like that one day,' she said.

'Who will?' he asked.

'Your friend,' she said.

At dinner, Beau placed David next to Nicola, but she never spoke nor looked at him.

A month later it was Lord's and Nicola was there again, wearing a small straw hat balanced on top of her dark curls. Jonathan overheard her grandmother talking to Julia.

'She won't be coming out for two more years, and later in the summer she's going to the States to visit that wretched father of hers. Why, I don't know. He's usually too drunk to recognise her.'

'Does she have to?'

'Her uncle, the good brother, likes her to come. He says she is, after all, the daughter of an American. When her mother was alive she'd never let Nicola go, but I thought she ought to see something of her American cousins. In September she goes to Paris for three years, to be finished.'

David covered himself in glory at Lord's, as he always did. He made a hundred before lunch. Both Beau and Richard Trelawney had been full of it.

'Hardly ever been done before, you know,' Beau had told everyone. 'That boy'll play for England one day.'

During the tea interval, after they had joined the promenade in front of the pavilion and were back at the coach the Playfairs were sharing with the Trelawneys, Nicola had whispered to Jonathan, 'Why does your father go on about David Trelawney. He's not his son.'

Jonathan had not said that Beau wished he had a son who made a hundred at Lord's and was President of Pop. All he said was, 'Our families are great friends. His father was with mine in the war.'

Rory joined them in the evening at a musical at the Adelphi. Beau nearly ruined the evening by complaining that the leading man had been at Cambridge in 1914 and the star of the Footlights, but had never gone to the war like everyone else. 'He said he'd varicose veins, but he spent four years prancing about the stage in the West End,' Beau grumbled. 'If I'd known that damn fellow was in the show, I'd never have come.'

It was Annette who calmed him down. Afterwards they went to supper at Nicola's grandmother's house in Kensington. Beau again made David sit next to Nicola, but Julia had pushed Jonathan forward to sit on Nicola's other side. At the end of the meal Beau stood up and tapped on his wine glass with his fork.

'I want to propose a toast,' he said, 'a toast to the hero of the hour. Not many fellows ever make a hundred at Lord's before lunch, and one day that fellow will be playing for England. And we'll all be proud to know him. So here's to David.'

He raised his glass, but before anyone could raise theirs there came another ring on a glass. It was Nicola. 'Not many fellows win scholarships to Magdalene,' she piped up. 'So here's to Jonathan.'

There was a momentary silence. Julia smiled across the table at her, and then at Jonathan, who could feel himself blushing. Then Nicola's grandmother broke the silence. 'Quite right. Here's to both of them. Here's to David and Jonathan.' And they all joined in.

Later, in the drawing-room Beau called out, 'Come on, Rory. Let's have one of your Irish songs – "Flanagan's Flying Machine" or "Slattery's Light Dragoons". One of those.'

'Not tonight, sir,' Rory replied. He went to the piano and began to play Cole Porter tunes from *The Gay Divorcée*. Beau and Annette leaned over him and began to croon 'Night and Day.'

Julia and Nicola's grandmother were together on the sofa; Richard Trelawney on a chair a little apart from them, his eyes closed. Jonathan followed Nicola over to the french windows open to the garden. 'When are you going to America?' he asked.

'Next week. Then to Paris.'

'Can I write to you?' he asked.

'Of course you can.'

He had written every month, and she had replied once or twice. He still had those letters. In one she'd written from Newport, where she'd gone to stay with a friend.

It's very grand. At dinner parties there's a footman behind every chair, and we play tennis at the beach club while a 20-piece orchestra plays dance tunes on the lawn under the trees. Rory would love that. But there's too much seaweed on the shore-line and it gets in my toes and I hate it. Daddy's very ill.

When she was in Paris, and he at Cambridge, he still wrote, but she did not reply. He did not see her again until two years later.

She was 'coming out' that summer Season of 1939 and Jonathan was asked by her grandmother to escort her to a pre-Season dance. When he saw her he hardly recognised her – hair long and curled at the back; lips and fingernails scarlet.

For him the evening had not been a success. Too many young men had swarmed around her, queueing to get her to write their names in her dance programme. What another world those dance programmes conjured up, Jonathan thought as he lay in his bed in the cold bedroom at Pembroke House. Little white booklets engraved in silver, the dances numbered, with a blank space for the names of the partners to be written with a small pencil attached on a ribbon. It was the supper dance that mattered most, because that was the dance immediately before supper and that meant longer together. He should have had the supper dance with her, but by the time he asked another name was in her programme. But in the taxi on the way home he asked her to come to Cambridge in the first week of June, to a May Week ball. She said she might.

He and Rory spent hours planning their May Week party. During the day, the river; in the evening, the Footlights revue and the May Week ball in the marquees spread over the garden beneath the floodlit sixteenth-century towers; at dawn, breakfast at Grantchester.

'After that,' Rory said, 'it's each man – and girl – for themselves. So make sure you book the girls separate rooms at the hotel.'

What was the name of the girl Rory had brought? Jonathan lay trying to remember, glad not to sleep lest his nightmare returned. He could picture her well enough – she had been short, with long, blonde hair and blue, china-doll eyes. But her name had gone. She was training to be an actress at the Webber Douglas School of Acting, though no one later had ever seen her on the stage. If she was still alive, Jonathan thought, she'd be an old lady now, and fat, because she'd been plump even then. He had seen her only once after Cambridge, fifteen months later, in October 1940, when the blitz on London had begun. She was at a crowded bar in a night-club with a naval officer, but by the time he'd crossed the room to her they had gone, and he'd never seen her again. By then she had long ceased to be Rory's girl. He'd had a string of girlfriends after her. One early in 1940 when both he and Jonathan had just been commissioned and were wearing the single star of a second-lieutenant, was a busty sergeant-major who was in charge of the uniformed ATS girls serving the officers' mess at the depot. An officer was not meant to have an affair with one of them, but Rory didn't care. He made her come to London and squeeze into some of the clothes his sister had left in her flat in Richmond and he took her away for weekends. When, eventually, he, and Jonathan, had been posted away, Rory said she'd wept. 'But she's a good sport,' he had said. 'She won't peach.' And she never had.

The blonde Rory had brought to Cambridge had been the same type, jolly, and rather plump, the kind Rory liked. What had she been called? Eve? Eleanor? Try as he might, Jonathan could not now remember.

He did remember how he had told himself it was bound to rain when Nicola came, but it had turned out a perfect June day. Was that summer of 1939 really so full of cloudless days and moonlit nights as he now remembered? For that was how he thought of his last summer of peace, just as Beau had of his last summer in 1914, golden days and velvet nights until, before the leaves had begun to turn, each had become a soldier. Rory had collected his girl off the London train and brought her to the boat-house. Nicola had come up earlier and had helped Jonathan prepare the picnic in his rooms in college. When they were cutting the sandwiches, she asked, 'Who's in our party?'

'Only you and me, and Rory and his girl. No-one else.'

In the punt on the river, he had taken the pole. Both girls – Nicola dark, the other blonde – lay on the cushions facing him, trailing their hands in the water. Rory lounged opposite them, his back to Jonathan. Nicola was in white, holding a large hat with a ribbon in her lap. Jonathan had to be careful to avoid water from the pole dripping on to the girls as he raised it before slipping it back into the river, leaning on it, pushing the punt slowly upstream. For this whole day and evening, he had thought, I have her to myself.

They had moored under some trees, and eaten cold chicken and cucumber sandwiches and played a portable gramophone, while they drank what Rory called hock and seltzer – but was a cheap white wine from the college buttery mixed with soda water from a siphon. Rory had punted them back in the afternoon.

More than sixty years later, lying in the darkness trying not to sleep, Jonathan could smell the mint and the sedge of the river, as he could the mown grass at that last Fourth of June. Mint and mown grass, and, at home, wallflowers. The scents of his youth.

For the ball, Nicola had worn a long, dark green evening dress, the hem of which got very damp when they walked through the dew to breakfast at Grantchester. Rory's girl wore black, which, she announced at dinner, set off her skin. Rory had agreed, patting her plump arm. At the Footlights revue, most of the music had been written by Rory, but Rory's blonde complained that there weren't any girls. There aren't any at the university, Rory told her – at least, no pretty ones; those who were up were uglier than the men playing the girls' parts. 'That's silly,' Rory's girl had said, and she was quite cross until he said that if she'd been up they would have made her the star. At the party backstage after the show she had flirted with the producer, a don, because he often produced plays in London and she thought he might get her a part. She didn't know that flirting with him was a waste of time – he was interested only in the female impersonators. At the ball, it was after midnight when, unexpected and uninvited, David had appeared. Jonathan saw him first, standing by the dance floor, very tall and dark, in a bottle-green tail-coat with brass buttons, the dress-coat of a dining club. He saw them and began to thread his way through the tables. As he came he brushed back his dark hair from his forehead.

'Here comes the bloody hero,' said Rory. 'He's meant to be at Pembroke with the flannelled fools at the wicket and the muddied oafs in the goal.'

David pulled up a chair. 'I've ditched my party,' he said cheerfully. He dusted down the sides of his coat. 'I had to climb over the wall to get in, so I'm a gate-crasher. What are you drinking? Champagne, good.' And he poured himself a glass.

'I thought you were with the rugger-buggers,' Rory said. 'What have you done with your girl?'

'Last time I saw her she was heading for the shrubberies with Michael Harrington, so I did a bunk to join you. And here I am. I hope you're pleased?' He was looking at Nicola, smiling.

'Only if you buy more wine,' Rory said.

'Of course,' David replied. 'Jonathan, be a good fellow and get hold of the waiter.'

Rory stood up. 'Come on,' he said, taking his girl's arm. 'Let's dance.' They disappeared on to the dance floor.

'I haven't seen you since the evening of the Lord's match two years ago,' David said to Nicola. 'Where've you been?'

'Abroad. I came back to London last Christmas.'

'Jonathan told me you would be here. That's why I came.'

A waiter appeared. Jonathan said, 'This gentleman' – he indicated David – 'wants to order.' But David wasn't listening. He was telling Nicola about the Trelawneys' villa on the Riviera. 'It's near Antibes, overlooking the rocks and the sea, with a frangipani tree on the terrace. Have you ever seen a frangipani tree?'

'Often.'

'And there's bougainvillaea and hibiscus. It belongs to my mother.'

'How is your father?' Jonathan asked, the wine list in his hand.

'Not well.' David had not looked round. He was leaning towards Nicola. 'I'm going there next week. You ought to come and stay.'

'I'm going to the States, to see my cousins.'

The waiter leaned over Jonathan and pointed to a wine on the list. When Jonathan turned to hand the card to David, he and Nicola were walking away. Jonathan ordered two more bottles and followed. He could see David's tall figure steering her through the throng. When they danced, Nicola held herself very stiff and away from her partner. Back at their table the waiter gave Jonathan the bill for the champagne. Then Jonathan danced with Nicola; David with Rory's girl. When David brought her back to the table she was puffing and laughing. Rory poured her more wine. 'You're meant to be with me,' he said.

At the gallop at the end, Rory manoeuvred the two girls next to each other so David was at the end of the line, his arm around Jonathan. When it was over David offered to drive them to Grantchester for breakfast. He had the family car, he said.

'At last you're making yourself useful,' Rory had said. David held open the front passenger door for Nicola, but she got into the back with Rory and the other girl. So Jonathan sat beside David.

At Grantchester the sun was already up. They ordered eggs-and-bacon and drank the last bottle of wine, which Rory had brought from the dance. Afterwards, with the dew heavy on the long grass, they strolled through the meadow to the river, the men in their tail-coats and white ties; the girls in their long dresses. As they walked Jonathan took Nicola's arm and David, when he saw this, wandered back to the car and lit a cigarette. Standing by the river with his arm around Nicola, Jonathan had bent his face and she had looked up and he kissed her clumsily on the cheek. Then she turned her head away.

Next day Nicola told Jonathan she'd been woken by the sound of the door opening. 'Sorry. Wrong room,' Rory had said, and disappeared.

A month later, in July, Jonathan had again been asked, by her grandmother, to be Nicola's partner. This was at the dinner party at the Savoy after Nicola's presentation at an evening court at the Palace. As well as Beau and Julia, three others were in the party – a married couple, the young wife a cousin of Nicola's, and an extra man for Nicola's grandmother, a broad-shouldered man with grizzled grey hair and very light grey eyes. Jonathan had then thought how old he was, but he could not have been more than fifty. A quarter of a century younger than I am now, Jonathan thought as he lay in bed remembering.

Nicola had arrived at the Savoy in her white ball-gown, with a string of pearls around her neck. For the presentation she had worn a diamanté band around her forehead with three feathers, but she had taken them off and was carrying them. It was in the feathers that she had appeared to him in his dream.

'How did it go?' Beau asked.

'Terrifying,' she replied. 'Especially the people gawking at us through the windows of the car while we waited in the queue in the Mall.'

'Did they cheer when they saw you?'

'No, one man shook his fist. But one or two blew kisses.'

'Did you fall over when you curtseyed?' Beau went on.

'Certainly not. Grandmama had to go to the loo when we got inside the Palace, which was a bit of a bore because we nearly lost our place in the line. Then off we went, I behind grandmama, in procession. The poor king looked frightfully bored.'

'I used to play tennis with him, at the old Melbury Club,' Beau said. 'He was quite good enough to get to Wimbledon, but when he did everyone rushed to the side court where he was playing to watch him. He got so nervous he couldn't hit a ball. Then everyone said he'd only got to Wimbledon because he was the Duke of York.' He stood up. 'Come and dance,' he said to Nicola. 'My privilege to have the first dance with the evening's princess.'

Jonathan watched his father and Nicola dancing, as he had watched David and her a month before at the May Week ball. But now, as she danced, Nicola was relaxed, laughing. Beau could always make any woman laugh. But I couldn't, Jonathan thought.

A week later Nicola had left on the *Queen Mary* from Southampton for the States and her grandmother asked Jonathan to come with them to the boat train at Waterloo to see her off. He kissed her goodbye through the carriage window, on the cheek she presented to him. The next time he saw her, the bombs were falling on London.

Jonathan was dozing now, and his sleep was untroubled by nightmares.

6

NEXT morning there was a foot of snow in the garden of Pembroke House.

'The lanes are almost impassable,' Mason said when he brought Jonathan his tea. 'They telephoned from the lodge. The drive's very bad. Better stay indoors today, Sir Jonathan.'

'I'll need some fresh air so I'll have a walk in the afternoon. I'm expecting the lawyers this morning.'

'I doubt if they'll make it.'

'I shan't be sorry if they can't,' Jonathan replied. 'It's not important.'

Mason paused by the bedroom door. 'I hope all's going well, sir,' he said. 'The way you want, that is.'

'It's going as I expected, Mason. Just as I expected. Will you see the fire's lit in my drawing-room.'

In the kitchen, Mason's wife, the cook, was preparing the breakfast for James and Mary.

'How is he?' she asked.

'Looking very old. I don't think he could've slept much.'

'It's a disgrace what they're doing to him. Ever since those police last summer banging on the door at that hour of the morning and taking him away like a criminal. Poor old man. Now it's all those lawyers. They've no right to do what they're doing to him. As for the newspapers and the cameras, I blame them, them and the police. Fancy running alongside the car to get pictures.'

'It's their job,' said her husband, as he picked up the tray to take to the dining-room. He looked out the window. 'The papers'll be full of it, so if we don't get them, at least he'll be spared that. Not that he often reads them.'

'Who was the man in the white hat walking with Mr Benson on TV last night?'

'He's the top lawyer, from London. Sir Jonathan's expecting him this morning. But I shouldn't think he'll turn up – not if he's got far to come.'

Later Harold Benson telephoned Jonathan. He sounded as agitated as ever.

'Shelbourne's snowed in and can't get to the conference this morning.'

'Never mind,' Jonathan replied.

'He should never have gone home, but he says he's certain he'll get out by Sunday evening. There's a tractor, he said, which would pull him out. But the forecast is the snow'll stop soon and thaw tomorrow.'

'Then that's all right. Our talk today was not important.'

'But it is important, Sir Jonathan. The evidence begins on Monday.'

'I know, Mr Benson, I know. But the first witnesses will be the formal ones and then there'll be the nurse and the doctor. There's no conflict over their evidence.'

'Shelbourne asked again about Major Lightwood and Mr Symes. He wanted to know if you'd changed your mind about not wanting them. He said if you had, I must let the prosecution know today.'

'No, I have not changed my mind. Their statements can be read to the jury.'

'I'm coming to see you,' said Benson. 'I'll be with you in an hour.'

Jonathan sighed. 'Very well,' he said.

Harold Benson, in his shabby duffel coat and Wellington boots, arrived at half past eleven. He had left his car by the gate and walked up the drive.

In his drawing-room, Jonathan stood waiting. 'It is good of you to make the effort, Mr Benson. Come and have that glass of sherry I promised you. The decanter is on the table by the chair.'

Harold, his nose red and his grey hair still tousled from when he had pushed back the cowl of his coat, so that it stood straight up around the crown of his head like a halo, poured himself a glass and then sat in the chair by the fire. He pulled his papers and a notebook from his inside pocket, then patted his pockets and began going through them.

'I've mislaid my pen,' he said apologetically.

'There's one over there.' Jonathan pointed to the desk.

As Benson went to fetch it he dropped his notebook. When he returned he began to search for it among his papers.

'It's by your feet,' said Jonathan. Benson picked it up and tried to write.

'My hands are still too frozen.' He put his hands out to the fire to warm them.

'There's no hurry. Drink some more sherry.'

They both sat for a moment in silence. Then Benson said, almost pleading, 'Mr Shelbourne asked that I should go through with you once again what was said between you and the nurse.'

'We know what she will say from her statement. She seemed a very pleasant young woman.'

'I'm sure she is, but is what she says in her statement all that was said? I have it somewhere.'

He began to search through his papers, but without success. Jonathan watched him, smiling faintly. 'Never mind,' he said. 'I think I remember. What she says is generally correct. We may have said a little more, but nothing important.'

'Mr Shelbourne says we must know so that when she gives evidence he can, as he calls it, put it to her.'

'Yes, that is what counsel should do, if there's any disagreement.'

'Well, is there?' Then Harold added plaintively, 'I've been asking you this, Sir Jonathan, for weeks.'

'I know you have, Mr Benson. I know you have, and you've been very patient.' He paused. 'But, as you can gather, I'm not at ease with Mr Shelbourne.'

'That may be so, Sir Jonathan, but he says he can't defend you if you don't tell him exactly what happened in that house with Colonel Trelawney.'

'Mr Benson, I have spent a lifetime in the courts. I know what counsel has to do, but I have my reasons why I shall not say more just at present. The time will come, and then I'm sure you'll understand. Mr Shelbourne enjoys this kind of trial and I fear he may want to probe into matters which are not relevant. That is why I have told him so little.'

Benson sighed. 'He is your counsel,' he said weakly. 'If you won't tell him everything that happened, how do you expect him to defend you?'

Jonathan reached for the poker and stirred the logs on the fire. 'The facts which the early witnesses speak to are not disputed, so there is no challenge to the greater part of the prosecution evidence and no scope for the kind of performance in which Mr Shelbourne excels. Now, is there anything else?'

'After the nurse, they're to call the doctor and the technician who checked the apparatus on the next day; after that there's the autopsy result, the fingerprint evidence, and finally the police evidence.'

Jonathan had risen and gone to the window, where he stood looking out at the snow. 'Ah, yes, the police,' he said over his shoulder. 'I am still pondering about the evidence of the police.'

'Still pondering, Sir Jonathan, when the trial has already begun!'

Jonathan turned back to Harold Benson, who was now standing in the centre of the room. He looked so forlorn and woebegone that Jonathan smiled and took him by the arm. 'You'd rather be talking to me about first editions and early folios, wouldn't you?' He patted Harold Benson's shoulder. 'You must trust me, Mr Benson. Your task is to handle, or at least to distract, Mr Shelbourne – whom, I remind you, I hope not unfairly, you chose.'

When Harold began to protest, Jonathan went on, 'But come. The snow has stopped. It is growing warmer. There will be a thaw. Monday is thirty-six hours ahead, and the sun is shining.'

At about the same time on that Saturday morning as Jonathan was with Harold Benson, Richard Bracton, the prosecuting counsel in the trial of Regina v. Playfair, was walking in the ploughed field behind their house with his wife, Joan. The children, the ten-year-old twins Thomas and Eleanor, had run on ahead. The snow was quite deep, and they all wore boots and were well wrapped up against the cold. But the sun began to shine and soon Bracton grew warm. He stopped to unbutton his oilskin jacket. 'It'll thaw soon,' he said.

'Have you finished all your preparation?' Joan asked.

'Yes, although I keep thinking up fresh points.'

'When will the evidence begin?'

'Mid-morning Monday, with statements by two witnesses. For some reason the defence doesn't want those two witnesses called, which surprised me.'

'Why?'

'Well, what they swear to is damaging for Playfair. The first, a Major Lightwood, got a letter from Trelawney which shows Trelawney was pretty scared of Playfair, who had insisted on visiting him. The other is a lawyer, Symes, who speaks about the money Playfair has lost. I expected the defence would want them called so as to cross-examine them. But they don't. That means that they don't challenge what Lightwood and Symes say. It's rather mysterious. I suppose Shelbourne's up to something.'

'What's he like?'

'You saw him on television. An actor, but effective with a jury. I've never been in a case with him before.'

It was important for Richard Bracton to do this prosecution well, for he was in line for an appointment to the circuit bench which he much wanted. There was a vacancy on the bench in the city and it was expected he would fill it.

They walked on in silence until Joan said, 'Could anyone except Playfair have caused Trelawney's death?'

'The nurse who was looking after Trelawney – but that's inconceivable. I can't imagine they'll suggest that. No, the real question is: was Trelawney's death murder, accident or suicide? The defence don't have to show their hand until later.'

She took his arm. 'It's all very sad,' she said.

'It is. Sad for Playfair – and, because of what he was, sad for the law.'

'And it'll be the last case you'll ever do as a barrister?'

He laughed. 'It isn't definite I'll be appointed.'

'Will you have to travel when you're a judge?'

'No, I'll only sit here, in the city.'

'What do you think of Graham Harris?'

'He's said to be very clever. He had a large commercial practice.'

'Does he know much about criminal law?'

'I shouldn't think so. He probably thinks being in a criminal court surrounded by all of us criminal hacks is slumming. In fact, criminal law is more difficult than the commercial boys think.'

He picked up a stick and threw it for the Labrador, which had left the children and come bounding back to them, his black mask covered in snow.

'But they had to find a High Court judge who didn't know Playfair. So they chose him, the newest and the youngest. He'll handle it all right.'

They had reached a stile at the end of the ploughed field. The children had knocked most of the snow from the top rail where they had clambered over, but at its foot the snow was deep. Joan called to the twins not to get too far ahead. She and Richard started to skirt the next field along the hedgerow.

'I shall be glad to be finished with barristering, if they do make me a judge,' Bracton said as they set off again. 'Simon Templar, the Presiding Judge of the circuit, has a considerable influence and he seems to think that I ought to get it.'

If I do the case right, he thought to himself.

She put her arm through his. 'You'll make a very good judge. You'll be your own man, as you always have been.' But that, she thought, might be a problem. He was often too much his own man. Once he'd made up his mind, no-one could get him to change it. And he had never been deferential to those older and senior, and sometimes wiser. But he was a good man, she loved him dearly and she hoped he'd get what he wanted. He deserved it.

'There'll be less money,' he said.

'I know,' she said.

She saw the children flinging snowballs at each other at the far corner of the field. 'Do you think you'll get a conviction?' she asked.

'Yes, unless Playfair has some very convincing explanation, which so far he's not given.'

'When I first read about it I thought it had all been blown up by the papers.'

'Well, Playfair's fingerprints are on the medical equipment

72

which pumped into Trelawney the drug that killed him. What was Playfair doing touching that? Then there's the letter Trelawney wrote about Playfair coming to visit, which came to light after Trelawney was killed; and there's the money. While Trelawney was alive, quite a lot of money was kept from Playfair and Playfair needs it. He's been ruined by Lloyd's. Then he left the house without telling anyone Trelawney was dead. He has a lot to explain.'

They trudged on in silence. Then he said, 'But before it's all over we'll have some fireworks from Shelbourne. This is the kind of case he enjoys. But then, he's counsel for the defence. I'm only the prosecutor. What I have to do is present the facts – fairly.'

She took his arm again. 'Which you will do, and when it's over you'll be His Honour Judge Bracton—'

He laughed. 'And we'll live happy ever after.'

'We're happy now,' she said.

In the afternoon, despite what he had said to Joan, Richard Bracton went back into his study to work on the final part of the opening statement he had begun on Friday afternoon. It was the most important case he'd ever done and he was conscious of his responsibility. What was more important than securing a conviction was to show to the world that Playfair had received no favours. So he had to prosecute hard. But prosecuting counsel, as he had said to Joan, was not like defending counsel. The prosecutor was meant to be more an officer of justice, fair and impartial, and that part of his duty Richard Bracton took very seriously. He was determined to do the case well, and be seen to have done it well. Then, when it was over, he could expect to get what he wanted, a seat on the circuit bench in the city in which he had lived all his life.

Jonathan lunched with James and Mary in the dining-room. Then they walked on the snow-covered terrace so that he could get some fresh air.

'It's going to thaw tonight,' James said, 'and tomorrow there'll be the devil of a mess. Slush and mud, epecially on the path to the church.'

'I won't be going to church,' Jonathan said.

Mary knew why. The photographers would be there. 'Neither shall we,' she said.

She and James set off into the park and Jonathan went into the house. He sat at his desk making notes for what he intended to say to the court – what he had told neither Shelbourne nor Benson. To check a date he opened a drawer, looking through a bundle of bank statements. When Mason brought a tray of tea and drew the curtains, he said without looking up, 'I won't need any supper tonight.'

'Are you sure, Sir Jonathan,' Mason said. Then he repeated what Mary had said the evening before: 'You must keep up your strength.'

But Jonathan waved him away and went back to his notes. After a time he rose from the desk and went to his chair by the fire. He could not get out of his mind his dream of Nicola and the ostrich feather.

He had only heard from her once after she had left for the States just before the war had broken out. It was only much later that he learned she had gone across the border to Canada and after the fall of France, in the summer of 1940, got a passage to Liverpool. By then he was at Dover, his battalion living above and around the castle in the tunnels and redoubts built to defend the coast from Napoleon. The town and the heights were shelled daily by the German long-range guns in Calais, the harbour strafed by dive-bombers until the Royal Navy's Dover Patrol was driven from the port to shelter in harbours farther down the coast. He was in Scotland when his mother wrote and told him Nicola had joined the Wrens and that her grandmother had moved to Shropshire. Then, early in 1941 when the bombs were still falling on London, he saw her again.

He had gone to a flat in Old Church Street in Chelsea, to a wedding party of a Cambridge friend with a snug job at the Ministry of Information. The sirens had not yet gone. It's a clear night, people were saying. So perhaps the bombers won't be coming tonight. But they had, a little later.

There were so many crushed into the small flat, with people sitting on the stairs and on the landing outside the sitting-room, that he hadn't noticed her at first. He was talking to a woman who was already rather drunk and who was swaying and pushing her body against his, and he had looked up over the woman's head and seen Nicola at the other end of the room in her dark blue uniform. He shouldered his way across the room. She saw him and smiled. But there was a tautness around her eyes and the corner of her mouth.

'I heard last autumn that you were back,' he said. 'It's been such a long time, I must hear all your news. Are you doing anything this evening?'

She shook her head. 'Let's get out of here then,' he said.

The guns had begun, but the bombs were falling away to the east in the City. They found a taxi in the King's Road and were driven to Soho, the old taxi-driver talking over his shoulder, unconcerned by the difficulty of driving in the black-out amid the noise of the guns. When they found a table in the second restaurant they tried, Nicola told him how she had got back to England and joined the Wrens. She spoke rapidly, hardly letting him say anything, not eating, drinking only water, although in those early wartime days there was still some wine. The bombing had now moved nearer. The Cypriot proprietor wanted to close and went from table to table urging people to leave and go to the shelters or the Underground. Some did, but most stayed. When a bomb fell a few streets away Jonathan asked, 'Do you want to leave?'

She shook her head. 'No, I'd rather be above ground, and I like to talk during a raid.'

'If I can hear anything you're saying,' he said as the doors and walls rattled. By now the proprietor had abandoned his attempts to shift the remaining customers and, shrugging his shoulders, he went to the little bar near their table and took down a bottle of brandy from the shelf.

'Bring us some,' Jonathan called out. The man came over and poured some into their glasses. His hand was shaking. 'Why don't you go away?' he said to them. 'You ought to go away.' He disappeared through a curtain and down the steps to the cellar, calling to his wife. The lights flickered each time a bomb fell, but Nicola sat quite still, both hands now around her glass of brandy.

'I shall be out of this tomorrow,' she said.

'Where are they sending you?' he asked.

'They are not sending me anywhere,' she said. 'I'm just going.'
He looked at her. 'What do you mean?'

'I'm going to grandmama in Shropshire. I'm leaving the Wrens.'

'Why?' he asked.

'Because I'm going to have a baby.' Then she drank. She saw him glance down at her finger. 'No, I'm not married. It began in September – that is, the baby began in September.'

He could hear the whistle of a stick of bombs and then the doors and windows rattled and shook from the explosion. That was near, he thought.

'In the early days,' she said, 'I was more frightened than I am now.' Still he remained silent. 'I'm four months gone,' she went on. 'It'll be born in June.'

Two years, he thought, exactly two years after the May Week ball. 'And . . .' He paused. 'The father? Where is he?'

'He's gone away. Gone back to war.'

'Do I know him?'

She looked at him, and at first did not reply. Then she said quietly, 'Oh yes. You know him very well.'

Then he knew. It was David.

'Are you going to marry him?'

She smiled. 'He hasn't asked me,' she said.

The raid was dying away by the time they came out into the street and into the cold of the January night. There were no cabs on the streets now – only ambulances and fire engines. She was staying with a friend in Chelsea.

'We'll have to walk,' he said.

'Let's go down to the Embankment,' she replied.

On the way he once had to pull her down the steps into the shelter of a basement as a house collapsed into the street. Skirting the burning buildings and the ARP workers struggling with the chaos and the casualties, they made their way down to the river, where the fire engines were drawing water to pump on to the fires. She had her arm through his. At the entrance to the house in Cheyne Walk she turned to him.

'I'm sorry I didn't tell you before,' she said. Then she was gone.

He walked back to Waterloo and sat on a bench waiting for a

train. Three hours later he was sitting beside the driver in his three-ton lorry as the battalion left on the long drive to Yorkshire.

Jonathan got up from his chair and went back to his desk. Then he took up the sheet of paper on which he had been making his notes and went back to his chair. He worked on them for a long time. Later he went to his small kitchen and filled the electric kettle to make tea. He dreaded the night. He didn't want to dream again. He took his tea back to his chair. Before he went back to his work, he thought again of Nicola and David.

Everything had always been Nicola and David. Even now, it was still David.

7

BY Monday the snow had mostly gone and the forecourt to the castle was wet and muddy as the old daimler delivered the judge to the Great Door. There were no trumpeters or police in full dress but there were still marksmen on the roof for the threat to the court and the judge remained.

Thanks to the interest of the Saturday and Sunday newspapers, the court was even more packed than it had been on Friday. In Counsels' benches, the prosecution team, Richard Bracton and Brian Graves, were sorting their papers. Virginia had secured a seat to the side but well in the front. She and Shelbourne had driven to the city early that morning, mostly in silence for by then she had become more responsive to his tastes and moods. When Harold Benson had learnt that Shelbourne was not expected back in the hotel on Sunday night, he had spent a sleepless night worrying that Shelbourne would not be there in time on Monday morning. But he sauntered in as cool as ever after the jury had taken their places, and while they waited for the entry of the judge, lounged in his place, talking loudly to Benjamin, indicating that as far as he was concerned everything the Prosecution had said and were going to say was unimportant and absurd.

'All rise,' the usher called and when the court settled, Richard Bracton rose and in his pleasant voice continued his opening address on behalf of the prosecution. It was well past eleven o'clock when he was approaching the end of his opening statement, that he came to the letter. He had kept it to the end deliberately, and to emphasise its importance, he once again set the scene.

'Let me remind you of what I told you when I first began to address you on Friday. David Trelawney was lying on his bed suffering from a broken ankle caused by a fall, and from cancer of the prostate with traces of bone cancer. To alleviate the pain he was from time to time experiencing, he had been fitted with an apparatus called a syringe driver. This consisted of a syringe with a plunger resting horizontally on a rectangular syringe barrel holder placed on the bedside table to his right. From the syringe a thin tube led to what is called a 'cannula' or small tube inserted beneath the skin of Colonel Trelawney's right breast and taped to his breast. The syringe was loaded with an analgesic, an opiate called diamorphine, and a small and strictly regulated dose of this drug flowed hourly through the tube and the cannula into his body. The syringe, held in position by a thin strap, sits on a shallow v-shaped recess on top of the syringe driver which prevents the barrel being accidentally pushed back over the plunger and the syringe contents emptied, while the plunger has also a clamp assembly which prevents the plunger from being accidentally advanced. Recessed dials set the rate of the supply of the drug – which in this case was set at 2 milligrams each hour. But, members of the jury, were the plunger assembly to be lifted, the syringe raised and the plunger determinedly pressed and held against the head of the syringe and held there until all the contents in that syringe emptied, a massive, indeed fatal, dose would be discharged into the patient.'

Bracton paused, then he picked up from the desk beside him the syringe driver, an object no more than six inches long with the syringe lying along its top.

'You will have the chance a little later in examining this for yourselves,' he said. He put it back on the desk beside his papers. Next he told the jury that it was the duty of Colonel Trelawney's young nurse, Miss Sylvia Langley whom they would shortly see and hear, to supervise the dose of diamorphine which the apparatus caused to flow automatically from the syringe into her patient. On June 21st, he said, she had been with the Colonel for several days and by then she and her patient were on very friendly terms, the Colonel ragging her and teasing her with great good humour.

'On this, the morning of June 21st,' Bracton went on, 'David Trelawney was in particularly good spirits. But the good humour of the early morning did not last. At about half past ten he received a telephone call, and thereafter his mood changed. He became depressed and anxious, for now he was expecting a visitor, a visitor whom he did not wish to receive; a visitor who had forced himself on him; a visitor of whom the nurse will tell you, David Trelawney was scared.' Here Bracton paused. 'The telephone call came from the accused. The visitor was the accused, who came at about two o'clock and at once engineered that the nurse should leave him alone with her patient. When the accused left that house between the hours of four and five on that afternoon, David Trelawney was dead.'

Bracton paused again. 'But before the visit of the accused, David Trelawney had written a letter which was posted by Mrs Jackson, his daily cleaner on her way home. It bears the postmark of this city, 12 noon on June 21st, some four hours before Colonel Trelawney's death.'

He held up a letter in his hand. 'It was written,' he continued, 'to an old friend, a Major Lightwood who, however only read it several days after David Trelawney was dead. Major Lightwood was so concerned with what that letter contained that he took it to a solicitor, a Mr Symes who in turn gave it to the police. In a moment I shall read that letter to you.'

Bracton laid down the letter as he went on, speaking now gravely and slowly.

'The case for the Crown is that at some time on that afternoon when the two men were alone together, perhaps when David Trelawney was dozing as the drug at that time often caused him to do, the accused went to the syringe driver on that bedside table, raised the plunger assembly and the syringe from the syringe driver and pressed that plunger so that the whole of its contents were emptied into the body of David Trelawney. He did that, the Crown say, with the deliberate intention of murdering David Spencer Trelawney. That at some time he handled that apparatus, there can be no doubt, because his fingerprints were on that syringe driver and on that syringe. So you will ask yourselves, why should his fingerprints be on that apparatus? Why should the accused, Colonel Trelawney's unwelcome visitor, have tampered with that syringe which fed the drug that was flowing in strictly limited and regulated doses, if it wasn't as the Crown contend, to accomplish the murder of David Trelawney?'

Bracton paused again. 'The next question you may ask yourselves is why? Why should the accused want to murder David Trelawney? What was his motive for wanting to kill?'

Bracton bent forward and picked up the letter again. 'This letter, members of the jury, written by David Trelawney only a few hours before his death, may supply you with the answer. In short the answer is that Trelawney alive stood between the accused and the accused's family money, money the accused needed. To get that money, he needed Trelawney dead.'

Then in more matter-of-fact tones, he told the usher to give to the jury type-written copies of the letter so that they could follow it as he read it to them, and in complete silence, the usher distributed the documents. Graham Harris took his copy from among his papers.

Shelbourne looked more bored than ever. Virginia studied the impassive figure in the dock. What was he feeling, she wondered. All she could see of him was his profile, the head bent, his face a mask.

When the jury were ready, Bracton began to read. 'Letter addressed to Major Francis Lightwood, 12 Belvedere Mansions, Kensington, SW8, dated Friday June 21st, inside a plain white envelope postmarked twelve noon June 21st:

My dear Frankie,

I'm sorry I haven't been in touch before but I've been rather poorly lately. I'm still not too good – but the quack has promised I'll soon improve. At the moment I'm in bed because like a fool I tripped and broke my ankle – a damn nuisance, as I'm waiting to go into hospital, the Georgie 6th, for treatment. They've fitted me out with a confounded contraption strapped to my chest which pumps some bloody drug into me to keep down the pain – which I must say had been getting pretty bad, particularly the ankle. All very Heath Robinson, but it seems to be helping – and it's only for a week until there's a room in hospital where they'll give me the works, which should do the trick and buy me some extra time. Anyhow I'm looking forward to getting there and starting it. Afterwards they're packing me off to a Home, as they say I oughtn't to live on my own. I said I'd be damned if I'd be shoved into some suburban villa stinking of stewed cabbage, so I came up with St Edward's at Send – pretty grand and bloody expensive. So my number's not yet up, Frankie, altho' I know you'll say it's about time it was! Meanwhile I'm guarded here by a plump little nurse – quite pretty. You'd fancy her – not that you're capable at your advanced old age!

But if you're ever near Send in a few weeks time, pop in to St Edward's so that we can have a gossip. I haven't encouraged visitors here with this confounded thing on my chest, but this morning I heard from Beau's son, Jonathan Playfair. He's just telephoned and bloody well insists on coming this afternoon, damn him.

Indirectly, he's paying the bills, which is rather a joke, because the money comes from Beau's trust through a solicitor, Symes in Lincoln's Inn Fields. Under old Beau's will, if ever I got really ill the trust has to pay the bills. Beau knew I'd never have the cash to pay for it myself. He was very fond of me and I of him. The net of it is that a hefty chunk gets switched from JP to me, much to his lordship's annoyance, particularly as I've heard he's lost a packet at Lloyd's. Half a million, I'm told! So now he's broke and through me being ill he's losing the trust money, which is going on my quack's bills and will cover my costs at St Edward's. He's bloody sore and I expect he's coming to check on how much longer I can last and how long the trust will have to go on paying. He'll be in for a shock when I tell him I'm good for some time yet. So he'll probably stuff a pillow over my face to hurry me off!'

Bracton paused in his reading and looked at the jury. Some of them raised their heads from the copies of the letter which they were following and looked up at the dock. Then Bracton went on with his reading:

'If you hear I've snuffed it while he's here today, you'll know what to do! It's funny to think that he and I grew up together, and we became sort of connected when Beau and Ma lived together. But if he tries to get funny about the money because he's broke or tries to overturn the will or something, I've a bundle of letters here which will stop his nonsense. Some are from his lady-love and are about him. Some about the war, also about him. I've held on to them for years, as a kind of insurance. I want to keep them safe, so before I go to hospital next week, could I send them to you at Belvedere Mansions until I've moved into St Edward's? Give me a call here if that's all right and I'll have them sent. I just don't trust JP not trying to get his hands on them – or doing me some harm, and I feel pretty vulnerable with this contraption wired to me. He's a malevolent old bastard under that smooth, respectable appearance, and it would suit him bloody well to have me out of the way.

When you read this, I can hear you say old Trelawney's gone paranoiac in his old age! I probably have, but all I know is I'm scared of what JP might get up to and I feel pretty helpless. Once, in the war, I saved his precious skin – and more than that. But that's half a century ago! God, we're old, Frankie. Remember our first show, the raid on that radio station in 1941? The war wasn't such a bad time, was it? We did our bit all right, and we had some good times. It seems another world now, a long way from all this politically correct balls!

Well, I'm scribbling much too much, but it will be good to hear from you. Let me know if I can park my 'insurance' with you – and look after yourself, Frankie boy. See you at Send.

Yours, David'

Bracton waited until the heads of all the jury had lifted as they finished reading. Then he again held up the letter. 'As I said, Francis Lightwood received this letter after David Trelawney was dead. Because of what it contained, Major Lightwood took it to Mr George Symes, the solicitor. Mr Symes in turn handed it to the police.' Bracton placed the letter back among his papers.

'The defence have informed the prosecution that they do not require the attendance at this court to give oral evidence before you of either Major Lightwood or Mr Symes. They are content that their formal statements be read to you. As a result, these statements will then become as much evidence as if Major Lightwood and Mr Symes had attended and given evidence here before you this morning.' He paused again. 'With those final observations, members of the jury, I conclude all I wish to say to you at this stage. It is time now for the evidence, starting with the formal statements of Major Lightwood and Mr Symes, which will be read to you by Mr Graves, who appears with me for the prosecution.'

He sat and Brian Graves rose. 'Statement,' Graves began, 'of Major Francis Mulleneux Lightwood, holder of the Military Cross, Major retired, company director, of 12 Belvedere Mansions, Kensington, London, SW8, who says:

I have known the deceased, David Spencer Trelawney, since we served together in the Special Forces in 1940 in World War Two. We were friends for fifty years.

After I left the army in 1955 I went into business and had many interests in Sydney, New South Wales, Australia, where I visit regularly.

David Trelawney was at one time living in Paris, but he used to come and stay at my flat in Belvedere Mansions. Later, when he moved back to the UK, we used to meet and kept in touch by telephone or letter.

I had not seen so much of him over the last eighteen months and then in May I heard he was ill. I wrote to him, but I had no reply before I left for a trip to Sydney on June 8th. I returned to London on July 6th. At my home, among my unopened mail, I found a letter from David Trelawney.'

Graves here held up the letter which Bracton had just read and then continued:

'I look now at a manuscript letter dated June 21st. I recognise the handwriting as that of my friend, David Trelawney. I first saw it on July 7th when I opened my post after my return from Sydney. On that day, and before I had a chance to reply, I went to the Special Forces Club for lunch. While waiting for my guest, I saw a notice pinned to the notice board of the club which announced the death at his home in Hampshire on June 21st of Colonel David Trelawney DSO, MC and Bar. I had the letter in my pocket and I saw at once that David Trelawney had died on the very day on which he had written to me about the visit to him of Jonathan Playfair.

That afternoon I took the letter (Exhibit 6) and handed it to Mr George Symes of 29 Lincolns Inn Fields.
Signed, Francis Lightwood.

'That,' said Graves, 'is the statement of Francis Lightwood.' He put down the document, took up another and again began to read. 'The statement of George Walters Symes Esquire, Solicitor to the Supreme Court, senior partner of Symes and Lester, Solicitors, of 29 Lincolns Inn Fields, London, WC2, who says:

I am a trustee of a trust established under the will of Captain Merryworth 'Beau' Playfair, Villa des Pins, Antibes, France, who died in 1965. Under the terms of that trust, the income was to be paid to

Mrs Annette Trelawney during her life, and on her death to Captain Playfair's son, Jonathan Playfair (now Sir Jonathan), his heirs and successors. However there was a feature in the provisions in the will establishing this trust, namely that the trust should remain in existence until the death of Mrs Annette Trelawney's son, Colonel David Trelawney, and only then would the capital pass to Sir Jonathan Playfair; or, if Jonathan Playfair had predeceased David Trelawney, to Jonathan Playfair's heirs and successors. This was because the will provided that, in certain circumstances, the income of the trust which Jonathan Playfair was to receive after Mrs Trelawney's death was to be switched from Jonathan Playfair to David Trelawney.

For, in his will, Captain 'Beau' Playfair declared that he had always had great affection for Colonel David Trelawney, and had helped him generously in the past, but was making no immediate provision for him because, if he did, he knew that David Trelawney would inevitably squander it. However, if the trustees at any time were satisfied that, by reason of war wounds or serious illness or by the onset of old age, Colonel Trelawney was in urgent need of major medical treatment or residential care in a home, the costs of which he was unable to bear himself, the trustees were required to discharge all such bills and medical fees as a first charge on the income of the trust and before any of the income was paid to the testator's son, Jonathan Playfair. In discharging this obligation, the trustees were also empowered to advance capital.

Since 1978, when Mrs Annette Trelawney died, the income of the trust had been paid to Sir Jonathan Playfair, but in April of last year the trustees received notice from Colonel Trelawney that he was seriously ill and in need of urgent medical attention and that he had not himself the means to pay for it. In May and early June the trustees investigated Colonel Trelawney's financial situation and received medical reports and estimates of future cost of treatment at the King George VI Memorial Hospital and an estimate of the weekly cost of residing in St Edward's Residential Home in Send, Surrey.

After satisfying themselves that the colonel was virtually destitute, the trustees duly paid his immediate medical bills out of the income of the trust, and set about accumulating monies to meet the further anticipated costs. As a result, from May of last year, all income from the trust which had hitherto been paid to Sir Jonathan Playfair ceased.

On June 18th last year I visited Colonel Trelawney at his home and interviewed his doctor, Dr Oliver Mitchell. On June 19th I saw Sir Jonathan in London and explained to him that he could not now expect to receive any more income from the trust. I was apologetic, because he told me he had sustained very serious losses as a result of his membership of a particular syndicate at Lloyd's, as had other members of his family. Sir Jonathan told me that he had received an account from his members' agent and that in this very month, July, he had been called upon to pay £500,000. To raise this, he told me, he would have to mortgage all he had, including his judicial pension, and that he would be almost destitute. Thus, he said, the loss of income from the trust arising from Colonel Trelawney's illness would be a severe blow. While I expressed regret, I had to warn him that, having regard to the estimates, substantial inroads might have to be made into the capital of the trust and that, were Colonel Trelawney to survive for long, I feared that there would be very little of the capital of the trust remaining.

On June 23rd I was informed of the death of David Trelawney. As I have said, the consequence of this would have been that the Playfair trust would have been wound up, and the capital would have reverted to Sir Jonathan, but before this had been completed Major Francis Lightwood came to see me on July 7th and handed to me the letter (Exhibit 6). I had read in the newspapers about a police enquiry into the death of Colonel David Trelawney, and when I had received the letter I considered it my duty to inform the police about its existence. Accordingly, on July 8th I handed it to Detective-Inspector Johnson. Signed, George Symes, Solicitor of the Supreme Court.'

Brian Graves resumed his seat. Bracton said, 'Call Miss Sylvia Langley.' And, amid a rustle of expectancy and interest as the spectators turned to look towards the entrance, the first witness in the case was led by the usher into the court.

9

A DUMPY figure, with fair hair and a pleasant, open face, she climbed the half-dozen steps to the witness-box unsteadily, not because she was old or infirm, for she was in her early twenties, but because she was nervous and very conscious that every eye was upon her. In the box she gripped the rail with both hands to stop them trembling, holding it so fiercely that the whites of her knuckles showed.

'Take the Testament in your right hand and repeat after me . . .' The voice came from slightly below her and she stared uncomprehendingly at the man in the wig who had spoken. From behind her the usher came forward and handed her the book. She took it. 'No,' he whispered, 'the right hand.' She transferred the book from her left hand and read from the card: 'I swear to tell the truth, the whole truth and nothing but the truth.' Her voice was shaking, hardly carrying across the court. The usher took the book from her and she waited, her knees tensed, her hands back on the rail.

She had been told by the detective outside the court that the judge would be on her left, and now she looked towards the wigged head bent over the documents in front of him. When he looked up she was surprised by the young face. She had expected someone older, fiercer. She did not look to her right, for there she knew would be the man she had not seen since the day her patient had died. Facing her, across the well of the court, was the jury-box and the twelve jurors. The five women and seven men.

Starting on Friday afternoon and during most of this morning they had been listening to Richard Bracton, and now, at last, a person had appeared who would give substance to a name and put flesh on the bare bones of the story Bracton had told them. They eyed her expectantly as they waited to hear from her lips what had happened on Midsummer Day over eight months ago.

'Is your name Sylvia Langley?' Richard Bracton began.

'Yes,' the witness answered, her voice hardly audible.

'Where do you live?'

No-one could hear her reply. Bracton smiled at her encouragingly. 'Miss Langley, you must speak up. The ladies and gentlemen here' – he waved a hand towards the jury-box – 'must be able to hear what you say, as well as my lord on the bench – not to mention defence counsel sitting beside me. So please raise your voice. We all want to hear what you have to say.'

'I'm sorry,' the girl said, louder, but her voice shaking.

Poor child, Jonathan thought. It is always an ordeal giving evidence. He had not looked at her when she had been sworn, but he remembered what she looked like. Now he raised his eyes as, for the second time and more loudly, she gave her address. She is plumper than I remember, he thought, and dropped his eyes again.

Virginia made a note on her pad: hardly out of her 'teens, round face, fair hair – dyed.

Shelbourne studied her, brooding over her, noting her figure and the soft mouth. I wonder, he thought. It would be a risk but it might come off.

She was, she said, her voice gradually increasing in strength and confidence, a state-registered nurse of five years' experience and in June of last year had been engaged by Dr Oliver Mitchell to nurse an elderly man, Colonel David Trelawney, who was bedridden from a broken ankle and was awaiting admission to the King George VI Memorial Hospital for Officers at Windleshot for treatment for cancer.

'Would you please look at this?' said Bracton.

The usher handed her the syringe driver, a flat rectangular object, about six inches long and two or three inches deep, with a syringe laid along its top.

'What is that?' Bracton asked.

'It is the syringe and barrel holder of a powered syringe driver which automatically injects a drug, in this case diamorphine. The doctor had fitted this up for Colonel Trelawney, with a cannula strapped to his chest beneath the skin below the right breast. It was to keep him free from pain, from his ankle as well as his cancer, while he was awaiting admission to hospital.' She pointed to the pencil-like object. 'That is the syringe. From this the drug, in this case diamorphine, flows down the tube and beneath the skin. The amount is controlled by a dial which was set to allow only 2 milligrams an hour to enter the patient's body.' The gadget was handed to the jury. The middle-aged woman next to the youngest of the men who sat on the end of the front row looked at it with distaste and quickly handed it on.

The doctor, the witness was saying, filled the apparatus daily with 50 milligrams of diamorphine. As 2 milligrams entered the patient each hour, that lasted for just over twenty-four hours, but because the doctor was to be away for a few days attending a conference in Bristol, and so unable to pay his daily visit, on Friday June 20th he had filled the apparatus with 220 milligrams, enough to last for the four days he expected to be away. She was in charge of monitoring it and ensuring that only the prescribed 2 milligrams an hour passed into the patient from the syringe to the cannula taped to his chest. This was, she added, until he got to hospital.

'Did Colonel Trelawney ever say anything about his admission to hospital in the presence of the accused?' Bracton asked. Jonathan looked up at the witness and smiled. For the first time she looked at him, but she did not return his smile.

'Yes,' she said. 'When he came to visit on the afternoon of June 21st. I heard the colonel explain about the apparatus and say he wouldn't have it for long because soon he was going to hospital for proper treatment, to which he was much looking forward.' She stopped, and then said in a rush: 'The colonel was alway saying how much he was looking forward to getting to hospital. He said he wasn't ready to die yet and—'

'We can't have that,' Bracton interrupted. 'We can only have what was said when the accused was present.'

Shelbourne, seated beside Bracton, sighed heavily and shook his head. 'We can't have it,' he whispered, loud enough for the jury to hear him, 'but of course we have.'

Bracton paused, and looked at him. Then went on: 'On Friday June 21st, did you bring him breakfast at eight-thirty?'

'I did.'

'And was he at that time quite cheerful, his usual cheery self?'

'That's a leading question.'

It was the voice of Shelbourne, very sharp, loud enough for everyone in the court to hear him. 'Please do not lead the witness,' he said.

The heads of the jury swung round and twelve pairs of eyes stared at him. He had decided it was time to make his presence felt and Bracton had given him the chance. Graham raised his eyes from his papers.

'Is my friend really suggesting,' exclaimed Bracton, 'that this is important?'

Were they going to start squabbling already, Graham thought nervously. Shelbourne was on his feet.

'Mr Bracton,' he said, 'must not put words into the mouth of his witness, not at this time nor at any time. If he does it once without correction, he'll do it again. We've already had from the witness alleged remarks by the deceased not made in the presence of the accused.'

'I did not understand,' Bracton replied, slightly flustered, 'that there was any conflict over whether Colonel Trelawney was looking forward to being admitted to hospital or not, nor what his mood when he was brought breakfast that morning. But since my learned friend appears to attach importance to it, I shall of course re-phrase the question.'

'Please do, Mr Bracton,' Graham muttered.

'Tell us, Miss Langley,' Bracton resumed, 'how did your patient seem when you brought him his breakfast that morning?'

'Quite cheerful, his usual cheery self,' she replied, repeating Bracton's words.

'Was there at this time a telephone – ' Bracton stopped. He turned to look down at Shelbourne. 'But perhaps my friend considers that a leading question?'

Shelbourne waved his hand dismissively. Bracton turned back to the witness. 'Was there anything, apart from the apparatus and his medicines, on the table by his bed?'

'Yes. A telephone.'

'At any time that morning, did your patient in your presence use that telephone?'

'When I came into the room at about ten o'clock I saw him replacing it, as though he had just been speaking.'

'Just answer this 'yes' or 'no'. Did he then say something to you?'

'Yes.'

'When Colonel Trelawney spoke to you after you saw him replacing the telephone receiver, did he seem the same as he had been, what you described as 'his usual cheery self'?'

'Not after the telephone call. He'd changed.'

'In what way had he changed?'

'He was not at all jokey. He seemed – ' She paused and then added, 'He seemed worried.'

'Did you have a visitor that afternoon?'

'Yes, him.' She nodded her head towards the dock. 'He came at about two o'clock. I took him to Colonel Trelawney's bedroom.'

'What did Colonel Trelawney say?'

'He said hello and explained about the syringe and the diamorphine and his broken ankle. It was after that that the colonel said how keen he would be to get rid of the apparatus and get into hospital. But he seemed very nervous and unhappy, very different, as if – ' She paused again.

'Go on,' said Bracton quietly, 'as if what?'

'As if he was scared,' she said.

'Of what?'

'Of the accused.'

After a pause Bracton went on briskly: 'Had you had any conversation with the accused before this?'

'Yes, when I let him in. He seemed very interested in how Colonel Trelawney was and enquired about the treatment and said he'd be happy to stay the afternoon with the colonel as the two of them had much to talk about, and that if I liked I could go out for a few hours.'

'Were you pleased at this?'

'Well, I was quite pleased at the chance of getting some fresh air, but not with him for suggesting it. I wasn't going to take it from him, knowing that the colonel was so worried about seeing him.'

'Did he say anything about how long he'd remain with Colonel Trelawney?'

'He said until I got back.'

'And did he?'

'No. He was gone when I got back at four o'clock.'

'Did that surprise you?'

'It did, very much. The colonel said I could go out, but he was prompted by the accused.'

'Before you left the house, did you—'

'Please do not lead the witness.' It was Shelbourne again, very loud. Bracton cursed himself silently for his slip, cleared his throat and corrected himself. 'What did you do?' he asked.

'I checked the apparatus and the dial which regulated the flow of the drug and also the syringe and saw it was all normal and in proper working order. Then I left and returned at four o'clock, as I had promised.'

'Was the accused still there?'

'No. When I let myself in there was no one downstairs and I thought he must be upstairs, but when I went to the room he wasn't there. He'd told me he'd stay until I got back, but he hadn't.'

'What did you find when you went into Colonel Trelawney's room?'

'The curtains had been drawn – to keep out the sunlight, I supposed.'

'What was the first thing you did?'

'I went to the table on which the dial stood and turned on the bedside light to check it. It was as I had left it. Normal. I didn't then notice the syringe was empty.'

Bracton looked down at his papers and paused. Then asked, very quietly, 'But your patient, what of your patient?'

She raised her hand to her throat. 'I could see he was very still, lying on his side. I thought he was sleeping, but when I took a closer look I saw he wasn't breathing. He was dead.'

There was silence in the courtroom. Bracton looked up at the clock on the wall to his left, and then at the judge. Priestly, sitting beside the judge on his left, leaned over and touched Graham's arm, indicating the clock. It was ten past one.

'We'll adjourn now,' Graham said. 'Ten past two.'

He rose and, followed by the High Sheriff and Priestly, left the bench.

It was mid-afternoon by the time the examination-in-chief of Nurse Langley was concluded. 'Wait there, please, Miss Langley,' Bracton said and sat down.

Shelbourne rose to his feet. Virginia could see his face under the grey wig. It was very dark and grim. For a time he remained looking down at the papers on the desk in front of him; then he hitched up his gown around his shoulders, raised his head and looked across the court at the woman in the witness-box. Still he said nothing. No note had come to him from the dock during her evidence so he had no instructions from Playfair to challenge anything she had said, but she was the first witness in the case and he was not going to let her leave the witness-box without some questions.

'I'm going to chance my arm', he had said to Benjamin at the lunch adjournment. If it didn't come off, he'd said, they'd be no worse off.

Suddenly he began. 'Whom did you meet on the afternoon of June 21st?'

She did not answer immediately, and because she hesitated Shelbourne knew instinctively that he was all right. He waited, standing very still, looking at her. Then she said: 'A friend.'

'A man friend?' he asked.

More hesitation. 'Yes,' she replied.

'His name?' The girl looked at the judge. 'His name?' Shelbourne repeated, still very quietly.

'Do I have to – ' She looked at Graham, who in turn looked at Shelbourne, but he was standing, rigid, his face turned away from the judge, facing the witness. Graham saw Shelbourne was not going to give way.

'Yes,' he said to the witness. 'You must answer counsel's question.'

'His name?' Shelbourne repeated, this time even more sharply.

'Matthew Barnes.'

Shelbourne decided to risk it further. 'Is Mr Barnes your boyfriend?'

'Yes.'

'By that, do you mean he's your lover?'

She coloured slightly and again turned towards the judge. Graham said to Shelbourne, 'Is this relevant, Mr Shelbourne?'

'It is,' Shelbourne replied shortly, still not looking at the judge. Only after a pause did he add, 'my lord.'

Graham, his heart beating fast, looked down at his papers. 'I must rely on you, Mr Shelbourne,' he said.

'You may,' Shelbourne said, smiling slightly. And then, again after a pause, 'my lord.'

Graham said to the witness, 'You must answer.'

'He is,' she said very quietly.

Benjamin knew Shelbourne had gambled. As he had gone on to say during the lunch break: 'She's very young. She must have had good reason to have slipped out and left Trelawney alone with Playfair. And she looks the type. Look at her mouth.'

Benjamin scribbled away in his notebook. Behind him a bemused-looking Harold Benson wondered what this had to do with it.

Shelbourne went on: 'So, on Saturday June 21st last, you had arranged to meet your lover?'

'I hadn't arranged it. I telephoned from a call-box when I left the house.'

'Where to?'

'To where he was working. The White Hart hotel.'

'What does Mr Barnes do at the White Hart hotel?'

'He looks after the bar.'

'Mr Barnes is the barman?'

'Yes.'

'Had the barman expected you to call him on that afternoon?'

'No.'

'Why not?'

'Because I didn't know I'd be free.'

'So it was only when the accused said he'd stay with your patient that you were able to leave the house. Were you surprised at this?'

'Yes.'

'And pleased?'

'Yes.'

'And excited?'

The woman paused. 'I wanted to see him.'

'Why?' She did not answer. 'Why did you want to see him? Not, I'm sure, to play billiards or darts or the other games they get up to in Mr Barnes' bar? But perhaps other games, with Mr Barnes himself?'

He's very sarcastic, thought the young jurywoman who had appeared on Friday in pink but had changed to a dark blouse and skirt for today. However two of the younger jurymen smiled.

The woman did not reply. She looked down at her hand gripping the rail of the witness-box. Shelbourne went on: 'At any rate, Miss Langley, on the afternoon of the 21st, before you left the house, you were feeling very excited at the prospect of a meeting which had come about so unexpectedly?'

She had coloured again. 'Yes,' she said, so quietly that the jurors could hardly hear her.

'And where did you meet Mr Barnes?'

Again she paused. Then she said, 'At the White Hart.'

'In the bar?'

'No, he met me at the door.'

'And after he'd met you at the door, where did you go?' She did not reply. 'To his room?' Still no answer. 'To his room in the White Hart hotel?'

'Yes,' she whispered.

'His bedroom?'

'Yes.'

'And when you got to his bedroom, what did you do?' Again she did not reply. 'Well, you hadn't gone to his room just to talk, had you?' Again she did not reply. 'Oh, come, Miss Langley. You went to his bedroom to do what lovers usually do in bedrooms, didn't you? You went to make love, what you hoped you were going to do from the moment you left the house. Isn't that what you were doing on the afternoon of June 21st – making love?' The witness nodded. 'Please answer,' Shelbourne said cheerfully. 'The shorthand writer has to take down your evidence and he can't record a nod, can he?'

'Yes,' she whispered.

'Yes, the shorthand writer can take down a nod, or yes, you did make love on the afternoon of June 21st?'

The middle-aged jurywoman with blue-rinsed hair shifted uncomfortably in her seat. The youngest of the juryman at the end of the front row put his hand to his mouth to hide a grin.

'We made love,' the witness said.

'Earlier in your evidence, in answer to my learned friend, you said you were pleased to have the opportunity to get out of the house. He paused. 'In order to get some fresh air.' He paused again. 'Not much fresh air in the barman's bedroom in the White Hart was there, Miss Langley?'

She didn't reply and Shelbourne looked at the jury. Then he changed his tone. 'Was that why you were so late in getting back to your patient, because of your love-making with your barman?'

At this she flared up. 'I was not late back.'

'Weren't you? Had not the accused said he could stay only until four o'clock?'

'He may have. I got back at four – or soon after.'

'I suggest it was nearer five o'clock when you got back to the house and returned to your duties.'

'No, it was nearer four o'clock.'

'Was it?' Shelbourne consulted a sheet of paper on the desk in front of him. 'I see that it was at five-forty-five you telephoned the doctor's office and reported that while you were out your patient had died. What were you doing for the hour and three-quarters from when you returned from – ' he paused, 'from your tryst . . . from your tryst with the barman?'

When she still did not answer he said: 'You told us this morning you were surprised to find the accused was not in the house when you returned and that you went to the sickroom, which was dark because the curtains were drawn. You turned on the bedside lamp and immediately checked the dial of the apparatus.'

'And I found it was normal, as I had left it,' she replied, defiantly. Shelbourne stared at her. Then he threw down the paper he was holding. 'Did you,' he asked quietly, 'did you check the apparatus when you returned?'

'Yes, I did.'

'Miss Langley, on that afternoon, quite unexpectedly, you had been presented with the opportunity of seeing Mr Barnes. You were pleased and excited. Are you certain you checked that apparatus before you rushed away to arrange – how shall I put it? – a tryst with your lover?'

'Of course I am. It was my duty to do that. I wouldn't neglect my duty.'

'But you did, didn't you? You neglected your duty by going out at all, and by getting back later than you had promised. Isn't that right?'

'No, it is not. I wasn't back late.'

'Then what were you doing between the time when you say you got back – soon, you say, after four o'clock – and five-forty-five when you telephoned Doctor Mitchell's office?'

'I – I was trying to revive my patient. Then I couldn't get through to the doctor. They couldn't find him. I was terribly shocked when I found the colonel was dead and I, I sort of panicked and—'

'Panicked? You, a trained nurse, panicked? Is that what you want us to believe, in order to explain away why it took you one hour and three-quarters before you reported that Colonel Trelawney was dead?'

'I told you, I was very shocked when I saw he was dead.'

'Oh, yes, I'm sure you were, for Colonel Trelawney died when you were making love to your barman. Was that why you panicked?'

'No, no. I was very upset. He was quite all right when I left and when—'

'I suggest, Miss Langley, you knew perfectly well that under no circumstances should you have left your patient that afternoon?'

'I told you, when I left he was all right and—'

'You left him with a massive dose of diamorphine in that apparatus, and when you got back he was dead. When you saw he was dead, what did you think had caused his death?'

'I knew it was the diamorphine that had killed him, an overdose of diamorphine.'

'And from where had that overdose of diamorphine come?'

'From the syringe. He must have received more of the diamorphine than he should, so when I saw him lying there I rushed to the dial and—'

'Miss Langley,' Shelbourne interrupted sharply. 'You told us that the very first thing you did when you returned was to check the apparatus. Why do you now say you rushed to the machine after you had found that your patient was dead?'

'Because – because, when I saw what had happened to him I rushed back to the machine to see if there'd been any fault. – It was then I saw that the syringe was empty.'

'Miss Langley, you told us that the prescribed dose administered by that machine from that syringe was 2 milligrams per hour, just enough to relieve pain; and that the doctor supervised the amount daily. You also told us that the syringe was normally filled only with 50 milligrams, not enough to cause death even if the whole of the contents were pumped into the patient.'

'Yes, I did.'

'And you told us that on this weekend, as Dr Mitchell was unable to visit because he was attending an important medical conference in Bristol and would be away for several days, he had loaded the apparatus with 220 milligrams.'

'Yes.'

'Which meant that over those few days it was very important that you should remain on duty to check that the machine was working properly and only supplying the appropriate amount of diamorphine?'

'Of course, that was why I checked it.'

'Because you knew that if all the diamorphine in that syringe had been pumped in one dose into your patient's vein that could have killed him. Isn't that right?'

'It is, but—'

'And, knowing that the apparatus was loaded with far more of the drug than was usual, and knowing how vital it was to keep checking regularly, nevertheless you abandoned your patient so that you could go to your barman. Isn't that what you did?'

By now her eyes were filled with tears. 'Yes. No, no.' As she struck the rail of the witness-box with her hand clenched into a small fist, the tears began to run down her cheeks. 'Before I left the house I checked everything.'

'Did you? Do you swear to that?'

'Yes, I do. I checked it before I left and the flow was quite normal. It was working perfectly, as it had been all week, injecting 2 milligrams an hour. But someone must have interfered with it and pumped the whole of the diamorphine into him. That must have been done by hand. You know that was what happened, and you know your client's fingerprints are on the—'

'Miss Langley, we are at present dealing with your evidence, not that of anyone else—'

'But you know that your client must have touched it because his fingerprints are—'

'Miss Langley, others will give their evidence all in good time. At the moment we are listening to your evidence and that of no-one else. Now please answer my questions. Do you swear you checked that apparatus before you ran off to your lover's bedroom at the White Hart and checked it when you came back, almost an hour late?'

'I tell you, I did. When I left and when I came back. I knew it was quite safe to go out for a few hours and I was entitled to—'

'Entitled? Are you saying you were entitled to leave a patient like that and go off to your lover! Is that what you are telling the jury?'

'There was no danger and—'

'Wasn't there, Miss Langley? How can you possibly say there was no danger? Your patient died when you were with Matthew Barnes. Wasn't it a wicked thing to have done, to leave that man lying there with that potentially lethal dose in the syringe and the tube strapped to his chest? Wasn't that a wicked and irresponsible thing to have done? Wasn't it, Miss Langley, wasn't it?'

Without giving her a chance to answer his final barrage of questions, Shelbourne flung down his papers on the desk in front of him and sat down.

The woman was now leaning over the witness-box, sobbing. 'No, no, no. It was that man who did it while I was away. He touched the syringe. It was him who pumped in the diamorphine. You know it was him who did it.' She was pointing now at Jonathan. 'He pumped in that overdose. He killed him.'

She stopped, and the court was very silent. Graham looked at the clock. It was past four o'clock. 'We'll rise now,' he said, relieved. 'Tomorrow morning, half past ten.' And he left the court.

Shelbourne, accompanied by Benjamin and followed by a bewildered Harold Benson, sauntered casually over to the side of the dock. James and Mary Playfair were already there. Jonathan was just leaving. He looked at Shelbourne. 'I told you there was no challenge to the evidence of the nurse. Why did you treat her like that?' he said coldly. 'It was contrary to my instruction, and it was unnecessarily brutal.'

He walked away, followed by James and Mary. Shelbourne stared after him; then, with a growl, he swung away. Virginia came through the crowd. 'Hugo,' she began, putting a hand on his arm. 'That was—' He brushed off her hand. 'Not now, Virginia, not now.' He pushed past her and disappeared.

In the car, on the journey back to Pembroke House, Jonathan said nothing until they had entered the drive. 'Shelbourne had no need to do that to her,' he said at last. 'All he wanted was to make some kind of a show. And he did – at her expense.' He disappeared into his rooms. James and Mary stood in the hall. 'What was he on about?' said James. 'What was so wrong with what Shelbourne did? I thought he made the girl look pretty irresponsible. She could have been wrong about checking the dial and so on. Why's he so bloody angry?'

Mary shook her head. 'I don't understand him,' James went on. 'I never have and I never will.'

And the two of them went into their own part of the house.

10

I N the robing-room Shelbourne tore off his wig and almost flung it at his clerk. Isles caught it and helped Shelbourne off with his gown and court coat. Not a word was said. Benjamin watched the grim expression on Shelbourne's face – he had heard a lot about Shelbourne's temper. For once Shelbourne brushed aside the photographers when he emerged from the building and crossed the courtyard to the wicket gate leading to the path down the hill to the city which was reserved for the use of court officials and lawyers. Benjamin trotted along beside him.

'What the devil did he expect?' Shelbourne said at last. The cold of the late afternoon had not cooled his temper. 'His only chance is for me to throw some doubt on the evidence, and that's what I was doing – had the girl really checked the apparatus before she ran off to her barman? When I do, the bastard ticks me off!'

Benjamin kept quiet. At the hotel they pushed through the swing door and came face to face with Harold Benson, obviously waiting for them, in the foyer. Behind him was a group of journalists.

'Keep that buffoon out of my way,' Shelbourne said as the rumpled figure, looking even more like a shabby schoolmaster than usual, advanced toward them. But there was no way they could avoid him.

'Mr Shelbourne, I'm glad I've caught you,' Harold began. 'I wanted—'

Hugo Shelbourne stopped, glared at him, then raised his right arm and shook a finger almost under Harold's nose. 'I don't care a damn what you want. It's what I want that matters.'

'But, Mr Shelbourne—'

'No buts, Mr Benson. Just listen to me – and then do what I tell you. What I want is for you to go out of that door, get into your car, drive to Pembroke House and—'

'I expected to have—' Harold began again.

Shelbourne shouted at him: 'Don't interrupt me. Listen to me. You're to go to Playfair and tell him from me that if he wants to see himself hanged, I don't.' He paused, and then went on sarcastically, 'I'm speaking metaphorically, Mr Benson, in case you haven't heard they abolished hanging thirty years ago.'

'Well, really, Mr Shelbourne—'

'Yes, really, Mr Benson. And you can tell him from me that the case aginst him could not be stronger and his bloody-mindedness is making it stronger still. For some reason, known only to him and the Almighty, that appears to be what he wants. Well, I don't. Tell him that.'

'I don't think—'

Shelbourne advanced even closer. 'What you think doesn't matter a damn. You are to do what I tell you. Playfair refused – God knows why – to allow Lightwood and Symes to come and give evidence. As a result I had no chance of trying to reduce the effect of what they had to say – which, let me tell you, could be fatal. But oh no, he didn't want Lightwood or Symes called! There's no conflict over their evidence, he said! They were telling the truth, he said, and there was nothing to get out of them, he said! Do you remember that?'

'Yes, I do but—'

'Well, you tell him that the jury have got the picture all right, and a pretty ugly picture it is, of a ruined and malevolent old man with every possible motive for knocking off his old friend. So you go to him and make him understand the danger he's in. And do it now.'

Richard Bracton and Brian Graves came through the swing-door. Shelbourne and Benjamin, facing Harold Benson, were blocking their way into the hotel. Bracton tried to brush past them.

Shelbourne, seeing who it was, turned on him. 'What are you trying to do? Eavesdrop?'

Bracton, without a word, slipped past into the foyer. Benjamin took Shelbourne's arm. 'Let's go to your room,' he said. Shelbourne shook off his hand. 'Not until I'm sure' – he pointed at Harold – 'that he understands what he's to say to our stubborn and stupid client.'

Harold had taken off his glasses and began miserably to polish them. 'Have you understood what I've told you to do?' Shelbourne added.

'I understand perfectly that—'

'Then go and do it. And remind him he's briefed me to defend him and I intend to defend him in my own way and in his best interests, and if I believe it's right to attack a witness and challenge the evidence, I shall. Tell him that.'

He stalked past Harold to the staircase and mounted the stairs. Benjamin followed, resting his hand as if in apology on Harold's arm as he passed, shrugging slightly. Harold turned, looked back towards Shelbourne, and shook his head in disbelief.

Virginia was standing at the head of the staircase. 'What was all that about, Hugo?' she asked.

'I can't talk just at the moment.' He smiled at her. After Friday night she had sensed what he had been feeling and the weekend had improved. She was, as she had said, a pro, like him; and as a pro she had reminded herself that the purpose of her coming that weekend had not been just for pleasure – it had been to make sure that when he returned to the trial on Monday she would be with him. So she had made sure he enjoyed Saturday and Sunday nights as much as he had disliked the one before.

'I need the sitting-room for a conference,' he said. 'I'll see you later for dinner.' He knew the dining-room would be full of reporters, like the foyer in which he'd staged his very public row with Harold Benson. They'd have that for background too, as he had intended they should. When Playfair was convicted that scene would be remembered. Benjamin was on the stairs just below them – and behind him, others.

'Sure,' she said. 'I'll be in the bar.' She rested her hand lightly on the side of his face and went down the stairs.

In his sitting-room Shelbourne flung off his overcoat and jacket, loosened his tie and threw himself on the sofa, staring up at the ceiling.

'Was that wise?' Benjamin said quietly as he took a seat. 'A lot of people must have overheard.'

'I wanted them to.' Shelbourne stretched his arms above his head and clenched his fists. 'A senile ex-judge for a client and a half-witted solicitor! What a pantomime! But you and I, Andrew, have to take care we don't suffer. Between the pair of them, they could make fools of us.'

'So what do you propose?'

'I shall go on, and in my own way.'

'We'll have the doctor first thing tomorrow.'

'I may have something on him. Nothing much, but I'll know more tonight.'

'Will Playfair approve if you go for the doctor?'

'Probably not. But, whether he likes it or not, I'm going to give Playfair a run for his money – the money he's paying us.'

'He must surely understand you have to probe the evidence.'

'He ought to. But I have an uneasy feeling he's up to something.' Shelbourne again stretched out his arms above his head. 'He's playing some game – and we're a part of it.'

For a time Benjamin remained silent, thinking of the silver-haired figure in the dock who had sat either staring up above the judge's bench or down at his hands folded in his lap. Then he asked, 'If you get something on the doctor, will that help?'

Shelbourne shook his head. 'At best it might shake some confidence in him, but it won't get us round the fact that at some time, for some reason, Playfair handled that apparatus; and that it was the diamorphine from that syringe that killed David Trelawney.'

He swung his legs to the floor. 'All I can do is make a stir and confuse the jury. Isn't that the classic technique?'

'Is it?'

'Don't you do that on the Western Circuit? What else is there to do? Our man's pleaded Not Guilty, and the Crown has to prove that he is. Our job is to see they don't succeed. If the jury get confused we've created a doubt and we've done our job.'

He stood up. 'For the first time in a long and lucrative career I don't see any other way out. Now be a good fellow and ring for a drink.'

As Benjamin ordered two whisky-and-sodas over the telephone, he said, 'The lady on the stairs—'

'What about her?'

'You said you'd see her.'

'I know. Another complication in a very complicated affair, but at least a more agreeable one. But I'm beginning to regret getting involved.'

'With her?'

Shelbourne looked at him. 'With the whole damned case.'

In the Judges' Lodgings, Graham Harris was entertaining the High Sheriff and the Under-sheriff and their wives to drinks. High Sheriffs were chosen from prominent figures in the locality and changed every year. The Under-sheriff was a local solicitor. His was a permanent position, and he did all the work of the Sheriff's office.

'It'll be pretty sticky, I imagine,' the High Sheriff had said to his wife as they drove to the Lodgings. 'He's not easy, and his wife's not with him.'

'Why hasn't she come?' Susan Basildon asked.

'I don't know. He said on Friday he had to work over the weekend, and, God knows, the present case must be strain enough. As for tonight, he won't make much of an effort. We'll have to make the running.'

And that's what he was now doing, talking cheerfully in front of the fire around which all five of them were gathered. Graham said little. At least he's wearing a suit, the High Sheriff had noted, and, as far as he could see, socks. Susan Basildon, a handsome woman in her early sixties, with white hair carefully coiffed, dressed in black, with pearls at her neck and a regimental badge in diamonds above her left breast, was standing next to their host. On his other side was the Under-sheriff's wife, a small bird-like woman with a pointed nose. Graham was barely listening to Colonel Basildon's chatter. All he could think of was the figure in the dock and the plump nurse in the witness-box. Shelbourne had been pretty savage. And to what end? How had it helped Playfair? The jury were probably sorry for the girl.

'We had a good day on Saturday, despite the snow,' Graham heard Mrs Basildon say. 'The scent was excellent.'

The Under-sheriff's wife simpered. 'Do you hunt, judge?'

Graham thought of Anne and Francis Keating. 'No,' he said, 'I don't.'

'Jim and I are quite against it,' the Under-sheriff's wife went on blithely. 'We're against all blood sports, aren't we, Jim?'

'The High Sheriff enjoys his hunting, my dear,' her husband said reprovingly. His wife put her hand to her mouth. 'Oh,' she said. 'I didn't mean to—'

The drawing-room door suddenly opened and the butler announced, 'Lady Harris is here, sir. She has just arrived.'

Startled, they all swung round to face the door. Anne Harris, in a tweed topcoat, a scarf around her neck, her gloves and bag in one hand, walked into the room. When she saw the group by the fireplace she stopped. The butler closed the door behind her.

'Oh,' she said. 'I'm sorry. He didn't tell me anyone else was here.'

After a few seconds, while the others stared, Graham advanced towards her. 'Anne,' he said, 'I'm so glad you could come after all.'

He pecked her on the cheek. 'You're just in time to join us for a drink.' He turned back to the others. 'This is Colonel Basildon, the High Sheriff, and Mrs Basildon; Mr Whately, the Under-sheriff, and Mrs Whately. This is my wife, Anne.'

'How do you do,' said Colonel Basildon. 'Glad you could come, Lady Harris.'

Mrs Basildon smiled briefly, the Under-sheriff wanly. Mrs Whately looked as if she was about to drop a curtsey.

'I'm interrupting,' Anne began. Mrs Basildon noted her high colour, and the unkempt fair hair. It's a well-cut coat, she thought. An expensive coat.

'Not in the least. We were just talking over some of the court arrangements,' said Graham. 'Let me take your coat. Come over to the fire.'

'No,' said Anne. 'No. I'll – I'd rather wait. Yes, I'll wait outside until you've finished, if you don't mind. I can wait in the hall, or in some other room.'

'You're not interrupting, I promise. It's not important, is it?' Graham half-turned towards the group at the fire.

'Of course not,' Colonel Basildon said heartily. 'We're only talking shop, administrative shop, you know – and drinking the judge's whisky. You must be damned cold if you've driven down. Have you come far?'

'From London,' Anne said. 'But I'd rather wait outside until you've finished.'

No-one spoke. Then Graham turned again to the group. 'Forgive me if we leave you for a moment. We shan't be long. Do help yourselves to drinks.'

He took Anne by the arm and steered her to the door. When it had closed behind them, Colonel Basildon broke the silence. 'Well, that was a turn-up for the book. I understood he was to be on his own. I certainly didn't expect we'd see Lady Harris this evening.'

'Nor did her husband,' said Susan Basildon drily. The Whatelys said nothing. Colonel Basildon drained his glass. 'Funny she didn't stay and have a drink.' He looked down at the empty tumbler. 'As the judge invited us, I think I'll help myself.' He went to the drinks tray at the side of the room.

'No, Esmond,' his wife said. 'I don't think so. I rather think we ought to be going.'

He stopped. 'Going? Why?'

'I just think we should.'

'But we've only been here ten minutes.'

'Sir Graham and Lady Harris might prefer to be on their own and I think we might be in the way. Don't you agree, Mrs Whately?'

Mrs Whately started. 'Agree, Mrs Basildon?' she said.

'Yes. Lady Harris was obviously not expected by her husband, and they'll want to be alone. After all, she has just driven from London.'

'From London?' Mrs Whately said the words as if London were in outer space. 'Oh, yes, yes, of course. Perhaps we ought to slip away. As she's just arrived.'

'It would be good manners, Esmond, if we all left,' Mrs Basildon insisted firmly.

'But we have arrangements to make about court tomorrow.'

'You can do that on the telephone.'

Mrs Basildon gathered up her bag from the sofa and marched to the door. The others followed. In the hall there was no sign of their host. They began to pick up their coats, which were lying over a chair, when a door opened and Priestly appeared.

Colonel Basildon explained why they were leaving. 'I'll telephone later about the morning.'

'Very good, sir,' Priestly replied. He let them out. He too was wondering about the judge's wife. Why hadn't she telephoned?

Mrs Basildon drove her husband home. 'Did you see that man in the car outside the house?' she said.

'I did,' he replied. 'Was it the chauffeur?'

'No,' she said. 'It was not a chauffeur.'

Francis Keating had kept the engine of the car running to retain some heat. Anne had promised she'd only be long enough to tell her husband and then they'd drive on to Portsmouth. The ferry didn't leave until midnight so they had plenty of time.

In the small study opposite the drawing-room, Graham and Anne heard the others leave. They were still standing and Anne had not removed her coat. Graham said, 'Won't you sit?'

'No. I'm not staying. I thought I should tell you myself. Francis and I are going away – together.'

Graham crossed the room and stood facing the fireplace. The grate was empty and the room was cold. He heard the front door bang and the cars driving off.

'You must have expected it,' she said.

He had his back to her, but she saw him nod. 'Why now?' he asked, and turned to face her. 'The children—' he began, but she interrupted him.

'I know. Next weekend is half-term and I won't be at home. That's why I've come to tell you.'

'Can't you postpone your – your trip, even for a few days?'

'No. You can look after the children. It's about time you got to know them better.'

'I'm here, away from home, trying this case, a difficult and important case, my first on circuit—'

'It's always some case, and always the most important there's ever been. It always was and it always will be. The law, always the bloody law. I've had enough. When we come back I'm moving in with Francis at Sandlands and I've told the children. It will be better for them in the end, better than the atmosphere in the house over Christmas.'

'You told them when they were at school?'

'Yes, and I warned the headmaster, and his wife.'

'So it's all settled?'

'It is. And I don't want anything from you. I don't want any of your money.'

'That's what they all say,' he replied. 'In the beginning.'

She stared at him. 'Always the lawyer, aren't you? That's why I'm glad I'm leaving.' She went towards the door. Then she turned. 'I've told my family. Mother said she'd come up next weekend, if you needed her.'

He shook his head. 'No,' he said. 'I shall manage.'

'You'll have to. Goodbye, Graham,' she said. She turned on her heel. He remained where he was in the small, cold room and heard the front door close and the sound of the car as it drove away. He went through the hall and up the stairs to his room.

In Jonathan's room at Pembroke House, Harold began: 'I've come from Shelbourne.'

'I expected as much. He's angry because of what I said to him.'

'He is. He told me to tell you that while he's your counsel he'll do the case in his own way. He also said it could not be going more badly than it is.'

'That's his opinion. I didn't like what he did with that nurse. It was not necessary.'

'He said he has to cross-examine the witnesses. He has to challenge the evidence, he said, and he added that, even if you don't care what happens to you, he does.'

'Ah, yes, I'm sure he cares. But not because of me, Mr Benson. He cares about his reputation, his professional reputation.'

'But, Sir Jonathan, you must understand that he has to do

something. Otherwise you're going to prison for the rest of your life. You, Sir Jonathan, sentenced to life imprisonment.'

'It is a possibility.'

'It's more than a possibility.'

'If you say so, Mr Benson.'

'Mr Shelbourne says so.'

'I expect he does. But I have – and I know you won't mind my saying this – more experience of courts than you, and even more than he. So I can form my own judgement.'

'I can only report what Mr Shelbourne asked me to tell you.'

'Of course, Mr Benson.'

'He's the best, everyone said he was the best.'

'I'm sure he is, for the right kind of case.'

At the hotel in the city Hugo Shelbourne, preceded by Virginia, entered the dining-room. Richard Bracton and Brian Graves were dining together at a table in a corner of the room. 'Who's she?' Bracton asked.

'An American journalist,' Brian Graves replied.

Bracton watched as the pair gave their order to the waiter. 'He would turn up at a trial like this with a woman like that,' he said, 'while a few miles away that old man see his whole world crashing about his ears.'

But to Harold, at Pembroke House, Jonathan did not appear like a man whose world was falling about him. He seemed very calm. 'Well, you've delivered your message. You can do no more. And now I'll say goodnight.'

He took Harold by the arm and led him into the hall.

'We mustn't get too worried and excited, Mr Benson,' he said as Harold put on his greatcoat.

'Colonel Trelawney, you see, was not a good man, Mr Benson. Nor, I fear, is Mr Shelbourne, although not wicked like Colonel Trelawney. Just vain and difficult.'

As he drove back to his small house on the outskirts of the city, Harold Benson talked as he often did to his dead wife – silently when he was in company, aloud when he was alone in his house or in the car. Now he told her of his troubles with Jonathan Playfair and Hugo Shelbourne.

Harold and Margaret had married late, and Harold still wondered that she could ever have accepted him – he the ungainly, awkward, book-loving country lawyer, and she the matron at a local preparatory school, a friendly, pleasant-looking woman in her forties, with a comfortable figure and a round, cheerful face under a mass of brown hair which she kept in a well-disciplined bun at the back of her head. They had only been married two years when she'd gone on a coach trip to Glastonbury arranged by their local church. On the motorway the coach-driver had suffered a massive heart attack and the coach had careered off the road down an embankment. Margaret and two other women sitting just behind the driver had been flung through the windshield and killed instantaneously.

It had been six months after the tragedy that Harold had met Jonathan Playfair, and their polite, formal acquaintance had been a great comfort to him. But it had been that friendship which had propelled him into a world which he did not understand and with people he did not like. He was being tossed about like a battered shuttlecock, he told Margaret sadly, between two important men who ought to know better.

It had been on his initiative that Hugo Shelbourne had become involved, and when Shelbourne had been so impressive and effective in securing Jonathan bail Harold had been pleased at what he had done. He had chosen the right man, he had thought. But ever since leading counsel and the client had been at each other's throats, and tonight there'd been that shaming scene in the foyer of the hotel, with Shelbourne shouting at him in public.

It was after nine o'clock when, weary and despairing, he eventually got home. He had no garage and parked in the small drive beside the house, where his car was the regular target of local vandals – as was his garden, from which packs of small boys stole his fruit and laughed as they were chased by the wild-haired owner in his vain attempts to catch them.

He had had nothing to eat all day except a sandwich in the cafeteria at the court, and he opened a tin of soup and began to heat it on the stove, talking all the time to Margaret. It has become a nightmare, he told her as he stirred the soup; and I can do nothing, nothing to prevent two stubborn men from fighting among themselves when they ought to be fighting the prosecution.

He went to bed dreading what the next day in court would bring.

11

WHEN, on Tuesday morning, the middle-aged jurywoman who sat next to the young man at the end of the front row took her seat in the jury-box for the third time, and the accused was brought up the steps and had taken his place in the dock, she looked at him differently than she had on the day before. At the start of the trial she had felt rather sorry for the old man who sat so still and impassive while they said such bad things about him. He hadn't looked to her like a murderer. But during the past two days she had began to feel he didn't look quite so harmless as she'd thought. There was, she now considered, something rather sinister about him, and when for one brief moment he cast a glance in the direction of the jury she thought she detected a strange glitter in his eyes.

'Morning, luv.' The young juror squeezed into his seat beside her. 'I thought I wouldn't make it. What would they'd've done if I hadn't? Cut me head off?'

Everyone rose as the judge entered the court. He doesn't look well, the middle-aged jurywoman thought. His face was very pale, with dark patches under his eyes. Colonel Basildon, who had taken his seat on the judge's right, had also remarked to himself on the judge's pallor when he had collected him from the Lodgings in the official car. What had that bloody woman said last night? he wondered as they drove in silence to the castle.

At a nod from the judge, Richard Bracton called out: 'Dr Oliver Mitchell, please.'

The doctor was a large man with a rosy complexion, bald, but with some grey hair smoothed back over his ears. He was smartly turned out in a dark green tweed suit, check shirt and knitted yellow tie. In one hand he held a pair of heavy tortoiseshell spectacles, which he put on as soon as he had taken the oath, and in the other a file, which he placed on the ledge of the witness-box in front of him. After stating his qualifications, he said he specialised in the treatment of cancer, and that Colonel Trelawney, who was seventy-eight, had been referred to him by a local GP about a year ago. He had arranged for the colonel to be admitted to the Malmesbury General Hospital, but the colonel insisted upon being privately treated at the King George VI Memorial Hospital for Officers at Windleshot. No bed at the George VI was available until June 26th.

'How were the costs of this private treatment to be met?' Bracton asked.

The doctor replied that all the medical bills were submitted to a firm of lawyers (here he consulted his notes in the file), Messrs Symes and Lester of Lincolns Inn Fields, London, to whom was also sent a report on the patient's condition, with estimates for the future as well as the immediate costs.

'Did you ever meet and speak to the lawyer, Mr George Symes?'

'Careful now,' growled Shelbourne. 'We can't have what was said.' The judge heard him and looked up.

'I have no need to be warned by my friend about what I ought to do or not do, or what I may ask or not ask,' snapped Bracton.

'You did yesterday,' Shelbourne said loudly.

'I do not intend to ask the witness what was said,' Bracton replied. 'I shall ask him only what he did as a result of that conversation. That is perfectly proper.'

Graham rapped sharply on his desk. 'I won't have bickering between counsel. Mr Shelbourne, if you wish to object or make any submission,' he said with an asperity that he had not shown on the previous days, 'please make it on your feet.'

Shelbourne half-rose, bowed and then sat again.

'Testy young gentleman we are this morning, aren't we?' he said to Benjamin from behind his hand.

'As a result of that conversation, what did you do?' Bracton was asking the doctor.

'I prepared a report and prognosis on Colonel Trelawney's condition, the course of treatment he would have to undergo in hospital and the residential care he would need thereafter, which I considered would last for the rest of his life. At my patient's insistence I had reserved a place for him at St Edward's Residential Home at Send in Surrey, which is one of the most expensive in the country.'

'Were your fees subsequently paid, and if so by whom?'

'By Mr Symes' firm on behalf of the trustees.'

'While Colonel Trelawney was waiting to go to the King George VI Hospital was he in pain?'

'Yes, he was. He had fallen and broken his ankle and was confined to bed in considerable pain.'

'So what did you do?'

'I arranged that while he had to remain at home in bed he should be fitted with a syringe driver which would supply him intravenously with regulated but sufficient doses of diamorphine to alleviate the pain. These syringe drivers can be battery operated but, as Colonel Trelawney was bedridden, in his case the supply of the drug was managed by a dial on a syringe barrel holder positioned on the table by the bed. The syringe normally contained some 60 milligrams of diamorphine which were fed through a small tube cannula taped to his chest or vein, at the rate of 2 milligrams per hour. The apparatus was monitored by Nurse Langley, a trained state-registered nurse, an excellent nurse, in whom I had complete confidence.'

'Had Nurse Langley previous experience with this apparatus?'

'Oh yes, on at least three occasions with three other patients. That was why I was glad she was free to come to nurse Colonel Trelawney.'

He and Sylvia Langley had spoken on the telephone the night before, and she had told him about how Shelbourne had questioned her. He had also read about it in the morning newspapers, and he had spoken to her again outside court. It was a pity, he'd thought, that she'd gone off to the barman's bedroom on that afternoon, but he was not going to let her down. She was a good nurse. And, ultimately, she was his responsibility.

'She was thoroughly conversant with this apparatus,' the doctor said stoutly, 'and a very responsible, professional nurse.'

'On the weekend of June 20th to June 22nd were there any special circumstances which led you to adopt a different system with regard to the supply of diamorphine than you had on the three days prior to June 20th?'

'Yes. On the afternoon of Friday the 20th I had to attend a medical conference in Bristol. . .'

At this Shelbourne gently nudged Benajmin, who half-turned towards him. Shelbourne nodded.

'As a result I knew I'd be unable to pay a daily visit to Colonel Trelawney to top up the supply of the drug, so on the morning of Friday June 20th I charged the apparatus not with 60 but with 220 milligrams. This meant that the supply of diamorphine would last until I next saw him on Monday 22nd. It did not, of course, affect the passage into his system of the normal dose of 2 milligrams per hour. All it meant was that the system did not need the usual daily topping-up. Instead it contained a supply for three days.'

'Who was aware that you had done this?'

'Nurse Langley and Colonel Trelawney. She also knew that there is a mechanism which makes it impossible for more than 2 milligrams of morphine to enter the body every hour.'

'Was any of this said in the presence and hearing of Colonel Trelawney?'

'Yes.'

'When?'

'On Friday June 20th, during my morning visit.'

Graham tapped on his desk with his pencil. 'One moment, Mr Bracton,' he said. He looked at Shelbourne. 'Mr Shelbourne, I do not know if Mr Bracton is going to argue that what was said on this occasion was part of the *res gestae*, but are you proposing to object to this conversation being given in evidence?'

Shelbourne rose. If he did object he would be drawn into a technical argument on the rules of evidence for which he was not prepared. What passed between the doctor and Trelawney ought not do much harm. Better, therefore, to make a concession, and do it graciously. So, in a different tone than he had previously used when addressing the judge, he replied politely: 'I'm grateful to your lordship, but I have no objection. I think it would be best for the jury to hear all that was said by the doctor and the deceased on the Friday so that we know his state of mind when the accused visited on the Saturday. I have no wish that anything relevant should be kept from the jury.'

Two of the older jurymen nodded approvingly.

'Very well,' said Graham. 'You may continue, Mr Bracton.'

Shelbourne sat. 'I don't think it'll do much harm,' he whispered to Benjamin. 'The jury liked it,' Benjamin whispered back.

Bracton was going on. 'Tell us, doctor, what was said.'

'I must explain,' the doctor began, 'that he and I were on very friendly terms. He was a great one for jokes, and for pulling my leg and the nurse's. For instance, he was always joking about his prostate condition, and the particular organ involved in that. Not in very good taste, but good-humoured.'

The young juror smiled. The blue-rinsed jurywoman behind him looked stolidly to her front. She wasn't sure what 'prostate' was, but it didn't sound nice.

'For the court to understand what was said, I must explain that one of the colonel's jokes was always to call me "the quack". He called all medical men quacks, for he used to say that the quacks in his war, World War Two, had killed more of his own men than had the enemy. That was a joke, of course.'

'Of course,' said Shelbourne, loud enough for the jury to hear.

'On Friday morning June 20th,' the witness continued, 'he said, as he was always saying, that he was sure I was just experimenting on him with what he called my "bloody Heath Robinson contraption" so that I could write it all up in the medical journal and get what he called "a gong".'

'Another joke,' Shelbourne muttered. Bracton looked down at him but kept his temper. Graham looked up, but said nothing. To the witness Bracton said, 'So on this morning he was still quite light-hearted about his illness?'

'Oh, yes. He was a military man and during his life, he said, he had seen a lot of life and death and pain. He even made a joke of that.'

'Did he make a joke that morning of what you'd told Nurse Langley about filling the apparatus.'

'He did. But first he asked what would happen if all the drug went into him "in one go", as he put it. I replied, imitating, you understand, his jocularity, "You'd be a goner, colonel", or something like that.'

'What did you mean by that?'

'I meant that if by any chance all that diamorphine was pumped into him in his then condition—' the doctor paused and pulled off his horn-rimmed glasses – 'he would lapse into an irreversible coma, and would die.'

'Which,' said Bracton drily, 'was not a joke?'

'As it turns out, it was not. It was a prophecy. Because that, in the end, is what must have happened.'

'Could that have happened through the operation of the apparatus?'

'Certainly not. I explained to him that it was quite impossible for all the drug to be emptied in one dose by the operation of the apparatus.'

'But if that did happen, how could that have come about?'

'Only by it being emptied manually. In other words, by someone deliberately raising the clamp and pressing the plunger until all the diamorphine had been emptied into him. It couldn't have been done accidentally, and it was impossible for that amount of diamorphine to have been administered through the normal operation of the apparatus.'

Shelbourne got to his feet. 'My lord, I didn't catch the last part of the witness's answer. Could the witness repeat it?'

'Yes,' Graham said shortly. 'Will you repeat your last answer, doctor?'

'I said that couldn't have happened through the normal operation of the apparatus,' the witness repeated.

'Ah, yes,' said Shelbourne. 'That's what I didn't catch. The word "normal". It couldn't have happened through the *normal* operation of the apparatus. Thank you. Yes, I see.'

Bracton went on: 'Did Colonel Trelawney say anything when you told him, jocularly, that if all the diamorphine got into him he would be, as you put it, a goner?'

'He did. I remember it very well, for it amused me. He said, "Well, for God's sake, nurse, listen to the quack and make sure his damn contraption doesn't go ape." Those, I'm sure, were his exact words. I told him he need not worry.'

'What did he say?'

'He said, "Thank God for that", and something, as I remember, about his number not yet being up. It was all very light-hearted.'

'On Friday June 20th, did he say anything about going to the George VI for the chemotherapy?'

'Oh, yes, he repeated what he'd said before – that he'd been a fighter all his life and intended to fight the disease to the end so I was to make damn sure, and he said it again, that the machine didn't go ape before he got to hospital. I re-assured him that couldn't happen. At this he chuckled and said, "Jonathan Playfair won't thank you for that". I asked him what he meant.'

'What did he say?'

'He said the cash to pay me and the hospital and St Edward's would use up the money in a trust which would otherwise go to a connection of his called Jonathan Playfair. That's why, Colonel Trelawney said, he'd chosen St Edward's. This seemed to amuse him, because, as he said, Jonathan Playfair would now be kept from the money.'

'Tell me, doctor, what was the general condition of Colonel Trelawney at this time?'

'He was quite comfortable, but the drug might cause him to doze now and then.'

'Would he do this regularly?'

'Yes. He was often sleepy, and he'd drop off from time to time, sometimes even when I or Nurse Langley were talking to him. There was nothing unusual about that.'

'What was the last thing you did before you left him on June 20th?'

'I checked the machine. Then I drove directly to Bristol to attend the conference.'

'Did you ever again see Colonel Trelawney alive?'

'No, when I next saw him, which was at about midnight on June 21st, he was dead. It was a great shock.'

'At midnight on the 21st, when you found that Colonel Trelawney was dead, did you examine the apparatus?'

'I did. I at once realised that he had died from a massive

overdose of diamorphine. The syringe was empty and I saw that the strapping to the cannula on his chest had been interfered with. It was clear to me that the overdose had been administered manually.'

'Did you check the operation of the apparatus?'

'I did. I found it was in perfect operating order. The safety mechanism which prevented more than 2 milligrams an hour automatically being fed intravenously was working properly. There was no fault in it whatsoever.'

'You have told us, doctor, that he often used to doze off even when you were talking to him. Would it have been possible in your judgement for that syringe to have been emptied manually without rousing him?'

'Certainly.'

'How long would it have taken for anyone manually to have emptied the contents of that syringe into the body?'

'Just as long as it took to depress it. A mere second or two, no more. He would then have sunk into an irreversible coma and death was inevitable.'

Jonathan was no longer listening. Once again he was far away. When Dr Mitchell had said that David Trelawney had told him he had seen much pain and death during his life, Jonathan began to think of David during the war. He had cut a great figure then. Only once after Nicola had told him she was pregnant by him had Jonathan seen David in London. It was in the crowded bar at the Berkeley hotel, where you ran into everyone at that time of the war – friends back from the Atlantic convoys or from Cairo and the desert. Because there might never be a next time, money was for burning on those Saturday nights which began at the bar of the Berkeley in Piccadilly. From there, dinner at Quaglino's. Then on to the Four Hundred in Leicester Square, where the whisky bottles were labelled with each customer's name and the level of liquor marked when last it had been poured, and dancing to the small band on the small, crowded floor in the dim, shrouded light. Or it might be the Café de Paris. Rory had been there the night the bomb had hit and the bodies of dead dancers lay amid the debris while the wounded staggered about, covered in blood. Rory had escaped without a scratch. 'I've a charmed life,' he had said. 'Nothing can get me now.' But the machine-guns had, on the mountain two years later.

There were other places. The Suivi near Claridges, brighter, faster, louder, the place for the fighter pilots with the top button of their jackets undone to show they were the elite of the elite. Or the Nut House in Soho, seedier, less respectable, where the girls pirouetted wearing only two fans, one in front and the other behind, waving them cheerfully at the customers. But David, Jonathan was thinking, would never have taken Nicola there.

When he had met Nicola again the war was long over, her hair grey and his white. It had been in Connecticut, at a dinner party in a yellow clapboard house with black shutters, to which he had been taken by friends. The dinner guests were standing on the terrace overlooking the garden and the fields and drinking highballs in the warm summer evening. He was talking to his hostess when he looked up and saw Nicola coming out of the house, stepping over the sill of the wide ground-floor window that opened on to the terrace. She was followed by a stout, white-haired man wearing rimless glasses.

Jonathan's hostess had seen him stare over her shoulder. She turned. 'They've arrived at last,' she said, and went to greet them. Nicola had seen him. 'Jonathan,' she cried. 'Jonathan Playfair! It can't be!'

'You haven't changed a bit,' he said, kissing her cheek. She laughed. 'Oh, but I have. Ted.' she called out, 'come and meet Jonathan Playfair from England. The boy I grew up with in Sussex.'

The stout man came to them. 'Edward van Holtz,' he said.

There was a buffet, and when they had their food he and Nicola went into the garden. Ted, his plate in his hand, came and stood in front of them.

'Jonathan took me to my first dance,' Nicola said to him. 'A century ago.'

'You must have a lot to catch up on,' Ted said, and wandered away.

She told him she'd been married to Ted for fifteen years. He was a broker in Los Angeles and had been married before, so she was a step-grandmother several times over.

'Have you children together?' Jonathan had asked. She shook her head. 'I've only ever had Tom. He died, you know. Years ago.'

'I had heard, through Annette Trelawney.'

When he spoke the name, Trelawney, he wished he hadn't. She turned her head away. 'And you, Jonathan,' she asked, not looking at him. 'What about you? Are you married?'

'No. I'm an old bachelor, living in the Temple.'

'Alone?'

'Quite alone.'

He thought of her by the stream on the day of the accident with the tractor; and at Plimpton's when they had caught Beau with the headmaster's wife; and at the May Ball at Cambridge.

'Eve's just told me you're a judge. You'd make a very good judge, Jonathan. Except you'd hate sending anyone to prison.'

He smiled. 'Oh, but I have to. Lots of people.'

'You're so much a part of my early life, Jonathan,' she said.

'And you of mine.'

You're a part of all my life, he thought. And you always will be.

The van Holtz's had left early. 'Come and stay, Jonathan,' she had said when she kissed him goodbye. 'Come and stay in Santa Barbara. You'd love it. Do come.'

But he never had.

Jonathan looked up. The evidence-in-chief of the doctor was concluding. The cross-examination would follow. But the judge was rising for the lunch adjournment and Jonathan was taken below.

In their conference room Shelbourne said to his clerk, 'Fetch me a glass of claret from the canteen. I need it.' Isles disappeared.

'Not an early night?' said Benjamin drily.

'No,' Shelbourne replied. The American woman, thought Benjamin.

But last night with Virginia had been different. Now she was insatiable only for information. At their table in the corner of the hotel dining-room she had said, 'You will give me plenty of the background, won't you, Hugo? Some story which the others won't have. I don't publish until the end of the month,' she added, 'and by then the trial will be over. So you can tell me anything.' She stretched out her hand with its long, blood-red fingernails to cover his. From their tables scattered round the dining-room the other journalists watched. He's my property, her gesture had signalled. Keep off.

'What was that slanging match all about?' she asked.

'Just a row with Playfair's solicitor. I can't get them to do what I want about the evidence. It's as though Playfair wants to self-destruct. When I put up some kind of a show and attack the prosecution witnesses, he objects. There can only be one end to it. He'll go down and—'

'Go down?'

'He'll be convicted, and it'll be his own damn fault.'

Later, when Virginia had gone up to their room, Hugo Shelbourne had spent half an hour over a whisky-and-soda with the man from the *Western Gazette* who covered the Bristol area. As he climbed the stairs and went along the corridor to their room he was in a happier frame of mind. At least he had something now.

Isles came back into the conference room with the glass of wine. Shelbourne was sitting at the table, studying the note Benjamin had taken of the doctor's evidence.

'Make or break time?' asked Benjamin.

'Maybe,' Shelbourne replied and drank the wine in one gulp.

In his room Graham had removed his wig but was still in his robes. He said to the High Sheriff, 'I'm not going back to the Lodgings for lunch today. I have some telephoning to do.'

Colonel Basildon looked at him. 'Forgive me saying so, judge, but you don't look very well. Can I get you anything?'

'I slept very badly and I've a bit of a headache. Priestly's gone to get me something.'

'You're sure I can do nothing?'

'No, it's very kind of you.'

Colonel Basildon, in his uniform, walked down the hill to the

County Club to meet his wife. She had been in court in the morning. Over lunch she said, 'He doesn't look well.'

'No,' her husband replied, 'and this afternoon that fellow Shelbourne's bound to get up to something, so he'll need all his wits about him.'

'Her ladyship turning up last night can't have helped.'

'My old grandfather used to say there's no step a man may not take under the pressure of domestic disquietude.'

'Actually,' Susan said, 'it was William Lamb who said that, when he was married to Caroline whom Byron called "mad, bad and dangerous to know".'

'Oh, was it?' Colonel Basildon replied. 'Well, he ought to have known.'

When the High Sheriff had left him Graham picked up the telephone and rang the school. As he thought, half-term began on Thursday and lasted until Monday night. There was no conceivable chance he could get away before the court rose on Friday evening, and all weekend he'd have to spend preparing his summing-up to the jury. There couldn't be a verdict until late on Monday or Tuesday morning, but he couldn't leave the children at school. Someone had to fetch and return them. He put through a call to Anne's mother.

Yes, she said coolly, I was expecting you to call. Yes, she would collect the children on Friday morning and return them to school on Monday, although it would mean driving to and fro across the whole south of England and neither she nor the children's grandfather were getting any younger. It was a great pity, she added, that, as the children's father, he seemed to find it so impossible to pay any attention to his children who were now at the most formative time of their lives. She would explain to them that he would not be seeing them this weekend, and she rang off.

He sat with his head in his hands until he heard Priestly's knock.

'This should help,' his clerk said, putting the glass of water and the tablets on the table. 'I'll get you some tea.'

It was more than a slight headache; his head was splitting, and it would be a difficult afternoon. Shelbourne would be going after the doctor, and Shelbourne, as ever would need watching.

12

SHELBOURNE rose slowly to his feet and stood very still, looking down at the sheet of paper he held in his hand, his usual technique at the start of a cross-examanition. After some seconds Graham, irritated, said, 'Yes, Mr Shelbourne?'

Shelbourne looked at him, then nodded briefly. He wasn't going to be hustled by this young puppy of a judge. He turned to the witness and stared at him. At last he began.

'You shouldn't have done it, should you?'

The witness looked surprised. Shelbourne repeated, 'You shouldn't have done it, should you?'

'Shouldn't have done what?' the doctor said. 'I don't understand.'

'I think you do, Dr Mitchell, I think you understand very well.'

'I do not,' the doctor replied indignantly. 'What shouldn't I have done?'

'Then let us go through what you did on the morning of June 20th. On that morning you visited your patient, as you had visited him on the day before?'

'Yes.'

'And the day before that?'

'Yes.'

'And the day before that?'

'Yes.'

'Three visits on three consecutive days, and on each visit you filled that apparatus with enough diamorphine to last some thirty hours, 60 milligrams maximum?'

'Yes.'

'You were topping up what remained of the drug in his apparatus to a maximum of 60 milligrams?'

'That is so.'

'If that amount of diamorphine, the full complement of 60 milligrams, had, by some mischance, entered your patient's body in a single dose, would that have killed him?'

The witness paused. He began to suspect what was coming. 'No,' he said. 'It would not. It would have induced drowsiness, sleep. That's all.'

'But double that amount, almost triple it, say a single shot of about 168 milligrams, if that was pumped in to him in one dose, that would have killed Colonel Trelawny, wouldn't it?'

'Yes. As I explained, the effect of large doses of diamorphine varies, but in Colonel Trelawney's then state of health, in his condition, yes, a sudden injection of 168 milligrams would have killed him.'

'And it did, didn't it?'

'I explained to the court this morning that as I—'

Shelbourne snapped at him: 'I didn't ask you what you, explained to the court this morning. I repeat, did not that 168 milligrams pumped in one dose into your patient's body kill him?'

'Yes, but—'

'Now I repeat the first question I asked you. You shouldn't have done it, should you?'

'Done what?'

'Dr Mitchell, you know perfectly well what I am asking you. On Friday June 20th you should never have filled that apparatus with 220 milligrams of diamorphine. Isn't that correct?'

'No, it is not correct.'

'In what way is it not?'

'As I explained—'

'Answer my question.'

'My lord' – Bracton was on his feet. Shelbourne flung down his brief on the desk in front of him, pleased to have provoked Bracton so early in the cross-examination. As he said to Benjamin, all he could do was make a show, and Bracton's reaction would help the show along.

'My lord,' said Bracton, 'the witness is trying to explain his answer. He must be allowed to give his explanation. That was a trick question.'

'That is a singularly offensive comment,' said Shelbourne, even more pleased.

'Let the doctor answer the question first,' Graham replied. 'Then he may explain.'

Bracton sat down heavily. Graham said to the witness, 'Counsel has asked you, Dr Mitchell, whether you agree that if the syringe had never been charged with 220 milligrams on the Friday, a fatal dose could never have been administered on the Saturday. That seems a perfectly easy question to answer. Do you agree or disagree?'

'Put like that,' Dr Mitchell replied, 'of course I agree, my lord. It couldn't.'

'Now you may add what you wish.'

'As I have explained, my lord, the only reason why I charged the apparatus with 220 milligrams of morphine on June 20th was because I had to be away over the weekend, but it was wholly incapable of administering more than 2 milligrams in any one hour. So there was no danger when I filled it with 220 milligrams.'

'Did you say no danger?' Shelbourne leaned forward over the desk towards the witness. 'No danger in loading the apparatus with 220 milligrams?'

'No, none.'

'By that I suppose you mean there was no danger if, and only if, the apparatus was working normally.'

'Which it was.'

'So you say. No danger, provided' – he stressed the word – 'provided the apparatus was working normally?'

'Yes, which I know it was.'

'How do you know? You weren't there on the morning or afternoon of Saturday June 21st. Where were you?'

'I was in Bristol.'

'Ah, yes,' said Shelbourne slowly, 'you were in Bristol.' He paused. 'Attending a medical conference, I believe you said. Is that right?'

The witness nodded.

'As I've had occasion to point out to another prosecution witness,' Shelbourne went on smoothly, 'the shorthand writer has to make a record of these proceedings and he finds it difficult to show a nod. Please answer. Yes or no, Dr Mitchell?'

'Yes.'

There was another pause, before Shelbourne asked, 'Was it an important conference?'

'I thought so, at the time.'

'Sufficiently important for you to leave your patient?'

'Yes. He was perfectly properly provided for.'

'I'll come to your visit to Bristol a little later, but so that there can be no doubt about it, we have established, have we not, that if during that weekend the syringe had contained only 60 milligrams no fatal dose could have been administered by any means whatsoever?'

'I agree.'

'So do you also agree that you should never have charged that apparatus with the amount of diamorphine which you did on June 20th?'

'I do not, if by that you mean that what I did was wrong.'

'You don't deny, do you, that if you hadn't done that Colonel Trelawney would now be alive?'

'I don't know if he would have been alive or not. Your client—'

'I am not asking you about my client,' Shelbourne interrupted. 'If there hadn't been that amount of diamorphine on hand Colonel Trelawney would not have been killed. Isn't that obvious?'

'I am not prepared to answer a hypothetical question.' The doctor looked down at the closed file on the ledge in front of him. He took a deep breath and said slowly, 'But I will agree that it was to suit my obligations, to fit in with my commitments, that the syringe on June 20th was filled with 220 milligrams of diamorphine. I was, however, satisfied that there was no danger, as the apparatus still could not discharge, was incapable of discharging, more than 2 milligrams an hour into Colonel Trelawney's body.'

'Do you think it was a responsible thing for a doctor to do? To go away and leave a patient for the whole weekend with that amount of the drug in a syringe attached to an apparatus which was pumping the drug into his body.'

'Of course it was. The apparatus controlled the supply. There was a perfectly competent safety mechanism—'

'So you were quite prepared to leave your patient to the mercy of a safety mechanism? Have you never heard of even the most sophisticated and apparently foolproof apparatus failing to do what it is meant to do?'

'That is nonsense,' the doctor replied angrily, thumping the ledge of the witness-box so angrily that he knocked his file to the floor, scattering sheets of paper below the box. The usher collected them up and handed them to the doctor, who snatched them out of his hand and began to re-arrange them. 'It is a perfectly normal practice to do what I did,' he went on. 'I have done it before with other patients, and, to my knowledge, it is done by many of my colleagues. Before I left the house that morning I checked that machine. After I returned the next night when Colonel Trelawney was dead, I again checked the machine. Mr William Fraser, the technician from the manufacturers who was specially called next morning, checked the machine. There was no fault in it. The safety mechanism was in perfect working order. The mechanism is not capable of pumping more than 2 milligrams an hour through the syringe; 168 milligrams of morphia could never have entered the deceased's body through the operation of that machine.'

As he spoke the doctor's face had flushed an even deeper red than his normal high colour and he had gradually raised his voice until at the end he was almost bellowing. With a satisfied smile Shelbourne lolled back against the bench. He is enjoying himself, Virginia thought.

'Those 168 milligrams which were emptied through that syringe into Colonel Trelawney were administered manually,' the doctor continued. 'That is the only way they could have been. It was done by hand, by the hand of a person pressing the plunger – and there was only one person who could have done that. You have no reason to smile at me, because you know exactly who that person was.'

Shelbourne jerked forward and stood very straight, staring hard at the witness. The doctor pulled the handkerchief from his breast pocket, put it to his mouth and dabbed his lips.

'Gently, doctor, gently, please,' Shelbourne said, smiling again.

'That's outrageous,' said Bracton. Graham was about to intervene when Shelbourne went on rapidly, 'Two hundred and twenty milligrams of diamorphine left in that syringe while you drove off to attend to what you have called your obligations, your commitment to attend a medical conference.'

Graham lookd quickly through his papers. Dr Mitchell had spoken of William Fraser, and there was a statement by Fraser in the depositions. Fraser was the technician who was coming to give evidence, indeed he was to be the next witness. Graham found the statement. As he had thought, Fraser would swear he had examined the apparatus on the Sunday morning, June 22nd, the morning after Trelawney had died, and had found it in perfect working order. He decided to intervene.

'Is it part of the case for the defence, Mr Shelbourne, that the diamorphine entered the deceased's body because of some fault in the operation of the machine. Is that your case?'

'Good,' whispered Bracton to Graves. Shelbourne turned slightly to look at the judge, but said nothing.

'I'm not clear,' Graham went on, 'what exactly you are alleging? What is the defence on—'

Shelbourne interrupted him. 'Unlike commercial cases, in which your lordship has had so much distinguished experience, there are no pleadings in a criminal case and the defence does not have to state in advance what is or what is not the nature of the defence. But I can tell you, for your information, that the defence in this case is what it has been from the moment the prisoner was arraigned – Not Guilty. I am not, at this moment, prepared to say more.'

Graham flushed. In his chair beside the judge, Colonel Basildon crossed his legs uneasily. That was pretty offensive, he thought. There was silence for a moment, the judge staring at counsel. The tablets he had taken at the lunch adjournment had worn off. Graham's head was throbbing, worse than it had in the morning. I must keep my temper, he said to himself. I must.

'Then I think that you had better move on, Mr Shelbourne,' he said and dropped his eyes to the notebook in front of him and picked up his pencil.

'If,' said Shelbourne, emphasising the word, 'if your lordship pleases.' He paused and then said, 'I shall now turn to the nature of Dr Mitchell's so-called obligations or commitments which took him away from daily supervision of his patient's welfare.'

Bracton lumbered to his feet. 'Before my learned friend does so, in my submission he must make clear whether he is suggesting that the diamorphine found in Colonel Trelawney after his death was or was not caused by the operation of the apparatus.'

Shelbourne wagged his head, and sighed. 'All in good time. Perhaps my learned friend will allow me to conduct my cross-examination in my own way and' – he turned to Bracton and almost spat out the words – 'and without interruption.'

Graham held up his hand. 'Both of you, please be quiet. Mr Bracton, according to my papers your next witness is William Fraser, who examined the apparatus on the morning of Sunday June 22nd. Is that correct?'

'It is, my lord.'

'Then when he is cross-examined we shall hear what is suggested or what is not suggested to him by Mr Shelbourne. And when the jury have heard that doubtless they will remember what is presently being put, or – which is equally important – what is not being put, to Dr Mitchell.'

Bracton bowed and sat down, looking satisfied.

'You may go on, Mr Shelbourne,' Graham said coldly.

Shelbourne remained silent. Bloody young brat, he thought. But he said nothing and turned back to face the witness. 'What exactly was the commitment which made you leave your patient lying in his bed with a syringe containing a fatal dose of diamorphine?'

'I was to attend the weekend conference in Bristol of the West Country Association of specialists in the treatment of cancerous growths and leukaemia.'

'And this was sufficiently important for you to forego your daily visits to your patient and to leave him in the circumstances you have described?'

'Over the weekend, yes. I was quite confident that Nurse Langley would be able to watch over my patient while I was away and I needed to attend the conference.'

'Ah, yes, Nurse Langley.' Shelbourne smiled. 'And you were quite confident, were you, that your patient would be properly looked after during your absence by Nurse Langley.'

'I was.'

'Tell me, doctor, why were you so confident of her devotion to her duty?'

'I had worked with her before.'

'Were you aware of the existence of Nurse Langley's gentleman friend who works as a barman and occupies a bedroom in the White Hart Hotel?'

'I was not, but that is quite irrelevant.'

'Is it? Did you know that she had slipped away from the house on the afternoon of June 21st?'

'She told me when I saw her very late on the night of June 21st when I had been telephoned and I had returned from Bristol. In the circumstances it was quite permissible for her to take a few hours off. The condition of the patient was perfectly stable, the dial was set at the correct level and the apparatus was in perfect working order. She is entitled to some time off. Where she went or what she did was her own business. Moreover she had left someone whom she imagined was a perfectly responsible person in the room with the patient. She was not to suspect that that person—'

He was not permitted by Shelbourne to conclude his sentence. 'At what time did you arrive in Bristol on Friday June 20th?' he asked.

He's coming, Benjamin thought, to what he's learned from the journalist. He glanced at the jury. They were not, he thought, looking at Shelbourne with much friendliness, especially the middle-aged woman near the end of the front row. He's very rude, she was obviously thinking.

'I arrived at the hotel in Bristol where the conference was being held at about half past twelve on Friday the 20th and registered as one of those attending.'

'When did the conference begin?'

'At two-thirty that afternoon.'

'That was the opening session?'

'Yes.'

Shelbourne was examining a sheet of paper he held in his hand. 'I believe that the speaker at the opening session of the conference was—now let me see, who was it? Dear me, the name has slipped my mind. Can you remember, Dr Mitchell? Can you remember who was the speaker at the first session and what he had to say?'

The witness did not reply.

'Did he give a rousing opening to this important conference which you were so anxious to attend that you abandoned your daily visits to your patient?' Shelbourne was shuffling the pieces of paper. Then he held one almost to his nose. 'Ah, yes, I have it now. The speaker at the opening session was, I see, a Dr Stevens.' He smiled at the witness. 'Did you enjoy Dr Stevens' opening speech, Dr Mitchell?'

'I didn't hear it'

'You didn't hear it?' said Shelbourne. 'How do you mean, you didn't hear it? You had come all the way to Bristol, leaving Nurse Langley in whom you had so much confidence in sole charge of your patient who had a lethal dose of diamorphine in the syringe feeding the tube strapped to his chest, and you didn't hear the opening of this important conference which you were so eager to attend?'

Shelbourne paused, smiling. Then he dropped the paper and his mocking tone and snapped: 'Where were you on the afternoon of Friday June 20th, Dr Mitchell?'

'After I had registered and I had seen who was to be the opening speaker, I had lunch with a friend who was also attending the conference. A surgeon, Mr Lionel Black.' The witness hesitated. 'As we had both heard Dr Stevens speak at an informal meeting at Bath the month before—'

Shelbourne interrupted him. 'You and your friend decided to give Dr Stevens' talk a miss. Isn't that right?'

'Yes.'

'And instead you spent a jolly afternoon with your friend on the Royal Bristol Golf Course. Isn't that right?'

So that was it, thought Benjamin. The witness nodded.

'Come along, Dr Mitchell,' said Shelbourne cheerfully, 'Think of the poor shorthand writer. Yes or no?'

'Yes.'

'Tell me, when you and Mr Black went off and played hookey, or rather golf, did you have to hire golf clubs?'

'No. I had them with me, in my car.'

'You had your golf clubs in your car,' Shelbourne repeated thoughtfully. 'So, when you fitted up Colonel Trelawney's syringe with what turned out to be a fatal dose of diamorphine and left him, you had in your car your clubs which, presumably, you were intending to use when you got to Bristol. Tell me, Dr Mitchell, did you have any intention whatsoever of attending the conference?'

'Of course I did. My clubs were in the car because I had played at home on the previous evening.'

'How convenient! At any rate, on Friday afternoon you abandoned all chance of improving your medical knowledge to play a round of golf? Now tell me, on the following day, Saturday June 21st, the second day of your important medical commitment, did you attend the conference on that day?'

'I attended the morning session.'

'And the afternoon session, did you attend the afternoon session?'

'After attending the morning session Mr Black and I formed the view that we were not going to gain as much as we had expected from the conference. It appeared to be directed at those with less experience in the treatment of cancer than that of Mr Black and myself. Indeed we'd heard much of what was being said the month before at a conference in Bath, so—'

'So off you went to the golf course again?'

'Yes.'

'One out of three! You scored one out of three attendances at the first three sessions of this important medical conference. But tell me, do you think that on that weekend you displayed an appropriate degree of dedication to your profession?'

The witness remained silent, glaring at him. Shelbourne waited. Then he half-turned to the jury as he went on, 'To leave a seriously ill patient with a massive dose of a dangerous drug attached to him while you went off to play golf. Do you think that was a proper thing for you to have done?'

'I have explained—'

'You have. But consider for a moment, doctor. On the afternoon when the fatal dose of diamorphine with which you had loaded the syringe entered the body of Colonel Trelawney, and Nurse Langley was in bed with her barman, you were on the golf course.'

'You are distorting—'

'No, Dr Mitchell, I am distorting nothing. I'm asking you if on reflection you consider your conduct at the time when Colonel David Trelawney died was that of a responsible medical man in charge of a seriously ill patient.'

Shelbourne was leaning forward, bent over the desk. Virginia could see his face in profile under his wig. The light caught the flash in his eyes and when he spoke his lips pulled back in a sneer. Oh, yes, she thought again, he's enjoying himself.

'Do you think it was right to go off and play golf leaving Colonel Trelawney with that deadly amount of drug in the syringe and the tube attached to his chest?'

The doctor tried to speak but Shelbourne went on inexorably. 'You are not seriously suggesting, are you, Dr Mitchell, that on that weekend you behaved in accordance with the best traditions of the medical profession?'

'This is intolerable,' the doctor spluttered.

'No, I suggest that what you did was intolerable, Dr Mitchell. I suggest that by your behaviour on that weekend you failed in your duty to your profession, and above all' – Shelbourne bent even further forward and literally hissed – 'you failed in the duty which you owed to your unfortunate patient.'

'Stop!'

The cry was so loud and so sudden that at first no-one in that courtroom knew exactly from whom it came. It was only when it was repeated – 'Stop! Stop this, immediately!' – that everyone realised that it had come from the figure in the dock.

'Stop, I want this stopped.'

Jonathan was standing, brushing aside the restraining arm of the warder. From her seat at the side of the court, Virginia, like everyone else, craned forward to stare at the tall figure standing with one arm raised, pointing at Shelbourne.

Shelbourne swung round. A great murmur arose in the court and Graham began to bang on his desk with his gavel. The High Sheriff half-rose to his feet. A policeman and the usher came to below the dock, looking up at Jonathan, who had dropped his hand and was leaning over the edge of the rail, his white hair falling over his brow. The noise in the court increased. The usher bellowed, 'Silence, silence.' Graham's gavel fell again and again. Gradually the noise subsided.

'What is the meaning of this? You must not interrupt the proceedings,' Graham said. 'You must sit down and keep silent.'

'I dismiss my counsel,' Jonathan replied loudly. 'I no longer wish to be represented by Mr Shelbourne. I wish this cross-examination to cease. I withdraw all instructions from Mr Shelbourne. I dispense with the assistance of any counsel.'

Oh God, thought Graham. Not this, not this.

Shelbourne slammed the papers he was holding on to the desk beside him, looking up in astonishment at Jonathan.

'I gave no instructions for the doctor to be cross-examined as he has been,' Jonathan said. The whole court was very still. 'I disassociate myself from this cross-examination and I dismiss my counsel. I shall defend myself.'

Graham took a sip of water from the glass in front of him.

'That is a very grave statement,' he said, clearing his throat, 'and a very serious decision, especially at this stage of your trial.'

'I am aware of that, my lord,' Jonathan replied more quietly. 'But I do not need Mr Shelbourne's services any longer. I withdraw my instructions from him. I dismiss him.'

With what sounded like a growl, Shelbourne, two livid spots of red now on the cheekbones of his dark face, turned his back on Jonathan and sat down noisily.

'I must advise you,' said Graham, 'that you should not make a decision in a matter which affects you so gravely without very serious thought. If you wish, I shall adjourn so that you can speak with your advisers privately.'

'No, my lord, I do not wish to speak to Mr Shelbourne. I have nothing to say to him. I no longer wish to have his services as my defending counsel. Nor do I wish for any counsel to replace him.'

Some of the reporters started to move noisily from their bench. 'Stay where you are,' Graham commanded loudly. 'Be still,' and they stood or sat where they could. For a moment nothing broke the silence. Virginia bit her lip, watching Shelbourne. The eyes of all the jury were on the figure standing in the dock.

'I am aware,' Graham said at last, 'that for someone of your experience to defend yourself does not present the same problem as it would for a person ignorant of court procedure. Nevertheless what you say you have decided is very grave. I shall now adjourn and give you the opportunity of considering the matter overnight. But I must warn you that, whatever you decide, the trial will proceed tomorrow morning.'

'I shall not change my mind, my lord. From now on I shall defend myself and I shall be ready to continue tomorrow, without counsel.'

'I hear what you have to say, but you will now have some hours to reconsider. The court is adjourned until tomorrow morning at half past ten.'

Graham rose and, gathering up his white gloves and followed by the High Sheriff and his clerk, left the court.

Immediately the judge had disappeared, hubbub broke out. Some of the reporters made a dash for the door to get to the telephones; other crowded below the dock. 'Sir Jonathan,' they called up, 'Sir Jonathan, why have you done that, Sir Jonathan? Why have you dismissed your counsel? What are you going to do now?'

Jonathan ignored them and leaned over the rail of the dock, calling out, 'Mr Benson, Mr Benson!'

Harold pushed his way through the throng, James and Mary at his heels. Seeing they would get nothing out of Jonathan, the reporters moved away and crowded round Shelbourne and Benjamin. Shelbourne's clerk, Isles, was already gathering up Shelbourne's papers, tying them with pink tape. Virginia pushed her way towards them.

'Mr Benson,' Jonathan said briskly, 'come to the house immediately. I must speak with you.'

He turned, but the warder tried to restrain him. 'You'd better wait, sir, 'till the crush is less.'

'No,' said Jonathan, 'I must be going.' Then, to James: 'See the car is brought to the door, and warn the house that the press'll be outside the gates. Tell them to be ready. We'll leave as soon as the judge has got away.'

'What does it all mean?' Mary asked James. 'What has he done?'

'God knows,' James replied, starting for the door. 'He's gone mad.'

Shelbourne approached. 'Sir Jonathan . . .' he began.

'No,' said Jonathan. 'I have nothing to say to you. I have dispensed with your services.'

'But this is intolerable—'

'It was you who were intolerable. I have nothing to say to you.'

'We must speak in private. We cannot talk here.'

'I have nothing to say to you, Mr Shelbourne. Mr Benson will make all the necessary arrangements with your clerk.'

'Damn Mr Benson and damn my clerk! You must listen to me, Playfair. I insist you listen to me. You've publicly insulted me in front of the whole court, in front of the whole world—'

'You left me no alternative. Now, if you please, I am leaving. I have nothing more to say to you.'

Shelbourne lost control. 'You bastard,' he said, white with fury. 'You bastard. To dismiss me publicly! You planned this, didn't you? You planned this.'

Jonathan looked at him but did not reply.

'You know what'll happen to you now, don't you?' Shelbourne snarled. 'You'll be convicted and you'll go to prison for life. You've disgraced yourself and the whole of the judiciary. And after the way you've behaved I shan't be sorry.'

Benjamin took him by the arm. 'Hugo,' he said, 'come away, Hugo.'

Virginia and some of the reporters were standing just behind them. James returned. 'The car is here,' he said. Benson had disappeared. Jonathan gave Shelbourne one final stare and then turned, left the dock and, with James at his side, made his way to the door, refusing to say a word in answer to the questions shouted at him as he went. There were photographers and television cameras as they got into the car and drove away.

Ahead of them, in the judge's car on it's way back to the Lodgings, the High Sheriff turned from the jump-seat in front of Graham.

'That was very sensational, judge. Has that ever happened before?'

Graham shrugged.

'Not in my experience,' said Priestly.

'What happens now?' Colonel Basildon asked.

'We shall go on with the trial tomorrow,' Graham replied. 'With or without counsel.'

'He won't change his mend,' said Priestly.

'Probably not.'

'Shelbourne was pretty offensive to the doctor,' said Basildon. And to me, thought Graham.

'How's your headache, sir?' asked Priestly.

'About the same. Not helped by what happened this afternoon.'

At six o'clock he spoke to the Lord Chief Justice in London and told him what had happened.

'It was on the five o'clock news,' said the Chief. 'Well, you must go on tomorrow as if nothing has happened. Do you think Playfair is all right, mentally?'

'I don't know,' said Graham.

'Well, if he goes down for murder, as it sounds as if he will, you have to sentence him to the mandatory life sentence and they'll have a medical report on him later.'

'What if it's a verdict of manslaughter?'

'Could it be?'

'Unlikely, but I suppose conceivable, if the jury for some reason think he didn't know the dose would kill Trelawney.'

'Then remand him in custody for a medical report and look at that before you sentence him.'

'When he's defending himself, how does that work?'

'Make him do it from the dock, and have his solicitor or someone help him with his papers and documents. At least Playfair will know what to do. It was always a difficult case, Harris, and now it's more difficult. But just get on with it, and do your best.'

As he replaced the receiver Graham thought about what Anne's mother had said about him and the children. A failed father, a failed husband, perhaps now a failed judge. He took some more tablets and went to his room.

13

FROM the window of the robing-room Andrew Benjamin saw the reporters gathering in the forecourt. 'Best not say anything, Hugo,' he said. Shelbourne nodded. He would say nothing now – not here. But when he got back to London he would say plenty.

'Why the devil did you get me involved with this madman?' he growled at his clerk. Isles did not reply. You got yourself involved and you know why, he said to himself as he put the wig in the wig-box and folded the gown and court coat. You thought there'd be plenty of publicity – and there has been, though not the kind you expected.

'You're well out of it, Hugo,' said Benjamin. 'No-one can blame you when he's found guilty.'

'The way the bastard did it – that's what I can't get over. Shouting at me in the court. If he wanted to get rid of me he could have asked the judge to adjourn, talked to me in private, and I'd have withdrawn, gladly.'

'I think something snapped. I don't think he could stop himself.'

'Because I was asking the bloody doctor why he'd buggered off to play golf, leaving his patient in the care of that randy little tart who went off to fuck in a pub?'

Isles was a lay preacher in Wembley and did not care for that kind of language. He cleared his throat noisily and snapped shut the catches of the suitcase. Shelbourne, knowing he was offended, ignored him. 'I hope to God they convict the bastard.'

'The *Western Gazette* man put you on to what the doctor had been doing?'

'Yes. He'd been playing himself on the Saturday and knew Mitchell by sight. I thought it worth getting him to check at the club to see if Mitchell was also there on the Friday afternoon.'

'And you were right.'

'I was.'

'Shall I collect your things from the hotel and pay the bill?' Isles asked.

'Yes, and when you get back to chambers send in a fee-note to that bloody solicitor. Make it as heavy as you can, and tell him we want the cheque before Playfair's in prison.'

'Will you be coming straight back to London?' Isles asked.

Shelbourne shook his head. 'No, I'll go to the country. I should be back tomorrow or the day after.'

It depended on Virginia. He would take her home this evening and bring her to London when she needed to be back at her office.

The cameras and the reporters crowded round them as they went from the court to the hotel, but Shelbourne just shook his head and shrugged his shoulders, as much as to say, 'What can you expect? The man's mad.'

In the foyer they ran into Richard Bracton. 'I'm sorry, Shelbourne,' he said.

'I'm not. I'm bloody glad to be out of it. You'll get him now and it serves the bugger right. You just make sure you pot him.'

Bracton walked away. Shelbourne had good reason to feel sore, for it had been a very public humiliation, but it was typical of him to talk like that with the place crawling with the press. He joined Brian Graves at tea in the lounge.

'Do you think Playfair will go into the witness-box?' Graves asked.

'No, my guess is that he'll make a statement from the dock which can't be challenged.'

'Then you won't have to cross-examine him.'

'No, I don't think I shall. It should be plain sailing for us from now on.'

At the reception desk Shelbourne was told that Miss Katz was up in their suite. On his way through the foyer he pushed past several journalists. 'Sorry,' he said. 'No comment now. Plenty later.' He put as brave a face on it as he could, grinning as he bounded up the stairs, waving to them cheerfully.

The door of the sitting-room was open. Virginia was standing by the fireplace. 'Poor old Hugo,' she said. 'Has he gone mad?'

Shelbourne kicked the door shut behind him. 'No more than he's ever been. A crazy client, a half-witted solicitor and a judge hardly out of short pants! I'm glad to be shot of the whole bloody case.' He went to the telephone by the bed. 'I'll ring down for a drink while we're packing. Let's get going as soon as we can.'

'Get going, Hugo?'

He was on the telephone, his back to her. 'A large whisky-and-soda, a double, and' – he looked over his shoulder – 'a vodka-and-tonic?' She shook her head. 'Just a large whisky-and-soda. No vodka – and send it up immediately.'

He replaced the receiver, picked it up again and started to dial. 'I'll warn Mrs Green at the house to expect us. I told her we wouldn't be back until Friday evening. We can stop for dinner on the way.'

She walked to the window and drew the curtains. 'Hugo darling,' she said over her shoulder, 'you know I can't leave here tonight. There's a lot I have to do.'

He turned and faced her, the telephone to his ear. 'What do you mean?'

'I'm covering the case for the magazine, remember? I've already been on to New York, and they're calling me back here.'

He replaced the receiver, staring at her. 'I can't stay here,' he said.

'Of course you can't. No, you slip off, darling. You go home and lick your wounds and—'

'Lick my wounds?'

'You know what I mean, Hugo. I understand what you're feeling and I'd love to come with you, but I have a job to do.'

'A job?'

'Of course. I have a story to write.'

'So you won't come with me?'

'I can't darling. I have to stay.'

He put the telephone back on the table and looked at her. She was in a white blouse and dark skirt, very smart. She looked very cool. 'Of course,' he said at last. 'You have to stay here, and to hell with everything else, including the friend who might, just at this moment, need you.'

'Darling, be reasonable—'

'Oh, I am. I'm trying to be very reasonable.'

He walked over to the writing-table. On it was his brief-case and some of his papers. He threw them into the case. 'Well, today will have given you some good material. How will it go? Ex-judge sacks Brief in murder trial. Dismissed lawyer slinks off in disgrace.'

'Oh, come off it, Hugo! What happened today will have to be in the story, but it's only a part. The trial's not over.'

He snapped shut the briefcase and turned. She was facing him, both hands in the pockets of her skirt. 'I'm a journalist, Hugo. I told you, I'm a pro like you, and I've a job to do. I can't leave here tonight. I've got to stay around. I've got to talk to the others, pick up the buzz—'

'The buzz about me?'

'No, darling, not about you. But about what Playfair will do now. I just can't run off to—'

'To be with me?'

'Now listen Hugo.'

'That's what I said to Jonathan Playfair. Listen, I said. Listen to me. But he wouldn't.'

He walked past her towards the door, his briefcase in his hand. 'And I don't think I'm going to listen to you.'

'Hugo, don't get mad at me. You must understand I *can't* leave now.'

'I'll send Isles to pick up my things.' He was at the door. 'Write a good article, Virginia. Make it as bitchy as I'm sure only you can make it. Make it very bitchy about the sacked barrister. And while you're writing about him, put in what he was like in the sack. They'll like that in New York.'

He slammed the door behind him. A quarter of an hour later he was in his car driving fast for London.

At Pembroke House Jonathan was seated at his desk when Mason showed in Harold Benson. James and Mary were sitting side by side on the sofa.

'Come in, Mr Benson,' Jonathan said. 'We're having a family conference.'

Mary was looking down at her hands, twisting the rings on her fingers.

'About that bloody awful scene in court,' said James.

'It had to be done, James.'

'I don't see why. The fellow came all the way from London and everyone says he's the best there is. Now you've got rid of him. I really don't understand you, Jonathan. Do you, Mary?'

'What'll happen now?' Mary said, still looking down at her hands twisting in her lap.

'As I told you, I shall conduct my own defence.'

'Isn't there something they say about a damn fool being his own lawyer?' said James. He shot out his legs and thrust his hands deep into his trouser pockets. 'The whole thing's hell, and it's getting worse.'

'I had always planned to conduct my own defence, even after Mr Benson brought in Mr Shelbourne.'

'It was essential to have counsel,' Harold said.

'It was. You were right. I needed counsel to get bail. I couldn't, in person, have applied for the exceptional step of being granted bail on a charge of murder. That would have been too difficult for my former colleagues on the bench. Only counsel of standing could do that. That was why I didn't veto his coming. And Mr Shelbourne did it very well. But I was never going to keep him and I could not dispense with Mr Shelbourne's services before the trial because I knew the application for bail had to be renewed at the trial. So I had to choose my time. I suspected that Mr Shelbourne, in order to make a personal show, would not resist attacking the prosecution witnesses, which was quite unnecessary. I might have dismissed him after the nurse's evidence but I thought he'd probably also attack the doctor. At what I judged was the appropriate time I stopped him.'

'You certainly did. You had everyone jumping out of their skins,' said James. 'Basildon nearly fell off his chair. That at least would have made for a laugh.'

'Don't be silly, James,' said Mary.

'Well, you certainly made a public ass of Hugo Shelbourne,' James added.

'It had to be done in the way I did it in order to mark, as I hope it later will, the difference between the advocate and' – he looked at Harold – 'myself. I hope that will help me with the jury.'

Harold shook his head. 'So it was quite deliberate?'

'Yes, Mr Benson, it was quite deliberate. I know that Mr Shelbourne will suffer, but I couldn't help that. For me the stakes are very high.'

'They are for all of us,' said James. 'And what was all that in Symes' statement about us all being ruined because of Lloyd's? First I've heard of it.'

Jonathan stood up. 'Later, James, later. It's not important now.'

'It's bloody important, if it's true,' said James.

'I shall explain, I promise you. But later. Now, Mr Benson and I have some technical matters to discuss. I'll see you, both at dinner.'

'Well, you seem to have got back your appetite,' James grumbled. 'I hope you can make some sense of what he's up to,' he said to Harold as he and Mary went to the door. 'I can't.'

Jonathan led Harold to his desk, 'I want you to take care of these and bring them to court tomorrow.' He handed Harold a bundle of documents and a small square box. They talked for some time, and then Harold returned to his office.

At half past eight he entered the dining-room of the hotel and walked across the room to where Richard Bracton and Brian Graves were still at their dinner.

'Good evening, Mr Benson,' said Bracton, half-rising. 'Will you have a glass of wine with us?'

'I will, thank you.' Benson sat. 'I can confirm that Sir Jonathan will be defending himself from now on, and I shall be helping him.'

'I expected that.'

'He asked me to tell you that there'll be some more cross-examination of the doctor, but none of Mr Fraser, the technician who examined the apparatus on the day after Colonel Trelawney died.'

Bracton looked at Graves. 'So he doesn't challenge the evidence that the apparatus was working properly?'

'No, there's no challenge to that.'

'That means,' added Graves, 'that he accepts that the apparatus had a mechanism which made it impossible for more than 2 milligrams an hour of diamorphine to pass through the syringe?'

'That is so.'

Bracton and Graves again exchanged glances. 'Which means . . .' Bracton began. Harold Benson completed his unfinished sentence. 'Sir Jonathan accepts that the drug could only have entered Colonel Trelawney's body by someone manually pressing and emptying the syringe.'

Bracton drank some of his wine. 'He understands criminal law and procedure well enough, so I don't need to spell out the implications of that admission.'

'No. He understands. He also told me to say that he would like Nurse Langley recalled for further cross-examination.'

Bracton nodded. 'Very well.'

'There's no challenge to the evidence of the cause of death nor to the fingerprint evidence.'

'Then we shall be galloping along.' said Bracton. 'All that remains of the prosecution case is the police evidence.'

'Yes,' said Benson. Bracton and Graves waited but Harold said no more. Bracton asked, 'Is that everything?'

'He would like Mr Symes, the solicitor, to attend for cross-examination because he has, after all, one or two questions he would like to put to Mr Symes.'

'I believe Mr Symes is abroad on a business trip, in Japan I seem to remember. He arranged the trip when he was told he was not required to give evidence.'

'Sir Jonathan said that if you can't get hold of Mr Symes immediately he would be quite content for Mr Symes to be interposed during the evidence for the defence.'

'We'll get him here as soon as possible. From what you say, it sounds as if the defence may take some time?'

'It may, yes. He has some witnesses.'

Bracton again exchanged glances with Graves. 'You look tired, Mr Benson,' he said.

'I am. I'm not used to all this. I shall be very glad when it is over.'

No-one spoke. Harold seemed to be lingering, looking over his shoulder, waiting for something. They heard voices, and Virginia with a party of three men came into the dining-room. Talking noisily, they went to a table in the corner. Harold turned to look at them. 'I have one more task before I go home,' he said. Then he rose from the table and bowed. 'Thank you, for the wine. It was very welcome.'

Bracton and Graves watched as he crossed the room to Virginia's table. As he approached she was throwing back her head, laughing. They saw Harold stop at her table, but they were too far away to hear what was said. 'Shelbourne's lady friend,' said Bracton, 'hasn't lost much time in finding consolation.'

'Excuse me interrupting.' Virginia and her companions looked up at the untidy figure in the shabby duffel coat and college scarf. He took his spectacles from his pocket and put them on. 'Could you tell me,' he asked, 'where I might find Mr Leslie Bramley, the crime correspondent of the *Globe* newspaper?'

'That's me,' said Bramley cheerfully. They had just come from several hours in the bar. 'What can I do for you, old son?'

'I am to give you this,' said Harold, handing Bramley a paper. 'Goodnight,' he added as he shambled out of the dining-room.

Bramley was studying the document. 'What is it, Leslie?' Virginia asked.

'Christ!' he said. 'Playfair requires me to give evidence! It's a subpoena.'

14

NEXT morning Virginia took her place early. She watched Bracton and Graves standing in the front row of counsels' benches talking. Today there would be no sauntering entry by Hugo Shelbourne acting his part for the jury; no Isles laying out his principal's papers on the desk; no neat and tidy Andrew Benjamin trying to keep the peace. Without Shelbourne the court seemed empty.

When the judge had taken his place he looked at Jonathan in the dock. 'I understand you have decided to defend yourself,' he said stiffly.

'I have, my lord.'

'And you wish your solicitor to assist you?'

'I do. He is a Mr Benson.'

'Then Mr Benson may take a place in counsel's bench immediately below the dock.'

Harold, briefcase in hand, left the solicitors' table where he had been sitting next to Patrick Trent, the Crown Prosecution Service solicitor for the prosecution. He slid past Bracton and Graves to the place the judge had indicated. To hand anything to Jonathan, or take anything from him, Benson would have to stretch up and Jonathan to lean over the edge of the dock. He placed his papers and the box Jonathan had given him on the desk in front of him.

The judge went on: 'And you want Miss Langley recalled for further cross-examination?'

'I do.'

Bracton stood. 'My lord, Miss Langley cannot be here until after the luncheon adjournment. After the doctor, I propose to call the police evidence, Inspector Johnson, if that is aceptable.'

'Well?' Graham said to Jonathan.

'Yes,' Jonathan replied.

'But first you have some questions for the doctor?'

'I have.'

'Very well, you may proceed.'

Dr Mitchell was already in the witness-box, leaning against one side, his file on the ledge in front of him. He looked with hostility at Jonathan, who turned towards him. Virginia leaned forward, her chin upon her hand.

'May I say at the outset, doctor, that I am sorry you were questioned as you were yesterday?'

'You must ask questions and not, at this stage, make statements,' Graham said sharply, not looking up from his notebook.

Graves whispered, 'It was a question.' Bracton shrugged.

'Will you take it from me, doctor, that to question you, as you were yesterday afternoon was not in accordance with my instructions?'

The doctor nodded briefly.

'You said yesterday that the apparatus itself could not have discharged the amount of drug which led to the death of the deceased?'

'I did.'

'So the discharge must have been by a human hand deliberately pressing the head of the syringe?'

'Yes.'

'And on Friday June 20th you informed the deceased that if all the drug in the system was pumped into his body he would be, as you called it, a goner?'

'I did.'

'Did you tell him the amount of drug which would make him a goner?'

The doctor thought for a moment. 'Yes, we were talking, laughing almost, about the amount of drug that was in the system. I think I said that if all of three or even two days' supply of drug was pumped into him that would make him, as I said jocularly, a goner. Colonel Trelawney had only been receiving 2 milligrams an hour, so I was sure that a single sudden dose of, say, 168 milligrams would have killed him, as indeed it did.'

'He knew, did he not, that the apparatus of itself was only capable of discharging 2 milligrams an hour into him?'

'He did. I told him so.'

'At noon on Friday 20th you filled the system with 220 grams, so by two o'clock on the afternoon of Saturday June 21st he would know that 168 milligrams remained.'

'I imagine he would, if he had chosen to make the calculation.'

'Who else had you told that 168 milligrams emptied into him in a single dose would, in his circumstances, have been fatal?'

'There was no-one else there to tell, except of course Nurse Langley,' said the witness, puzzled. Then, indignantly, 'You're not suggesting—'

'No, doctor, I'm not suggesting that Nurse Langley had anything to do with the discharge of the diamorphine.'

'Then I don't understand.'

'You and I, doctor, have never met, have we?'

'No, of course not. I have never seen you before in my life, except in this court.'

'The deceased knew from what you had told him that the system contained what could amount to a fatal dose of diamorphine. But you never told me that, because we had never met. Isn't that right.'

'Suicide,' whispered Bracton to Graves.

'No, I'd never seen you so I couldn't have told you,' the doctor replied testily, 'but any reasonably intelligent person must have appreciated that the sudden infusion of such a massive amount of drug would have had very serious consequences. Obviously such a dose is likely to be fatal.'

'What do you mean by "obviously"?'

'Well, you could have known. Colonel Trelawney could have told you what I had told him.'

'Could have?'

'Yes. And may I say that if you're suggesting Colonel Trelawney administered that drug himself with the intention of doing away with himself, I can only say that, during the time I was treating him, he never evinced the slightest indication that he contemplated taking his own life.'

'Not to you?'

'Certainly not. And he said to the nurse, in my presence, that she must make sure that the apparatus, as he put it, did not go ape.'

'At any rate we can be certain, can we not, doctor, that on June 21st Colonel Trelawney was well aware that the amount of diamorphine available if administered in a sudden, single dose, could be fatal?'

'Yes.'

'Thank you.' And Jonathan sat down.

Bracton rose to re-examine. 'It is now being suggested, as I understand it, that Colonel Trelawney might have administered the fatal dose himself. Tell me, when you left Colonel Trelawney at 1.00 p.m. on Friday June 20th, what kind of mood was he in?'

'Hearty, cheerful. As he always was with me.'

'Did he appear to you to be in any way depressed?'

'Not in the least. In fact the opposite. He was in excellent form, making jokes, teasing.'

'When you left him on the Friday, was he expecting a visitor on the next day, Saturday?'

'Not that I was aware.'

'Did he say anything about seeing you again?'

'Yes. He said he'd see me on Monday and hoped all was set for him to go into hospital on Thursday June 26th as he was looking forward to getting there and later to St Edward's, especially as he said that now all the bills would be paid and he had no financial worries.'

'So he never gave you any indication that he was contemplating taking his own life?'

'Never, ever. He was brave and cheerful about his illness, and optimistic about the treatment in hospital and his future.'

'Would he have been capable in his condition of pressing the syringe and administering that dose to himself?'

The doctor did not immediately answer. Then he said, 'Yes, he would have been capable of doing that, but I have absolutely no reason to think that he did.'

'It has been pointed out to you that on June 21st, after Miss

Langley had gone out, the accused was alone in that house with Colonel Trelawney?'

'Yes.'

'And you said that any intelligent person would have known that a sudden injection of a massive dose of diamorphine can be fatal?'

'Certainly. To receive instantly 168 milligrams in a single shot when the normal dose had been 2 milligrams an hour would obviously have the very gravest consequences. No-one could contemplate pumping into another that amount of opiate unless they had in mind inflicting death, or at the least very grave harm.'

That disposes of manslaughter, thought Graham. For murder the prosecution needed to prove that Playfair had the intent either to cause death or grievous bodily harm. By that answer the doctor had shown that if Playfair had pressed down the head of the syringe he must have had the requisite intent to cause death or sufficient harm. That would warrant a conviction for murder.

'I'd like to repeat, with all the emphasis that I can,' the doctor added, 'that I am quite convinced that when I left him at lunchtime on Friday he had not the slightest thought of committing suicide.'

To Bracton's irritation the judge now intervened. 'We have heard from Nurse Langley that she had the impression that, when Colonel Trelawney told her on the Saturday that Sir Jonathan Playfair was going to visit, his mood changed, and he appeared to her to be alarmed at the prospect. Tell me, what kind of tone had he used when he spoke to you about Sir Jonathan and the trust funds?'

He shouldn't have asked that, there could be objection to that, Bracton thought. But none came. Jonathan, now sitting in the dock, merely smiled. Virginia noticed the smile.

'I got the impression,' the doctor said, 'that he did not like Sir Jonathan Playfair.'

'If,' said Bracton hastily, lest the judge continue, 'that syringe was emptied manually on the afternoon of Saturday June 21st during the time the nurse was out of the house, it could only have been done by the deceased himself or . . .' And he paused. 'Or by whom?'

'Or by the only other person who, I understand, was then in that house. The accused,' the doctor replied emphatically.

Bracton turned to the judge. 'I have no further questions.'

'Thank you, doctor. You may leave the witness-box,' Graham said. 'But please stay in case you are needed further.'

'Detective-Inspector Johnson,' Bracton said.

The inspector was a square, heavily-built man in his early forties, with sandy hair and a fresh complexion, rather over-weight, and short so that when he stood in the witness-box he appeared truncated. He gave his evidence professionally with an air of bluff and open frankness, beginning with a description of what he had found when first he had been called to Colonel Trelawney's house. Then, with constant reference to his notebook, he gave details of the investigation and the interviews he had with the accused. Although the accused had admitted being with the deceased before and when Colonel Trelawney died, he said nothing of what had happened while he had been with Colonel Trelawney, except that the deceased had fallen into a deep and heavy sleep and, in the accused's words, 'ceased to breathe and passed away.'

Nor had the accused given any explanation of why he had left the house without informing anyone that Colonel Trelawney had died. When the cause of Colonel Trelawney's death had been confirmed by the post-mortem, and when he, the witness, had confronted the accused and told him that the post-mortem showed that death was due to diamorphine poisoning as a result of a massive discharge of the drug, the accused had merely nodded. When he told the accused that his fingerprints had been identified on the dial of the regulator on the bedside table, on the apparatus and the syringe as well as on the black tin box which was standing on the dresser in the deceased's bedroom, the accused again made no reply. Later, on July 7th, as a result of a message from Mr Symes, he took possession of the letter, Exhibit 6, which bore the postmark noon on June 21st. The papers were then passed to the Director of Public Prosecutions, and the decision was reached to charge Jonathan Playfair with the murder of David Trelawney,

Bracton sat down, and Jonathan rose to cross-examine. To get to his feet he had to pull himself up, using the rail of the dock and his stick to help him.

'We had met before you came to my house to interview me about the death of Colonel Trelawney, had we not?'

'We had not met before, although I'd seen you in the course of your previous official duties.'

'You are right. We had not actually met, but we had seen each other, had we not?'

'I had seen you on the bench, yes.'

'On at least one occasion you were witness in a case in which I was the judge?'

'I was.'

'Was that the case of Regina v. Joseph Stringer, which was tried at the Crown Court at Iddersley five years ago?'

The witness put his notebook back into his inside pocket of his smart blue suit and straightened the sides of the jacket. 'It was,' he said.

'Were you then a detective-constable?'

'I was.'

'Was Joseph Stringer accused of murder?'

'He was.'

'The murder of whom?'

The witness looked at Graham on the bench, and then straight ahead of him, his face firmly turned away from his questioner. 'A police officer.'

'Was that police officer called Simon, Stanley Simon?'

'He was.'

'Was Police-Constable Simon brutally hacked to death with an axe in the course of attempting to quell a riot on the James Maxton estate in Southampton?'

'That is correct.' The detective-inspector still had his face turned away from Jonathan.

'Was Joseph Stringer charged with PC Simon's murder?'

'He was.'

'Was the name of the lawyer from the Crown Prosecution Service in charge of assembling the evidence and preparing the prosecution of Joseph Stringer for the murder of PC Simon, Patrick Trent?'

'It was.'

'The same officer from the Crown Prosecution Service who is in charge of this case and who is sitting in front of Mr Bracton?'

'Yes.'

'To return to the case of Joseph Stringer, was the murdered police officer a colleague of yours?'

'He was.'

'An intimate, personal friend?'

'Yes, we joined the Force at the same time. I was the best man at his wedding and godfather to his daughter, who was born three months before he was murdered.'

'And were you gravely distressed by the brutal, vicious murder of your friend?'

'I was. It was a horrible death – and a terrible crime.'

'What is the relevance of all this?' said Graham abruptly.

Jonathan did not at first reply. 'The relevance,' he said at last, 'will become clear in a moment – if your lordship will allow me to continue. I am nearly finished with the case of Stringer.'

'I shall certainly not permit you to continue this line of questioning unless you explain to me the relevance of all these questions. So please do so.'

Graham had spoken very sharply. Behind his hand, Bracton winced. He'll alienate the jury if he appears to be bullying. But the judge went on. 'I wish to know to what issue these questions are directed before I allow this line of questioning to continue.'

Jonathan was silent for a moment. Then for the first time he raised his voice. 'These questions, as you will learn if you bear with me for a further moment,' he said, almost in the same tones as those used by the judge, 'are directed to the issue of this witness's credit and veracity. There is a conflict between this witness and myself as to what was said during one of his interviews with me. So I am perfectly entitled to ask these questions. It goes to his credit.' He paused and then said, equally sharply, 'Now may I go on?'

Brian Graves, sitting beside Bracton, bit his lip. Bracton stared stolidly to his front. The Stringer trial. He was beginning to remember.

'Very well,' said Graham after a pause.

'The trial of Joseph Stringer for the murder of your colleague and close friend, PC Simon, did not run its full course, did it?'

'No, it did not.'

'It never went beyond the conclusion of the evidence for the prosecution?'

'No, it did not.'

'The defence was not even called upon because the judge ruled at the end of the prosecution's case that there was no case to answer and directed the jury to bring in a verdict of Not Guilty. Is that not correct?'

'It is.'

'The judge decided that the prosecution had not established by their evidence – their admissible evidence – that Stringer had been the person who struck the blows which killed Simon nor that Stringer was present when PC Simon was murdered. Isn't that what happened?'

'Stringer had confessed he was there and that he had done it,' said the witness stolidly, still not looking at his questioner. 'He confessed. He made a statement.'

'I did not ask you whether Stringer did or did not make a statement. Did the judge at the trial, in effect, direct there should be an acquittal?'

'Something like that.'

Graham was about to interrupt again, but he thought better of it. I should keep quiet, he said to himself. It's better if I keep quiet.

'You say Stringer confessed to the police?' Jonathan continued.

'He did.'

'Was that in the course of a series of interviews with police officers?'

'Yes.'

'But the judge excluded that evidence, ruling it inadmissible, because the interviewing by police officers had been oppressive and irregular?'

'He did, but it wasn't. It was perfectly proper.'

'That is your opinion. But the fact remains that the statement, or confession, did not become part of the evidence.'

'No.'

'And Stringer, on the direction of the judge, was acquitted?'

'Yes.'

'Were you one of the team of police officers engaged in the

investigation and the questioning which the judge held was oppressive?'

The witness paused. 'I was,' he said at last.

'Were you very angry at the result of that trial and at that ruling by that judge?'

Again the witness did not immediately reply but remained staring straight ahead of him. 'Please answer.'

'I was.'

'And that case, in which Mr Trent was in charge on behalf of the Crown Prosecution Service, and in which you were one of the police officers involved, ended with Joseph Stringer walking free. Isn't that right?'

Still the witness remained silent. 'And I,' Jonathan went on, again raising his voice, 'I was the judge at that trial who was responsible for those rulings which led to Joseph Stringer being freed and acquitted of murdering your friend?'

'You were.'

'You were bitterly resentful of my conduct?'

'I thought you were wrong. I knew you were wrong. Stringer should never have gone free.'

'You held me responsible for letting go free the man you thought had brutally hacked to death your colleague and personal friend?'

'I did.'

Jonathan paused. 'Now,' he said, 'I come to July of last year, when you were in charge of the police enquiry into the death of Colonel Trelawney. During the course of that investigation did you have several consultations with Mr Trent?'

'I did. That was quite normal.'

'And eventually it was decided that an arrest was to be made?'

'Yes, after the papers in the case had been sent by Mr Trent to the Director of Public Prosecutions.'

'Did those papers include a recommendation by you and Mr Trent that a prosecution should be launched and an arrest made?'

'Yes.'

'Who made the arrest?'

'I did.'

'Was the arrest made at dawn on the morning of July 25th last, when you and your officers came to my home and woke the household by thundering on the front door?'

'We arrested you in the early morning, yes.'

'Why did you choose to come to my house at dawn to arrest me? Did you think that I would evade arrest?'

'I had my duty to do.'

'Did you?' Jonathan peered over the rail of the dock to the bench below him. 'Mr Benson,' he called out, 'will you please stand?'

Benson stood, facing the detective-inspector in the witness-box.

'You know this gentleman, do you not?'

'Yes. He's your solicitor.'

'At dawn on the morning of July 25th, when you and your officers hammered on my front door, you knew, did you not, that your superintendent, your superior officer, had arranged with my solicitor, Mr Benson, that Mr Benson and I would attend at ten o'clock at the police station when I would be arrested and formally charged? So why did you think it necessary to come five or six hours earlier and make the arrest which had been arranged for later that day?'

'There was a misunderstanding between me and the superintendent.'

'Was there? Or was it because you wanted to have the glory of making the arrest yourself and of making it as humiliating and as public as possible?'

'I know nothing about glory or humiliation. When a person is suspected of a crime, it doesn't make any difference who they are or what they once were. An arrest has to be made. That's all.'

'Why at dawn?'

'That is a time when I was certain we would find you.'

'You knew perfectly well where I was. There was no question of your having to find me. The arrangement for my arrest and charging had been made by your superior with my solicitor, who was to bring me to the police station at 10 o'clock that morning. Why did you interfere with those arrangements and take the matter into your own hands?'

'I've explained. There was a misunderstanding. I had not been informed.'

'Why were the press and the television crews at my home at dawn on that morning?'

'I have no responsibility for the media.'

'Weren't you responsible for the arrival of television crews and photographers at my house at dawn on that morning to witness and record my arrest by you?'

The witness did not reply but stared stolidly ahead of him.

'I repeat my question. Were not you responsible for the presence of the media at my home at dawn?'

'I am not responsible for the media.'

'They were there in force, weren't they?'

'I saw some of them there.'

'Only some?'

'Several perhaps.'

'And where did you see them?'

'At the gate to the drive of your house.'

'And, at the gate, did you not tell the police driver to stop so that photographs could be taken?'

'I did nothing of the kind. The driver had to stop.'

'The gate was open. Didn't you tell the driver to stop at the gate?'

'I do not recollect saying anything of the kind.'

'I suggest that you ordered the car to stop so that the press could get plenty of pictures of the former judge sitting in the police car beside you. Isn't that right?'

'No,' the policeman replied, but he shifted uncomfortably in the witness-box.

'Are you saying the press were there by chance? By coincidence?'

'I told you, I have no control over what they do and where they go. Perhaps they had a tip-off. There are always leaks when arrangements have to be made; officers have to be warned, cars booked. Many knew what was going to happen.'

'Your superior officer didn't, did he? He'd arranged for the arrest and charge to be made at ten o'clock in the police station, hadn't he?'

'He may have. I have said, three times, that there was an unfortunate misunderstanding between him and me.'

'The media had been told by you that you were going to arrest me at dawn, hadn't they? And it was you, Inspector Johnson, wasn't it, who tipped off the press to make sure the arrest was done with the maximum of publicity – for me, and for you?'

'Certainly not.'

'My lord,' said Jonathan, speaking now to the bench, 'I ask that Mr Leslie Bramley stand so that the witness can see him.'

As Jonathan spoke the name a flutter broke out in the bench reserved for the press. Bramley looked up, startled.

'Who is Mr Bramley?' Graham asked.

'He is the chief crime correspondent of the tabloid newspaper the *Globe*, and since the trial began he has been sitting in the press bench immediately beneath you.'

'If he is present,' Graham said to the clerk of the court, 'ask Mr Bramley to stand.'

But Bramley was already on his feet. Jonathan said to the witness, 'You know who this is, don't you?'

'I have met him, yes,' the detective-inspector replied.

'Thank you, Mr Bramley,' Jonathan said politely. Bramley sank back into his seat. 'Christ,' he whispered under his breath to his neighbour, 'what's the bugger up to?'

'Did you ever speak to Mr Bramley during the course of your enquiry into the death of Colonel Trelawney?'

'I may have spoken to him. He was interested in several cases we have under enquiry.'

'And the Trelawney case? Was he interested in the Trelawney enquiry?'

'He became interested, yes.'

'Because of what you told him?'

'I don't know how a journalist works. He became interested, that's all I know.'

'During the weeks prior to your dawn arrest, which was recorded so extensively by the media, were there not many references in Mr Bramley's newspaper to the progress of the police enquiry into Colonel Trelawney's death?'

'There may have been. The press became interested. That's all I knew.'

'And did not those references frequently refer to me?'

'I do not remember.'

'Did not the *Globe* call for an arrest, and suggest that someone was being protected, someone with important legal friends in high places?'

'I don't remember. I was busy doing my job. That's all I can say.'

'Is it, inspector? Was it not you who tipped off Mr Bramley and fed Mr Bramley daily with information because you were determined that you would, as they say, get me?'

'All I did was my duty. This was just another job.'

'Was it? The arrest of the judge who you thought responsible for the acquittal of the man you believed had so brutally murdered your friend? Was that to you just another job?'

'I acted as I thought right, and with advice from Mr Trent's office.'

'Does that mean that you and Mr Trent, both of whom were involved in the Stringer case, acted together in the Trelawney case, or the Playfair case, as it became?'

'As I said. I worked with Mr Trent. It was my duty to do so.'

'After the Stringer acquittal as a result of my direction, did you not widely complain about the result?'

'I may have said that I considered Stringer was guilty, if that's what you mean.'

'Did you say that repeatedly to your colleagues and to anyone who'd listen to you?'

'I may have said that to some of my colleagues.'

'And you blamed me, the judge at the Stringer trial.'

'Perhaps.'

'And you said this repeatedly to Mr Bramley?'

'I may have.'

'Mr Bramley is the chief crime correspondent of the *Globe*, a newspaper which I once had the occasion to fine £250,000 for contempt of court and which thereafter regularly criticised me as a judge. Did Mr Bramley tell you that?'

'They weren't alone in criticising you when you were a judge, but I can't remember if Mr Bramley spoke about that.'

Jonathan paused. Then he went on very quietly, 'So when you began the enquiry into the death of Colonel Trelawney, you had no love for me, had you?'

'I don't know what you mean, no love for you. I had my duty to do.'

'As did Mr Trent?'

'I'm sure he did his professional duty.'

'Did it give you great satisfaction to find yourself enquiring into and finally arresting the judge who had let go free the man you thought was the murderer of your friend?'

'It was certainly unusual, investigating the behaviour of a former judge.'

'You first came to interview me about the death of Colonel Trelawney on July 25th?'

The detective-inspector took out his notebook from his inside pocket and opened it. 'I did,' he said.

'By then you knew I was the last person to have been with Colonel Trelawney while he was alive?'

'Yes.'

'On that first visit you asked me what had happened when I was in the room?'

'I did.'

'I told you that I had arrived at 2.00 p.m., the nurse left the house at 2.30, the colonel and I talked and I left at 4.30.'

'You did.'

'And I told you that when I left Colonel Trelawney had by then passed away.'

'Yes, and I asked you why you had not immediately informed someone that David Trelawney had died. You replied that you didn't know why, that you just left. I then said that the death would be further investigated.'

'On that first occasion when you came to see me I told you that David Trelawney had dropped into a heavy sleep, his breathing had become very heavy, then stopped, and he passed away?'

'You did. I next returned on July 27th, accompanied again, as I had been on July 25th, by Detective-Constable Packer. By that time I had interviewed the nurse and the doctor and seen the solicitor, Mr Symes, from whom I had taken possesion of the letter, Exhibit 6, written on June 21st by the deceased. I had also identified that certain fingerprints were on the syringe and on the tin deed box which DC Packer took. I also asked you if you had removed anything from that house on June 21st and you replied, "Nothing".'

'Do you accept the police officer's account of that interview?' Graham asked Jonathan.

'I do. So far.'

'So far?'

'Yes, so far.' Jonathan turned back to the witness. 'When you were about to leave, when you were still with me and your colleague was already in the hall, did I not speak to you further?'

'I do not recollect your saying anything further.' He held out his notebook, pointing it at Jonathan. 'I have nothing in my book.'

'I didn't expect that you would. But I suggest that I told you Colonel Trelawney had been a very brave and distinguished soldier and I hoped it need not become public that he had taken his own life in my presence by injecting the diamorphine into himself.'

'I do not recollect your ever saying that, then or later.'

'No, inspector, I didn't think you would. In your determination to see me stand trial you have deliberately omitted that, haven't you?'

'I have not. I don't remember your saying that. In fact I'm certain you didn't.'

'I told you that Colonel Trelawney had killed himself, and you know that I did.'

'I don't and you didn't. Nor did you when I came the third time on July 30th.'

'Yes, your third visit. Let us see what you knew at that time. First, that David Trelawney had told the nurse that I had insisted on coming to visit him on June 21st, and the nurse had told you that that had disturbed him?'

'That it had scared him.'

'Second, you had the letter in which David Trelawney wrote that he feared me, even that I might put a pillow over his face to hurry him off; that he didn't trust me; that I'd like him out of the way?'

'Yes.'

'Third, my fingerprints were on the tin deed box, the apparatus and on the head of the syringe?'

'Yes.'

'And, knowing all that, you were convinced that I had killed David Trelawney?'

'I had good grounds for believing you were responsible for the murder of David Trelawney.'

'And when you came to interview me again on July 27th, I suggest, you made that perfectly clear?'

'I may have.'

'And you did not disguise your personal satisfaction at having gathered evidence which you thought pointed to my guilt?'

'At the time I was satisfied with the progress of the investigation. I may have made that clear.'

'At that third interview, because of your aggressive attitude and conduct, isn't it right that I said that I declined to answer any more of your questions?'

'I don't know the reason why you didn't say anything – that'll be for the jury. All I know is that you didn't provide me with any further explanation of what happened when you were with Colonel Trelawney before and when he died.'

'I told you I was not responsible for Colonel Trelawney's death.'

'You did not.'

'I had already told you at the second interview that Colonel Trelawney had killed himself by injecting the drug into his own body, and I told you at the third interview that I was not responsible for his death.'

'You did not.'

'I suggest you are lying.'

'I'm certainly not lying.'

'I suggest that then, as you are here today, you were motivated by the desire to see me brought to trial and convicted of murder partly because of your bitterness over what had happened during the trial of Joseph Stringer?'

'That is not so.'

'And I suggest you are lying when you deny I told you that David Trelawney injected himself with the drug that killed him?'

'I am not lying.' The detective-inspector now leaned over the witness-box towards Jonathan. 'And you tell us why, after the colonel died, you ran away. If you had nothing to do with his death, why did you run off without telling a soul what had happened? You tell the jury that. You ran away after that man died out of panic at what you'd done. Because you'd killed him.'

Jonathan lifted his head higher, then lowered it and looked at the policeman. 'You are right when you say I ran away, in so far as a man of my age with my legs can run away,' he said quietly. 'But you are lying when you deny that I told you that David Trelawney had killed himself.'

And then, very slowly, he sat down. Richard Bracton was whispering to Brian Graves sitting beside him. then he rose to his feet.

'The accused,' he said, 'has made some allegations, apart from those he has made about the conduct of the detective-inspector, which appear to involve the Crown Prosecution Service. I would like to take instructions about these allegations from the Director of Public Prosecutions. May I, therefore, postpone my re-examination of this witness until I have had instructions from the DPP in London? To avoid any waste of the court's time, at this stage I can in the meantime recall Nurse Langley.'

'I was about to adjourn for lunch,' said Graham. 'Would you be ready to re-examine after the adjournment?'

'I shall have to communicate with London. It may take a little time. I would prefer to postpone the re-examination until tomorrow.'

'Very well. I shall adjourn now, and Miss Langley can be recalled after lunch.'

Graham rose and left the court.

'Why the devil didn't they warn us Johnson had been one of the officers in the Stringer case,' said Bracton to Graves as they gathered up their papers.

'Trent,' said Graves.

As Virginia left the court she thought that Hugo, for all his swagger, couldn't have done that. Not like the old man had done it.

Colonel Basildon and his wife went again to the County Club. 'What did you think of that?' he said when he had ordered a pink gin.

'Rum,' she said. 'Nasty bit of work, that copper.'

Graham, alone in his room at the court, drank coffee but ate nothing. I must be careful, he warned himself. I must be careful.

15

AS Sylvia Langley mounted the steps to the witness-box on this
occasion she was still nervous, but not as nervous as before.
She was, however, very conscious that everyone now knew what
she had been doing in the White Hart on the afternoon of Saturday
June 21st. It's none of their business, she kept saying to herself.
When the police car had come in the morning and she'd been told
she had to return to the court, her heart had sunk. 'Why?' she had
protested. 'Why do they want me again?'

'All I know is I'm to bring you back,' the police driver had
said.

Detective-Constable Packer met her at the door of the court.
'They've broken for lunch. Do you want anything to eat?'

She shook her head. All she wanted was to get it over. 'What's it
all about?' she asked Packer. 'I've told them all I know. Why've I
had to come back?'

'He wants to ask you some questions.' Packer saw the look on
her face. 'No,' he went on, 'not the barrister. He's gone. It's the
old man himself, the man you met at the house before he did in
the colonel. Now he's trying to say the colonel did it himself.'

'Did what?'

'Killed himself, with the drug.'

'That's rubbish.'

'Well, you tell them that.'

Now she waited, her heart thudding, her hands gripping tightly
the edge of the witness-box as they had two days before. Graham
turned towards her. 'Thank you for coming back so promptly,

Miss Langley. There are some questions which the prisoner wishes to ask you. Remember you are still under oath.'

He turned towards Jonathan. The revelations concerning the behaviour of the police had disturbed him. He hadn't liked what he'd heard; nor, he thought, had the jury. But it couldn't alter the facts in the case against Playfair. So he addressed him in the same cool tone. 'You may begin,' he said.

Jonathan rose slowly and awkwardly from his chair. 'On June 21st, Miss Langley, when you let me into the house, you were not pleased to see me, were you?'

'No, I was not.'

'Why was that?'

'Because the colonel didn't want to see you.'

'Why did you think that he didn't?'

'Because of the way he spoke when he said you were coming.'

'What way was that?'

'As I said last time, he was upset. Before then he'd been laughing and joking as he always did. But not after he knew you were coming. He changed then. He was scared, I thought, because you were coming to see him. He didn't want you to come.'

Jonathan's voice was quiet, almost gentle. She wasn't frightened of him as she had been of Shelbourne. He looked, she thought, very frail, but she remembered what he'd done to the colonel. She'd do well this time, Bracton thought.

'And that happened, you say, after the telephone call?' Jonathan asked.

'Yes. Your telephone call changed everything.'

'The call he received?'

'Yes.'

'Did you hear him make a call that morning, an outgoing call?'

'No, but earlier, when he was reading the papers, he talked about the racing at Brighton and said he must phone his bookie. He loved the racing. But I don't know if he ever did.'

'You didn't hear him make a call?'

'No.'

'Did you yourself hear the telephone ring that morning?'

'I did. The colonel answered it from his bed. I was downstairs.'

'Did you come into the room while he was speaking on the telephone?'

'No. When I came into the room he had the telephone still in his hand and I could hear the buzzing. That was when his mood changed.'

'Why do you say that?'

'Well, when I came into the room he never said anything. Usually he made some kind of joke, about me or about what I was doing. I was over at the dresser tidying things when I heard him sigh and say something like "Oh, God". I turned round, and he was staring out of the window. I asked if everything was all right, and he didn't look at me but said something about not looking forward to the afternoon. "Why not?" I asked, and he said someone was coming whom he didn't want to see. Then he wrote the letter and asked me to get it posted and I gave it to Mrs Jackson.'

'When I arrived at the house at about 2.00 p.m. you and I had some talk and then you took me up to Colonel Trelawney's room and left us alone. Isn't that right?'

'Yes. I told you not to upset him.'

'So you did. Then, about fifteen minutes later, I came to your room?'

'Yes.'

'I told you the colonel had suggested you take a few hours off?'

'Yes, and I said I wouldn't take that from you, I'd want to hear it from his own lips. And you said there's no need, that he had sent you to tell me.'

'Didn't you want to have a few hours off?'

'Of course I did, but because I knew he didn't want to see you I said I'd only go if the colonel himself told me I could. So I went to his room, and you followed, and I asked him if he'd said I could go out and he said you'd said you'd be here with him. All the time he was looking at you. I said, "Are you quite sure?" And then you said "Yes, nurse, you take an hour or so off. I'll be here." And the colonel said to me, "yes, you go".'

'And you were very pleased at the chance of getting out of the house for a time?'

'Well' – she coloured a little – 'I was. I thought I'd be on duty all weekend.' Then she added fiercely, 'But it was you who wanted me out of the house. It wasn't him. He did it because of you. He was scared of you. I could see that by his face, and if you're suggesting he killed himself, that's rubbish, utter rubbish. He wouldn't have done that, not Colonel Trelawney. He kept saying to me he was going to fight his illness and he was going to win. That's what he said to me, often.'

Jonathan stood quite still and silent. Graham looked up from his notes. 'You think,' Jonathan said at last, 'that he didn't want me to visit him and that he was scared of me?'

'Yes. Scared before you came and scared when you had come.'

Jonathan smiled at her. 'Am I such a scary person?'

She stared back at him defiantly. Then she shook her head. 'Not to me – but you were to him. I just knew from how he seemed after the telephone call. He didn't want you to be with him.'

'Then why did you leave us alone?'

She didn't answer. For the first time she looked as she had when Shelbourne had been questioning her, as though she was on the point of tears. 'I never should have left you with him. I've told myself that, time and time again ever since it happened. If I hadn't left you with him, the colonel would be alive. It's all my fault. It's my fault for leaving you with him.'

She took a handkerchief from her bag and began to dab her eyes. Silly bitch, thought Virginia. Jonathan waited. Then he said very gently, 'No, Miss Langley, it was not your fault. It was not your fault at all.'

He waited while she put the handkerchief back in her bag. 'Would you be surprised to learn,' he asked, 'that it was Colonel Trelawney who suggested you go out because he wanted to be alone with me and didn't want to be disturbed?'

'I don't believe it. It was you who wanted to be alone with him, and now we know why.'

Jonathan looked at her sadly. Then he said, 'While you were nursing the colonel, had you ever looked inside the tin deed box which stood on the dresser?'

'No, never. I never opened it, nor saw it open.'

'Was it locked?'

'Yes. The colonel made some joke about it. He said I was to be careful of it when I was dusting as it was very precious. "There are

169

some," he said, "who'd like to get their hands on what's in it." I said, "Was it full of the Crown Jewels?" And he smiled and said it was something like that.'

Jonathan again was silent. Then he said, 'So you believe it all began, his change of mood, his anxiety or fear, after the telephone call he received. Is that right?'

'Yes. That's when it all began.'

'Before it, he was jolly and cheerful. After it, you say he acted as though he was anxious and—'

'He didn't act. He was.'

'Let me finish. He acted, I suggest, as though he was anxious and—'

'Scared. He was scared. And he wasn't acting.'

'So you keep saying. At any rate, it was after the telephone call that he wrote the letter?'

'Yes.'

'And when I came, you think it was I who suggested you slip off for a time and leave us alone?'

'Yes, I'm sure of it.'

'Quite sure?'

'Yes, I am. Quite sure.'

'As sure as you are that he was really scared when he saw me?'

'Yes.'

'As sure as you are that he didn't want to see me?'

'Yes. He didn't want you near him. I am sure of that too.'

'At the time of his death you had been with Colonel Trelawney for several days, looking after him, talking with him, joking with him?'

'Yes.'

'So you were quite used to hearing his voice?'

'How do you mean?'

'Well, you'd heard him talk so often. Do you think you'd be able to recognise his voice?'

'Of course I would.'

'If he'd been talking from the next room, you would recognise his voice?'

'Yes. What are you getting at?'

'Or when he was talking on the telephone?'

'I never heard him on the telephone. But I know his voice all right. Of course I do.'

'Then will you listen to this?'

Jonathan bent over the rail of the dock. Benson stood and handed him something. 'What have you got there?' Graham asked sharply.

Jonathan held up a grey rectangular object, about four inches long and two inches broad, held it close to his eyes and then said, 'It has stamped on it the words "Olympus Pearlcorder L 200 American microcassette recorder." It also has a cord attached to a small earpiece. When you place the recorder close to the telephone receiver, a telephone call can be heard and recorded without the caller knowing.'

Bracton stiffened. The journalists in their bench below the jury were staring up at Jonathan. A murmur arose in the court. The usher called out, 'Silence!' The noise subsided and the court became very still and quiet.

'I propose to play the tape in the recorder,' Jonathan said. 'I shall identify one of the two voices you will hear on the tape as mine, and I suggest that no-one who hears it will disagree. I shall ask the witness if she can identify the other voice. If she can, I shall ask that the recorder and the tape be admitted as an exhibit.'

Graham looked at Bracton, who rose and began, rather hesitantly, 'I am not sure of the relevance or importance of this, my lord, nor of the genuineness of the tape if there is a tape—'

Jonathan from the dock interrupted him. 'Then, before we argue about it, I suggest we see if the witness can identify the other voice on the tape.'

Graham, taken aback by the authority with which Jonathan had spoken, looked at Bracton, who shrugged and sat down. Graham turned to the witness. 'The accused, Miss Langley, wishes to see if you can identify the voice, or one of the voices, on a tape he is going to play on the recorder he has in his hand. So listen very carefully, and only speak when you are certain.'

He turned back to Jonathan. 'You may play the tape.'

Jonathan stood the small pocket recorder on the rail of the dock. He pressed the button. The courtroom was once again perfectly quiet. From the recorder, loud enough for everyone to hear, came the sound of a voice: 'Jonathan, are you there Jonathan?' There followed a pause. Then the voice again. 'This is David, speaking from home.' Again a pause. Then, again, the same voice. 'Jonathan? I want to speak to you.'

'Stop the tape,' said Graham loudly. Jonathan pressed the button and the tape stopped. The judge turned towards the witness. 'Do you recognise that voice?' he asked. She did not at first reply. Then she whispered something.

'Please speak up,' said Graham. 'Do you identify the voice that spoke those words on the tape?'

'Yes,' she said. 'It's the colonel. It's Colonel Trelawney's voice.'

'Do you say that because the voice on the tape said "This is David"? Or because you recognise the voice?'

'It's his voice,' she said. 'I recognise it.'

'You are sure?' She nodded. 'Please speak up,' Graham said.

'Yes. I'm sure. It's his voice all right. It's Colonel Trelawney's voice.'

Once again a murmer arose in the court. Graham tapped with his gavel and turned back to Jonathan. 'What do you wish to do now?'

'I wish to play the rest of the tape. It will identify when the conversation was held.'

Graham looked at Bracton to see if there was to be any objection. But Bracton stayed silent, staring straight ahead of him. 'Very well,' Graham said at last. 'You may play the rest of the tape.'

Jonathan again pressed the button on the small recorder. The same voice said again. 'Can you hear me? Is that you, Jonathan?'

Then came another voice, unmistakeably the voice of Jonathan Playfair. 'It is. What do you want?'

The first voice, the voice Nurse Langley had identified as the voice of David Trelawney, said, 'As you know, Jonathan, I'm ill, perhaps more ill than you think.'

There was silence. Then the first voice went on: 'I need to talk to you but I can't now. There's a nurse who keeps coming into the room. Will you call me back in two minutes? I'll see she goes downstairs. Call me back in two minutes. It's urgent. I must talk to you.'

Pause. Then Playfair's voice, very cool. 'Why?'

'I said I can't speak now. She's coming back into the room and I don't want her to overhear. Call back and I'll explain.'

Another pause. 'Why?'

'It's very urgent. Please call back.'

'Very well.'

Then followed the sound of the receiver being replaced. The court was now as still as the grave.

Graham broke the silence. 'Is there more?' he asked.

'There is,' said Jonathan. And the tape began again. First the ringing sound. Then Playfair's voice. 'This is Jonathan.'

'Thank you for calling back. I didn't want to be overheard and the girl's in and out of the room. She's downstairs now. I'm very ill, Jonathan, and I must see you. There's something I want you to have.'

Pause. Then. 'Are you listening, Jonathan? Are you there, Jonathan?'

'Yes, I am.'

'I've taken a lot from you over the years, Jonathan. Now I want to give you something, for a change. I've something you'll want to have.'

Pause. Again Playfair's voice, cool as before and distant. 'What is that?'

'They're planning to send me to hospital, but I am not going. Whatever the quacks say, I know I can't last much longer. And I don't want to. I don't want them messing me about. I've had enough. But before I go there are some letters, some documents I want you to have.'

'Why?'

'You should have them. I want you to have them as some return for what I've had from you. I'm sorry about all that.'

Another pause. Then Jonathan's voice. 'Why should I believe you?'

'You must. I'm not going to last, Jonathan, and these letters are all I have that I can give you. You'll want to have them. Anyhow, come and get them and judge for yourself. Some are from Nicola, and they are about you. You should have them.'

There was a long pause. Then Jonathan's voice again. 'When shall I come?'

'As soon as you can. Today would be best. The quack's away and I'll send the girl out.'

'Today?'

'Yes. I want you to come before it's too late. I'm pretty ill. I've put up a good show but I'm not going to have the quacks fiddling around and experimenting on me in the hospital. They can't do anything, I know that. Could you get here today, this afternoon?'

A pause. 'Very well, if it's so important. At what time?'

'Two o'clock?'

Again a pause. Then Playfair's voice: 'Very well. I'll come as near to two as I can.'

There followed the sound of the receiver being replaced. For a time, what seemed like a long time, the court remained silent. Then Jonathan said from the dock, 'That is all there is on the tape.' He pressed the button, turning off the recorder, and beckoned to the usher. 'I'd like this marked as an exhibit.'

The usher came and took the recorder from Jonathan and handed it to the clerk of the court sitting below the judge's bench, who passed it up to the judge. Graham turned it over in his hand, examining it. 'Mr Bracton,' he said, 'you may wish to have this checked.'

'Thank you,' said Bracton.

Graham began, now rather hesitantly, 'You are saying, Sir Jonathan' – this was the first time he had addressed the prisoner in this manner – 'You are saying . . . No,' he corrected himself, 'you will be saying that this tape is an accurate and true recording of telephone calls exchanged between you and the deceased on the morning of Saturday July 21st? Is that correct?'

'Yes. Whenever Colonel Trelawney wanted to speak to me on the telephone, I always recorded his telephone calls, for reasons I'll explain later. That was why I acquired this equipment. What you heard was the record of the last telephone calls between Colonel Trelawney and myself, on the morning of June 21st, a few hours before Colonel Trelawney killed himself.'

When he said this there was another stir among the spectators. 'Silence!' the usher called out. Graham said, 'Did you at any time play this tape to the police, or let them have it?'

Jonathan shook his head. Then he said: 'No. I had forgotten

that I still had it. At one time I had many others, but I destroyed them after Colonel Trelawney died. But this tape was still in the recorder and I'd forgotten it was still there. I only remembered after my arrest, and following my experience with the police over the arrest and having regard to the attitude of Detective-Inspector Johnson, I did not trust them.'

Graham fiddled with his pencil. 'Have the recorder and the tape ever been out of your possession since the conversation was recorded?'

'No. If the prosecution care to check they'll find it has not been tampered with, and I expect they'll also find there was only one outgoing telephone call from Colonel Trelawney's house in the morning of Saturday June 21st, and it was not to Colonel Trelawney's bookie.'

He turned back to the witness, who was again holding her handkerchief to her lips. 'That call was made to me, and you have just heard what was said.' He stopped and looked at her sadly. 'Do you understand, Miss Langley?'

She nodded and whispered, 'Yes.' Then she added, 'But why, why did he act as he did?'

Jonathan looked down. 'It all began,' he said, 'a long, long time ago.'

'That is a statement, Sir Jonathan, and not cross-examination,' Graham interrupted, but he spoke more gently than he had before. 'You will have the opportunity for explanation later.'

'You are right, of course, my lord, I shall. But as Miss Langley is here and because she blames herself, I thought Miss Langley deserved an explanation.'

He turned to the witness. 'You see, it was not your fault, Miss Langley. Nothing that happened on that afternoon was your fault. You must understand that. So, please, never, ever, blame yourself.' And, with his hands on the rail to help himself, he slowly lowered himself back on to the hard chair beside the warder in the dock.

No-one spoke. Then Graham asked, 'Have you any questions to ask the witness in re-examination, Mr Bracton?'

Bracton half-rose and said, 'No, my lord, none.'

Again there was a pause. Everyone in the courtroom, not only the lawyers, sensed that the tape had changed much, for now it was certain that it had not been Playfair who had forced himself on a reluctant and scared Trelawney; it had been Trelawney begging Playfair to come to him. But why?

Graham said, 'Who is the next witness, Mr Bracton?'

'It was to have been the solicitor, Mr Symes. The accused wishes to ask Mr Symes some questions on his statement, which has been read to the jury. However I was only warned of this last night and Mr Symes is abroad, in Tokyo. He cannot be here for at least two days, but the accused is content for him to be interposed during the case for the defence.'

'Very well. As it is nearly four o'clock, and since you may want to check the tape and consider the latest evidence, I shall adjourn now.'

In the conference room Bracton tossed his wig angrily on to the table. 'Why in heaven's name,' he said to Graves, 'did he only produce it now?'

'Do you think it's genuine?'

'It must be. I'll have it tested, but I'm sure it is.'

'Then why didn't he show it to the police?' Graves said.

'To Detective-Inspector Johnson or the superintendent Johnson had defied over the arrest? By then Playfair didn't trust any of them, and Johnson had got the press whipping up opinion against him. He must have thought if he let them get their hands on it he'd never see it again, or at least not in the same form!'

Bracton had flung himself into a chair. There was a knock on the door and Trent came in and stood uncomfortably just inside the room.

'I want to assure you,' he said, 'that I acted perfectly properly.'

Bracton got up from his chair. 'Why didn't you tell me that Johnson was one of the policemen in the Stringer case?'

'I didn't appreciate its significance—'

'You may have jeopardised the whole prosecution. Now get on to the DPP and tell him to ring me at my home in half an hour.'

As they walked to the car park Graves asked, 'Do you think Trent could've been involved?'

'I don't know. Johnson could've got at him, and I remember that the Crown Prosecution Service were as outraged as the police when Playfair directed the jury to acquit in the Stringer case. They bitterly resented his ruling on the oppressive questioning by the police which excluded the confession. That was the last case Playfair ever tried around here.'

In the Daimler on the way to the Lodgings the High Sheriff waited for the judge to speak, but as he said nothing the colonel could restrain himself no longer. He half-turned and said, 'I suppose that changes it a bit, doesn't it, judge? What happens now?'

'We just go on,' said Graham shortly.

But at the Lodgings he put through another call to the Lord Chief Jusice and told him about the latest developments. The Chief was irritated. 'I know it's a difficult case, Harris, but just get on with it. All you have to remember is that we mustn't have it said that Playfair was given any special treatment. Just see that the case takes its normal course, sum up impartially and get a verdict from the jury.'

And he rang off.

The Bractons' house stood in an acre of ground on the outskirts of the city. It was a medium-sized villa, a comfortable, ugly house. In the hall, when George Bracton and Brian Graves were hanging up their coats, they were greeted by the Labrador charging at them and then by the twins. Bracton hugged the children. 'Isn't it homework time?' he said.

'It is.' Joan was standing in the doorway to the dining-room. 'Come on, you two. Back to work.'

'We'll get ourselves tea,' said Bracton, leading Graves into the kitchen. They brought their cups into the large sitting-room, solidly furnished, well-lived-in, shabby. Joan joined them.

'I'm expecting the DPP to call,' Bracton said. Then he told her what had happened in court. Both, she saw, were anxious and unsettled. She prayed that when he talked to the DPP her husband would be sensible and not be stubborn. Brian Graves saw her look and smiled at her. She had cut her hair, he noticed, and it made her look much older.

'In justification of Trent, I expect Johnson never told him that Playfair had said that Trelawney had killed himself,' he said to Bracton.

'Probably not, and Johnson was feeding the press, who were putting pressure on an inexperienced DPP.'

'What'll you do now?' Joan asked.

'Just see how the defence develops.'

'You're going to speak to the DPP?' she asked.

'Yes, but the ultimate responsibility is mine.'

'What about the judge?'

'He can't interfere with how the prosecution is handled. Some judges have tried, without success. But Harris may not know that.'

It was not the DPP who telephoned. It was the Attorney General. Richard took the call at the table in the corner of the room; Joan and Brian were in the armchairs by the fire. 'James Tyson has been telling me what's been happening at old Jonathan's trial,' the Attorney boomed, 'and I thought I'd have a word. Of course, how you handle it, Richard, is a matter for you,' the loud voice went on, 'but we don't want any embarrassment, do we? I must say,' he added, 'that when James Tyson launched this prosecution he said he had the evidence for a conviction. I hope he was right.' He was not going to admit to Treasury Counsel that he himself had read the police reports. 'All I wanted to say, Richard, is go ahead and get that verdict and, as I said, avoid anything which could lead to embarrassment. You know what I mean.' I certainly do, thought Bracton. No awkward Parliamentary Questions about why a prosecution had gone off half-cock or been derailed; or, on the other hand, why one of the Establishment had been given an easy ride. Otherwise the press would be after the hide of the government's Law Officers.

'So the net of it is,' concluded the Attorney, 'leave it to the jury. But you're experienced enough, Richard. I leave it entirely to you.'

Of course you do, Bracton thought. So that if there's any trouble, you can blame Counsel for the Crown.

As he replaced the receiver, Brian Graves asked, 'What did he have to say?'

'Go on to the end of the road, no quarter, no favours, and mind my back. The Attorney wants no trouble, no complaint when it's all over.' He sounded angry. Please, Joan prayed, be sensible, be careful.

'Well. I'll do what I think's right,' he continued. 'And to the devil with them.'

If you don't do what they want, thought Graves, you can kiss goodbye to that judgeship.

Virginia ran the bath and emptied into it a cupful of aromatic bath-oil. She lay in the steaming water, playing with the froth, gently lathering her breasts. Limeys cock-up over judge prosecution. Perhaps that will now be the headline. But it wasn't over yet. Either way, she could make a story of it.

She thought again of Hugo. If the prosecution collapsed after he'd been sacked and Playfair had taken over his own defence, it wouldn't do Hugo much good. But Hugo, after all, was history, and tonight she was dining again with Leslie Bramley. She liked his crassness, more than she had Hugo's pretensions. And, she thought as she soaped herself langourously in the steaming-hot water, from Bramley she might get another piece of the jigsaw – the truth about the police and the press.

16

ON Tuesday evening the rumour had reached the journalists in the hotels and bars of the city that next day the defence would begin and that, contrary to what the prosecution had expected, the accused himself would go into the witness-box. As a result, on Wednesday morning the court was more crowded than ever before. Barristers in wigs and gowns who had slipped away from other courts to come and listen filled the back row of Counsels' benches. Solicitors and their clerks stood in every gangway; the press bench was crammed, and every seat in the public galleries taken.

As soon as the court sat Bracton announced he had no re-examination of the police officer. The technician, Fraser, came and went, his evidence, that he had checked the apparatus on the day following the deceased's death and found it in perfect working order, unchallenged. The post-mortem evidence proving the cause of death was read; it was agreed that the cross-examination of the lawyer, Symes, would be interposed whenever he arrived. At shortly after eleven-thirty the case for the prosecution was concluded.

It was the turn of the defence. Jonathan rose from his seat in the dock. 'I have no opening statement to make,' he said. 'What I have to say I shall say from the witness-box, on oath.'

It took him some time, using his cane and helped by the usher, to descend the steps from the dock and mount those to the witness-box. For this day he was dressed more formally than before, in a dark suit, with a cream-coloured shirt rather loose about the neck and a black knitted tie fastened in a large knot. He stood in the witness-box, a tall, slightly stooping figure, now directly facing the jury. Below them were the reporters, among them Leslie Bramley with the subpoena in his pocket. He tried to catch Virginia's eye across the court but failed.

When Jonathan had been in the dock, Bracton had his back to him. Now for the first time he could see Jonathan full-face and was struck by how frail the old man looked, as if a puff of wind could blow him away. He saw that Jonathan was carrying no note, no papers, nothing. In front of counsel, at the solicitors' table, sat an ashen-faced Trent, beside him Harold Benson, who had moved so as to be able to hand to Jonathan any documents he might need. In her seat in the front row of the jury-box the middle-aged jurywoman couldn't bring herself to look directly at him, so she kept her eye on the rail of the box, at about the level of his waist. But Virginia, in her usual seat in the front at the side of the court, did. Hitherto she had only been able to see him half-profile, or the back of his white head when he had stood and turned towards a witness. Now she too could see him full-face and she examined him carefully, noting the high cheekbones and the skin lined and crinkled like old parchment. He'll not live long, she thought, in prison or not.

While the usher was fetching the Testament, Jonathan once again glanced up at the wall high above the judge's bench to the wooden, painted wheel depicting King Arthur's Round Table – as he had when he had been brought into the dock on the first day of the trial. He remembered he had promised himself he would look up the role of Mordred, but he never had. Now he remembered the other names which, in his dream, had taken the places of Lancelot, Galahad and Percival; the names of Hartley, Trelawney, Connor, his own name – and, lastly, Willis. He looked down at the usher and took the oath.

'You may sit if you wish,' Graham said when Jonathan had been sworn.

'Thank you, my lord, but I prefer to stand.'

'Very well. But if you get tired, you may sit.'

Then Jonathan began, and the middle-aged jurywoman now raised her eyes. He looks very fine, she thought.

'I'm Jonathan Wentworth Playfair,' he said in a light but strong voice which belied his frail appearance and carried to every corner of the courtroom. 'I am nearly seventy-eight years of age and I live in rooms in my cousin's home, Pembroke House in Tildsley. David Trelawney, whom they accuse me of killing, was a few months older than I and we had known each other since childhood. At one time our families became linked because for twenty years my father lived with David Trelawney's mother.' He paused. 'So I knew David Trelawney all his life. I was with him when he died. But I did not kill him.'

When he said this the middle-aged jurywoman in the front row thought he was looking directly at her and she looked away to stop herself from nodding. Jonathan went on: 'We were at school together and at the same university, and soldiers together in the Second World War. Some of you may know' – he stopped and looked straight at the juror in the dark blue blazer with the brass buttons. Then he smiled. (It's a nice smile, Virginia thought.) – 'No, I don't imagine any of you are old enough to have personal experience of what I was going to say, which was that being together in war, in battle, forges a bond which is unique. It was one of the bonds which bound me to David Trelawney.'

He looked down at his hands gripping the edge of the witness-box – old man's hands, Virginia saw, mottled with age. Colonel Basildon, who knew about war, although a war later than that of which Jonathan was speaking, war in Korea, shifted in his chair beside the judge.

'I wish I was able to paint for you in words a true picture of how David Trelawney was in his prime, during the war of which I was speaking. He was a very handsome man and in his uniform, with the ribbons of his decorations for gallantry on his left breast, he looked very splendid. He had only to enter a room for every woman to fall in love with him.' He looked again at the same jurywoman, who again quickly looked away. 'In battle every man under his command followed him gladly, even into the greatest danger. That I am alive today is due to his heroism.' He paused. 'But that I am in this place today is due to his malevolence.' The court was deathly quiet as the light voice went on. 'He saved my life in battle at the risk of his own, and I owe to him all the years that have passed since that night on a hillside in North Africa over fifty years ago.' He paused again. Then added very quietly, 'And he never, ever, let me forget it.'

When he said this Bracton thought of what Trelawney·had said in the recorded telephone call. About all that Playfair had given him. What had Playfair given?

'When we were boys at school,' the voice continued, 'David Trelawney was the captain of everything, Head of everything. I was good only at my books, and my father, Beau Playfair as he was called, so much admired the young David Trelawney that he was unable to disguise his preference for David, the son of the woman with whom he eventually went to live, over me, the son of the wife he abandoned. And both David and I were aware of it. Later in our lives, during the war, David Trelawney fathered a child on a girl with whom I had grown up and whom I loved all my life. But he never married her.'

There had to be a woman somewhere, Virginia thought. Would he tell what happened to her?

'Because my father lived with David Trelawney's mother for the last twenty years of his life, David Trelawney at one time referred to us as step-brothers. I did not. During those years I saw little of him or my father. I saw more of my mother.'

Get on with it, thought the young juryman at the end of the front row, shifting restlessly. What happened in the room on that afternoon is what we want to hear. But the rest of the jury were listening, fascinated.

'When he left the army in which he had won such honours David Trelawney went to live in France – his mother was French. But there he became involved in some very dubious businesses, in what was then called the black market, and he only narrowly avoided prosecution by the French authorities. His business ventures failed and he lost what money he had. My father bailed him out, not once but several times. Then in 1970 my father died. In his will he made generous provision for Trelawney's mother and, as you heard from the statement of the lawyer, Mr Symes, he also made provision for David, but only if in old age David Trelawney was struck down by serious illness. After my father's death David Trelawney got money out of his mother. That was the kind of man he had by then become. When she too died in 1979, David Trelawney turned to me.'

Virginia began to make notes in a small notebook, but not like the court reporters in the press box, who had their heads bent over their pads, scribbling furiously as they took down every word. All Virginia needed for her piece was background, how he spoke, how he looked. Bramley too was taking notes, but by now he had become uneasy. Not only because of the subpoena in his pocket, but because he sensed that ever since Playfair had taken over from Shelbourne something in the atmosphere in the court had changed. He caught Virginia's eye and smiled, but she looked away.

'I had become a lawyer,' Jonathan was saying, 'and had been successful. Then I became a judge. Trelawney thought I was rich. He owed money, he told me; and I, as he also told me, owed him my life.'

Wasn't there something more than owing his life, Graham thought, something Trelawney had referred to in his letter to Lightwood? He leafed through his papers and took out the letter, Exhibit 6, and read it again. Yes, there it was. Trelawney had written: 'I saved his precious skin – and more than that.' What had Trelawney meant by 'more than that'?

'David Trelawney's failure after the war in which he had been such a hero changed our relationship. I, over whom he had lorded it at school, at the university and in the army – I, to whom he had so condescended as a youth and whose life he had saved almost contemptuously – was flourishing, whereas he was penniless, scrounging from friends. Our positions had reversed.'

Bracton whispered to Brian Graves, 'What was it Trelawney said on the telephone? Something about Playfair so often giving.' Graves handed him his note, and Bracton read: 'I've taken a lot from you over the years, Jonathan. Now I want to give you something, for a change.' Bracton handed back the note to Graves. That 'something' must be the letters. What Playfair had given must have been money. He looked up again at Jonathan.

'He demanded I invest in his business in France, which I did, reluctantly. Later he asked a second time, then a third. When the businesses all failed he said he was destitute and began to ask for money to save him from ruin. So I helped him. At this time the sums were not great, for until his mother died she was his main source of funds. He was quite blunt. I owed it to him, he used to say, because I owed him my existence. So I paid up.'

Why, wondered Bracton. Pay up once or twice for family reasons, yes. But why so often?

'I am telling you this, members of the jury,' Jonathan said, 'because it is true that when Trelawney died I had every reason to want him dead. So, yes, I had a motive for killing him.' He paused, looking intently at the jury. 'I had a motive,' he repeated, 'but I did not kill him.' He paused again. Then went on briskly, 'In the early summer of last year I learned he was ill and had applied to the trustees of my father's will for the funds which my father had provided. I was glad, for now he would get money from them, although I suspected that if he didn't get all he wanted he'd come back to me for more.'

He leaned forward and asked the usher for the tape recorder he had produced when he had been cross-examining Nurse Langley. He held it up in his hand. 'For many years, unknown to him, I had been recording what he said every time he telephoned. The tapes of these conversations I kept in a drawer in my desk and when I came home from his death-bed and I thought the story had ended, I destroyed them and put away the recorder, which I thought I'd never have to use again. I had forgotten that the tape of the last conversation was still in the machine.' He handed the recorder back to the usher. 'When I heard he had cancer I was not sorry, not only because I would be relieved of his demands on me, but also because, quite frankly, I hoped he would not have long to live. But I say again – I did not kill him, nor did I help him to die.'

Jonathan's voice was now less steady, and the usher brought a glass of water and placed it on the ledge of the witness-box. Jonathan took it and sipped.

'I had not heard from him for several months when he telephoned me on the morning of Saturday June 21st. As soon as I heard his voice on the telephone I reached for the small recorder which I had on my desk.'

Bracton turned back in his notebook to check again the note he had taken of what had been said on the tape. He kept it before him, following it while Jonathan spoke.

'You may remember he asked me to call him back and said it was urgent. He did that because he wanted to convince the nurse, as he did convince her, that it was I who had insisted on coming to him. This was part of a plan that he had devised, a plan to implicate me in the death he had planned for himself, for, despite what he said to the nurse and doctor, he had decided to end his own life. He was not prepared, he told me when I came to him, and I believed him, to allow himself to be eaten away by his disease. What I did not suspect was that by his death he planned to get his revenge on me, for by this time there had grown in his mind a canker of jealousy and resentment of me as great as the cancer which had grown in his body. Unknown to me, in ending his own life, he planned to pull down the figure which represented to him the success he believed his golden youth and young manhood so much better deserved. He thought of me, whom he despised, as the respectable, wealthy, self-righteous judge, and what could be more appropriate than to have me, the former judge, suspected, better still accused, of his murder.' Jonathan again sipped from the glass. 'And because the investigating officer was a police officer who had a bitter grudge against me and who used my enemies in the press' – here he looked down at Bramley – 'and partly, I admit, because I left that house when I did, his plan succeeded. But that came later. On June 21st, having prepared the nurse and written his letter to Lightwood, suggesting apparently facetiously that I might put a pillow over his face to get him out of the way, knowing that when Lightwood read it, he, Trelawney, would be dead, he told me on the telephone he wanted to see me urgently because' he was so ill and had not much time and wanted to give me some old letters from a person he knew I had always loved. This was the bait he used to get me to come to him. When I agreed he pretended to the nurse that he didn't want to see me, that I had forced myself on him and that he was scared of me, and he got me to tell the nurse she could go out. All this he did to make her believe that it was I who wanted her out of the way. So the stage was set for his final piece of play-acting, which began when we were alone.

'First, he talked about his disease, saying that he feared not death but dying slowly and painfully. He was not prepared to accept that, he said, and now he had the means to accomplish what he wanted. I asked what he meant, and he replied that soon I would see – and here he tapped the apparatus with the tube strapped to his chest and the machine with the syringe on the table beside him. "There's enough here to do what I want," he said. He then spoke of the past – of his mother's love affair with my father, of his regret at what he had done with his life after he had left the army, of the failure he had become. "The war," he said, "that was the time, the summit, the peak of my existence. Then I was a hero. When it was over, everything turned to ashes."'

Jonathan paused. Graham saw the beads of perspiration on his white face and that he was gripping the ledge of the witness-box in front of him as Nurse Langley had done the day before. The court was very quiet.

'He next spoke of his envy of me, of the success I had made of my life compared to his. It had begun to obsess him, he said, and created within him what he described as a devil which had driven him to prey on me. He did it, he said, more to injure me than to get money for himself – although, he added grinning, the cash had been useful. But now he was tired. He'd had, he said, a good innings and he knew the cancer was going to kill him. He was not going to face treatment in hospital which would only postpone what he knew was inevitable. "The chemotherapy," he said, "will make my hair fall out and I shall become as bald as a coot and none of the nurses will look at me." So he joked in his old way, the way I remembered so well. Then he repeated how sorry he was about his past behaviour towards me, and he spoke of what he called our salad days. He said he hoped I would forgive him for his bitterness and jealousy.

'As I have said, when I had entered his room I hoped to find he was dying, but now I was moved by what he was saying. So I told him that the treatment might cure him; that he might have more time than he thought. But he said, no. He'd made up his mind. He was going to die and he would not be sorry to go. But before he went he wanted us to end as we had begun, when we were boys seventy years ago. When he said this I also thought of our childhood, of his family and mine before my father had gone with his mother. Suddenly his body jerked and he gave a half-cry and said he was in great pain – would I help him with the apparatus and the tube at his chest, He said the strapping had slipped and he didn't think the syringe was feeding in the drug properly. He showed me where the dial was and asked me to adjust it slightly and shift the position of the syringe and the tube taped beneath his left breast. I did as he directed, and went back to my chair.'

Jonathan passed a hand over his face and Graham thought to ask him if he wanted to rest, but Jonathan had begun again. 'He got me to do that so that my fingers touched the apparatus and the syringe.' He paused once more. 'I then asked about the letters he wanted me to have and he replied they were from the girl I had known since childhood, the girl he knew I'd loved all my life. "You ought to have them, Jonathan," he said. "They will make you happy, for you will see from them whom it was she really loved." And when he said that, he meant me. She had really loved me. "Where are they?" I asked. He said they were in an envelope in the box on the dresser, and he held out to me a key. "Open it and take the envelope, but don't look at them now, not in front of me. Take them home," he said, "read them at home and keep them."

'I opened the box, and from it I took a large, sealed envelope. While I was doing this I had my back to him on the bed. "Don't open it until you're home," I heard him say again. I turned with the envelope in my hand and saw he was now smiling. Then he opened his pyjama jacket. He had his right hand on the apparatus on the table beside him and I saw him lift the syringe and press the plunger. "What are you, doing?" I said. "What I told you I was going to do," he replied. "What I want to do. End it peacefully." I watched, unable – no, unwilling – to move. Then, after almost a minute of silence, his manner changed. His smiling ceased. Suddenly he said savagely, almost in a snarl, "You're very pleased with yourself, aren't you? You're bloody smug, aren't you? But you won't be for much longer. I'm teaching you a lesson, Master Jonathan. I'm showing you how a brave man dies, Mister Lawyer."

'I thought this change in him must be because of the drug he had injected into himself, and I couldn't entirely follow what he was saying, for his words had become slurred. But I understood that suddenly, inexplicably, he had turned on me. "Why do you say that?" I asked. "Why are you speaking like that?"

'Then he changed again and smiled and spoke as he had before, gently, "Just a tease," he said. "Just a joke, just one last joke. You've never understood my jokes, have you, Jonathan? But this one you will. One day soon you will see how good a joke it is. Goodbye, Jonathan," he said, "You won't forget me. You'll never forget me." I had crossed the room and was standing by the bed, looking down at him and he up at me, and suddenly I saw a look of hatred and derision come into his eyes. I still thought it was the drug which was causing these sudden swings of mood. Then he closed his eyes and was silent and soon I suppose he sank into the coma, what Dr Mitchell called the irreversible coma, and I knew he had accomplished what he had wanted. To kill himself in front of me, when I was alone with him.'

Jonathan stopped and sipped again from the glass. For several seconds he remained silent. Then he continued: 'I knew I should do something, telephone for the doctor or an ambulance – but he had done what he wished and I decided I would let him be, let him sleep until he died. I went back to the chair and sat listening to the sounds of his breathing, waiting for the nurse to return. After a time I opened the envelope. Inside were several folded pages of writing paper. They were blank. All of them. All blank. Nothing.'

Again Jonathan lifted the glass of water and sipped, his hand shaking. 'There never had been any letters. That, I supposed, was part of what he had called his tease, his final, cruel joke, the pretence which he knew would bring me to him. But why, I thought, why had he wanted me to witness his death? Then I thought I knew. He had wanted to teach me a lesson, a lesson which he thought I needed to be taught. He had wanted me to see how a brave man dies. He had wanted to show me that he was not afraid of death, as he knew years ago I had been so afraid.'

At these words Graham raised his head and stared at the witness. Afraid of death, years ago? Jonathan looked at him. Then looked away, back to the jury.

'But I was wrong,' he went on. 'I had not understood what he had planned for me. I had not reckoned on the extent of the contempt he felt for me, nor of his plan for revenge. As I sat in the room while he was dying I thought only of what he had said before those last bitter words after he had injected himself with the drug.

I thought of what he had said about our childhood, when we were young and life lay ahead of us. I thought of how he was then, and of his gallantry in war; and I thought of our other friend, Rory Connor, the friend who grew up with us who had been killed in the battle when David Trelawney had saved my life. And I thought of how all the threads of my life had been interwoven with the threads of his. Now he was gone, and despite what he had taken from me over the years, and despite his lies about the letters, I was sorry I had wanted him dead, although I knew it was for the best that he was. Best for him; best for me.

'I must have sat there for an hour or so, still waiting for the nurse to return. But she did not come. His breathing had long since ceased and finally I went over to the bed and took a last look at the face I had known from boyhood to old age, and I thought of what I owed him – my life. And of how much thereafter he had made me pay. I did not then know how bitterly he had hated me for what I had become and what I was. Suddenly I had the urge to get away from him. I cannot explain it, but I felt as if driven by another's will, not my own, and I went from that house without a word to anyone. By doing that, by running away from his death-bed, I helped him achieve what in his hatred he had planned. By doing that I helped bring upon myself all that is now happening to me.'

He put his hand to his head and stopped speaking. Graham saw that he was swaying and his eyes were closed, as though he was on the verge of collapse.

'The witness needs a rest,' Graham said loudly. 'I shall rise early for the mid-day break. The court is adjourned.'

As the judge swept from the court Jonathan sank back into the chair, his head between his hands.

17

IN the conference room Bracton stared out the window. Graves, seated at the table, his wig on his notebook in front of him, pushed aside the plate with the uneaten sandwich and the empty plastic cup of coffee. It was not yet two o'clock but already the pale February sunshine seemed to be fading; soon it would be dusk.

'He impressed the jury,' Graves said.

'He impressed me,' Bracton replied.

Graves fiddled with the tail of his wig. 'London wants a fight to the finish,' he said. Bracton swung round and sat at the other side of the table. Neither spoke. Bracton broke the silence. 'There's more to the story than he's telling. But what it is I don't know.'

'More about what happened that afternoon?'

'No, not what happened. But why. Something in the past.'

'Does that matter?'

'No, but it interests me, although it may not be my business to find out.'

'It is if it provides a reason for murder.'

'Playfair has admitted he had reason. He's said so repeatedly. No, the issue remains: if it was Playfair who emptied that syringe, it was murder; if Trelawney, it was suicide.'

'What if Trelawney asked Playfair to help him?'

'Aiding and abetting suicide; or manslaughter. But, if you believe Playfair, his evidence rules that out.'

'But the jury might think that's what happened.'

'They have no evidence of it. No, it comes to this. If what Playfair says is true it was suicide; and if his story is a pack of lies he has some reason for lying, and the most likely reason is that he's a murderer. Either you believe him or you don't.'

'I think quite a few in court did.'

Leslie Bramley was in another conference room with a young in-house lawyer whom the management of the *Globe* had sent down from London when they'd heard about the subpoena. She was in her late thirties with short dark hair and large horn-rimmed glasses, in a black suit and white blouse. She looked as nervous as she felt. They could've sent a more senior lawyer, not this kid, Bramley grumbled to himself when he saw her. He had a large whisky-and-soda before he took her into the conference room.

'Why should they want me as a witness?' he said when the door closed behind them. 'Of course Johnson hates Playfair just as much as we do, and of course he fed me the story. It doesn't need me for the jury to see that.'

'Sources have to be protected and—' she began. He interrupted her. 'I know all that crap. They haven't sent you down to tell me that, have they? What I need to be told is what happens when the old bugger, Playfair, asks me who leaked the story and I tell them to get stuffed.'

'The judge will warn you that in law,' she recited, 'you have no privilege which allows you to refuse to answer and that accordingly you must.' She had rehearsed that in the train on the way down.

'And when I tell the judge to stuff it, what then?'

'He could threaten to send you to prison if you won't answer.'

'And if I still don't?'

'He could send you to prison.'

'They'd love that in London! Make a great front page. Judge jails *Globe* reporter. Liberty of the press threatened. The right to know! All that balls. Not a word about the right to know how the press got the story.' He lit a cigarette. She looked pointedly at the No Smoking sign on the wall but he ignored her. 'And the bloody foreigner who owns us will fly in from Palm Springs in his bloody private jet, hold a crappy press conference and fly back to the beach-house, while I'm in the Scrubs eating porridge and sewing mailbags. Thank you very much.'

'The judge can't send you to prison without giving you warning and hearing counsel on your behalf—'

'Are you counsel?'

'No.'

'Then why the hell haven't they sent counsel? No offence, I'm sure you're very bright, but I want someone who knows the ropes, someone who'll frighten the balls of that kid of a judge. And I want him quick. I don't fancy a spell in the clink. So tell them in London to get their finger out and get a heavy down here.' He opened the door.

'Perhaps the old buggar'll crack under cross-examination.' He stamped out. Where's Virginia, he thought. But she was nowhere to be seen.

The newspaper lawyer went off to telephone London, but it wasn't until the evening that a heavyweight silk was on the road to Bramley's rescue. By then he was no longer needed.

The jury had been led to their own room; a great crush was expected in the canteen. One of the younger men was the first to speak. 'What do you think?'

'I believe him,' replied the man in the dark blue blazer with brass buttons. 'I think it was wrong they ever brought it to court.'

The other older man in the suit said, 'It certainly looks a bit different now. But he'll be cross-examined when we go back. That might change it.'

'If it doesn't,' said the man in the blazer, 'I know what we ought to do. At least I know what I'll do.'

'It's the usual cover-up,' said the young man who had been nearly late the morning before. 'All the toffs looking after each other. But I didn't fancy that policeman.'

'Well, then, what are you on about?' said the young woman who had worn pink on the first day of the trial.

'He's very old,' said an older, motherly woman. 'He looked all in when the judge left the court.'

'Perhaps he'll kick the bucket and then we can all go home,' said the same young man.

'That's not funny,' said the man in the blazer.

*

Graham Harris had stayed in his room during the adjournment. Priestley came in. 'The Lodgings have been on the telephone. There's been a message from your son. The school want to talk to you.'

As if he hadn't enough to worry about without this! What could be wrong now? He'd told the headmaster that the children's grandmother would collect them tomorrow. He looked at his watch. 'We're due to start again in a minute. I've no time now,' he said.

Colonel Basildon came through the door. 'High Sheriff,' Graham said awkwardly. 'Could you do something for me, something personal?'

'Of course, judge. What is it?'

'I've had a message from my children's school. It's probably about the arrangements for their half-term which begins tomorrow. I've got to get back to court. Could you telephone and find out what they want?'

'Of course.' Graham gave him the number.

During the adjournment Virginia had stayed in the court watching Jonathan. Throughout the break he had sat on a chair in the witness-box, looking calm but very pale. He had refused coffee and was sipping from a glass of water. Once he glanced up and caught her eye.

Either he's been telling the truth or he's pretty smart, she thought. Listening to him she sensed that the story of the judge who was a murderer might be drifting away, unless they rocked him in cross-examination. Still, she had enough to make a story out of it either way. Last night she'd learned from Bramley some of what had gone on between the police and the *Globe*. She thought about Hugo Shelbourne. An acquittal wouldn't do him much good, but she couldn't worry much about him. He'd served his purpose.

In his chambers in London Shelbourne was reading the newspaper reports of what had happened in court the day before. The newspapers, except for the *Globe*, reported fully the evidence about the tape, of how the nurse had been misled, and the behaviour of Detective-Inspector Johnson. He flung down the newspaper and began to prowl around the room. He understood now. Playfair had held all this back so that when he took over his own defence it would make a greater impact. Playfair had set him up.

At lunch he telephoned a news editor on one of the broadsheets to ask how the trial had gone in the morning.

'Our fellow's just called in,' the news editor replied. 'He says Playfair's still giving evidence and is doing pretty well. Playfair's story is that Trelawney had been blackmailing him, then killed himself and made it look as if Playfair was implicated, helped by a particularly nasty policeman with a grudge. He was feeding the *Globe*, which old Playfair had once caned for massive damages for contempt.'

Shelbourne hung up and rang for Isles. 'I feel I'm getting a bout of flu. I'll go to the country to lie up. Cancel everything, will you.'

Isles was not fooled. And there was nothing to cancel.

In the court, Harold went up to Jonathan. 'Le Quesne is here. He arrived this morning.'

'Good. See he's ready to come into court when I call for him.'

'Is there anything I can get you?'

Jonathan shook his head.

'Will you be much longer?'

'No, I'm nearly done. I shall need the papers I gave you during the cross-examination.'

And he was nearly done, for, when the judge returned a little later and the trial resumed, he said he knew that by leaving the house without waiting for the nurse or telephoning he had brought the investigation on himself. When the police had come, he had not at first recognised Detective-Inspector Johnson, who from the start had been hostile and aggressive. On his second visit Johnson had been even more truculent, and when he had told Johnson that Trelawney had killed himself Johnson had just looked at him and walked away. He knew he had never been popular with the local police. They had always believed he had been too soft on the criminals they'd caught, but it was only after the second interview that it crossed his mind that Johnson might have been in the Stringer case. He had looked out his old court notebook and found that Johnson had indeed been one of the junior officers when he, as the judge, had ruled Stringer's statement inadmissible because of the oppressive questioning by the police. It was then that he knew what to expect. He trusted none of the local police, and the incident over his arrest at dawn confirmed his fears. He had not told the police about his family and his financial relationship with the dead man for he had destroyed the tapes of his conversations with Trelawney and had forgotten about the last tape. So at the time he had nothing to show them. He sensed Johnson's satisfaction at having him under investigation. Then the press campaign had started in the *Globe*. When the policeman returned for a third time he realised that Johnson was determined to implicate him. He had already told Johnson that Trelawney had commited suicide, and in view of Johnson's attitude he resolved to remain silent. When he heard that Patrick Trent, whose handling of the Stringer case had also come in for criticism after Jonathan's direction to acquit Stringer, was the lawyer in charge of the case for the DPP, and when Symes told him about Trelawney's letter to Lightwood, and when the pressure in the press mounted, he knew he would have to face trial.

Here he paused, looking down over the edge of the dock into the well of the court, his head bowed. Then he looked up at the jury, looking more tired and even older and frailer than before. 'So, whatever your verdict,' he concluded, 'David Trelawney got what he wanted. As I said when I began, it is due to his malevolence that I am here. But I say as solemnly as I am able' – and he said each word slowly, deliberately – 'when I went to that house on the afternoon of June 21st, I wanted Trelawney dead. But I did not kill David Trelawney. He killed himself.'

There was a long silence before he turned to the judge. 'That is my evidence, my lord.'

Graham nodded. 'Thank you,' he said. He looked at Bracton. 'Well, Mr Bracton?' Bracton rose, gathering his robe around him.

Joan Bracton had slipped into a place at the back of the court which Brian Graves had arranged should be kept for her. She could see Richard, but she didn't want him to know she was there.

'Why did you leave the dead man in that empty house and go

away without saying a word to anyone?' Bracton began very quietly.

Jonathan looked down at his hands gripping the ledge of the witness-box, then up at Bracton. 'I cannot tell you.'

'Why – to use your own words – did you run away?'

'I just felt I had to leave him.'

'Is that your only explanation?'

'It is the only explanation I can give. At the time I felt I had to leave, and I did.'

'But why not wait for the nurse?'

'I have tried to explain. I had been very moved by what he had said earlier, and I was very startled by what he had done. His death was for me the end of a long story. When he was dead I just needed to get away.'

'You had sat in that room for some time, with the dying man on the bed only a few feet from you. Why did you suddenly get up and leave? Wasn't that a strange thing to do, to run away?'

'It was. But I knew I had to leave.'

'Why?'

'I just knew I had to get away from him.'

'According to you, the man had just killed himself. You had watched him do it. Then, without telephoning anybody or waiting for the nurse, you went away. I ask you again: why?'

Jonathan shook his head. 'I cannot explain. I cannot remember what I thought at that time, except that once he was dead the story was over. So I left.'

'There was a telephone by the bed. Why didn't you summon help?'

'There was nothing that anyone could do and—'

Bracton interrupted him. 'How do you know? How do you know that someone might not have been able to revive him?'

'If you mean why did I not summon help immediately after he had injected himself, I was not prepared to do that. He said he wanted to die. That was his choice. He had done what he wanted to do.'

'To kill himself?'

'Yes.'

'When he was dead you knew his demands, his preying on you, would cease?'

'Of course.'

'And you were pleased.'

'When I went to that house on that afternoon I hoped he was dying of cancer. But after I had been with him, and listened to what he had to say, I felt differently.'

'Why?'

'Because I was thinking of what might have been. We ought to have been friends.'

'But you weren't, were you?'

'No, we were not.'

'You were not friends, even before he began making his demands for money, were you?'

'No, we were not.'

'Your father preferred David Trelawney to you, his own son?'

'Yes.'

'David Trelawney fathered a child on the woman you loved. Was that the reason why you weren't friends?'

'It was part of the reason. But there was also other reasons.'

'What other reasons?'

'Because of my father and his mother.'

'That was not his doing, was it?'

'No, but it had created a link I had not liked. By then we were certainly not friends.'

'You hated him.'

'Yes.'

'And his death suited you very well?'

'I have admitted that. From the time I heard he was ill I hoped he might die.'

'So you had a motive for killing him?'

'In the sense that he had harmed me and preyed on me, that is true.'

'And you had the opportunity, for you were alone with him in the house?'

'I had.'

'So you had motive, you had opportunity, and when he was dead you stole away without a word to anyone. Wasn't that because, deliberately, in a fit of temper provoked by something he'd said or done, you had killed him?'

'No, it was not. I have told you what happened.'

'The doctor told us that Trelawney at that time often dozed or dropped off to sleep, even when people were with him in the room talking to him. Did Trelawney do that when you were with him?'

'Not before he had injected himself.'

'You admit you touched the apparatus and the syringe?'

'Yes. Trelawney asked me to.'

'If he had been dozing would it not have been easy for you to have gone to the syringe driver on the table and injected him without waking him.?'

'That is your theory. I do not know if it is a sensible theory or not. All I can say is that it didn't happen.'

'I suggest that is what you did.'

'Then your suggestion is wrong. I did not kill David Trelawney, nor did I help him to kill himself – which is what he did.'

Bracton paused. 'You came that day because you expected to be given some letters?'

'Yes.'

'Were you not angry when you found you'd been tricked and only been given blank sheets of paper?'

'No, by the time I saw there were no letters I knew he was dying, if he was not already dead.'

'You came to him because you wanted those letters and you did not care whether he lived or died. Isn't that right?'

'No, I hoped he was going to die. I have never pretended to be sorry he was so ill.'

'When you were alone in the house and you found he'd lied to you about the letters, wasn't it then that you saw your chance of ridding yourself of him?'

'No, that is not right.'

'It was very easy to do, wasn't it – just go to the table, and press the syringe and inject him with a fatal dose?'

Jonathan shook his head. 'I have told you. I did not do that.'

'You could have, couldn't you?'

'That is what he wanted you and everyone to believe. But I have told you what happened.'

Colonel Basildon had slipped into his place beside the judge and passed him a note. 'The children are refusing to go with their grandmother for half-term,' Graham read. 'They wish to come to you.'

Not now, Graham thought. Not this now, at the most critical moment in the trial. How could he collect the children himself? How could he have them for the weekend? He whispered to the High Sheriff, 'Tell them I'll telephone at five o'clock.'

Colonel Basildon pushed back his chair. The heads of the jury turned and watched him leave.

'How many times did you pay money to David Trelawney?' Bracton asked, and the jury turned back to look at Jonathan.

'Many times.'

'Can you prove that?'

'Yes. Mr Benson has the documents which show the payments I made.'

He has deliberately kept them until now, thought Graves. He knew Bracton would have to ask about the money. Benson had risen from his place and was handing up a sheaf of papers to Jonathan in the witness-box.

'What do the documents show?' Bracton asked.

'That in 1964, 1974 and 1980 I made loans to the Continental and International Trading Cie, registered in Paris, of £20,000, on each occasion against personal guarantees from David Trelawney, who was the president and sole shareholder of that company. Later in 1980 the company became insolvent and my money was lost.'

Harold Benson was still standing below the witness-box, with more documents in his hand, waiting.

'I have here bank statements, not those which the police seized and examined. Those were my Coutts' bank statements. For the payments to Trelawney I used the Banque Nationale de Paris, the St Helier branch in Jersey in the Channel Islands. The name of the account is the Wentworth Estate account. My mother's name. I have the disposal of all the funds in those accounts and I am the sole signatory.

Bracton looked quickly down at Graves. Then he said, 'You didn't show these to the police?'

'No, I did not. The manager of the St Helier branch, Mr Le

Quesne, is here. He arrived from Jersey this morning and is outside the court, waiting to give evidence. Do you wish him to be called in?'

'Not yet.'

'Well, he will speak to the truth of what I'm saying. All the signatures on the cheques in this account are mine and in my proper name. Do you wish to see these accounts?'

'In a moment,' Bracton said, trying to speak coolly. 'Have you anything more to produce?'

Jonathan stretched down and took more papers from Benson. 'Oh, yes, much more. First, I have here Trelawney's acknowledgements of further personal loans. In 1985 he received from me £20,000; and again two more sums of £20,000 in 1987 and 1990. They appear in these bank statements.' He held them up.

'How do they appear in the statements?'

'As drafts for cash.'

'Is there anything to show the money went to David Trelawney?'

'Not in the accounts, no more than the £500 a month which I paid from 1979 until last year. From 1985 David Trelawney had no bank account. He had nothing, and only a life interest in the house in which he lived, which had been purchased by my father. After David Trelawney's death it reverted to me. But I have in my hand, as I said, Trelawney's receipts for the major sums in 1985, 1987 and 1990.' Jonathan looked at the judge. 'I have marked the relevant entries in the bank statements for easy reference.'

The judge nodded and they were brought to him. After he had looked through them he said: 'These accounts show a healthy credit balance, with a very substantial sum in the deposit account. Yet in his statement Mr Symes said you told him you had lost £500,000 at Lloyd's and were in very serious financial difficulties. Is that true?'

'It is true I told Mr Symes last summer that I had received notice from my agent at Lloyd's that I must pay £500,000. I wanted Mr Symes to believe that I and my family were in severe financial difficulties so that this information would reach David Trelawney. I wanted Trelawney to believe he could get no more from me because I had none, and that now he had to rely solely on what he could get from the trustees. I hoped this would prevent Trelawney from ever again demanding money from me.'

'So you had received notice that you had to pay £500,000 to Lloyd's?'

'Yes, but what I did not tell Mr Symes was that I had stop-loss arrangements—'

He turned from the judge and faced the jury, 'In other words I had taken out insurance to cover any losses from Lloyd's except for the last £50,000. As a result my loss was limited to £50,000. When certain tax consequences are taken into consideration my actual loss was estimated as no more that £4000.'

'You did not tell Mr Symes about these stop-loss arrangements?' Graham asked.

'No, nor was he aware of my bank accounts in Jersey. I had also told others that I had to pay Lloyd's half a million pounds. I did this because I hoped it would get back to David Trelawney. It did, for Trelawney told Mr Symes, as he also wrote to Lightwood, that I was ruined. But, unknown to me, this fitted the impression he wanted to create – that I desperately needed to get my hands on the money which the trustees were about to pay out in respect of Trelawney's illness. That was part of his plot. So my plan to deceive him aided his plan to implicate me.'

He leaned again over the rail of the witness-box and took more documents from Harold Benson.

'This is the notice from my Lloyd's agent calling on me to send a cheque for £500,000 in July of last year; and this the stop-loss policy and letter which shows that my loss is limited to £50,000. Neither I nor my family are ruined. We are fortunate in still having very considerable financial resources.'

He handed the documents to the usher, who took them to the judge, then to Bracton and lastly to the jury. Jonathan broke the silence. 'You will also see that the monthly drawing from my account of £500 ceased in May last year. It was in that month that David Trelawney approached the trustees.'

Bracton asked quietly, 'Why were you paying him all this money?'

Jonathan did not immediately reply, Then he said, 'I have explained. I paid him because I owed him a great deal.'

'Because you owed him your life?'

'Yes.'

'Fifty years ago?'

'Yes.'

'Was that sufficient reason to make you pay him scores of thousand of pounds?'

'I thought it was.'

'Was that the only reason?' asked Graham from the bench. 'In his letter to Major Lightwood, David Trelawney wrote that he had saved your life – and something more. What did he mean by that?'

Jonathan turned towards him, and for a moment was silent. Then he said 'I do not know. I suppose it was part of the plot to denigrate me and involve me in his suicide.'

'But how could that further involve you in what you say was his suicide?' Graham continued. 'Why does he refer to something more? What could he mean?'

'I have said. I do not know.'

'But he must have meant something when he wrote to his friend that he had saved something more than your life. What could it have been?'

'It could, I suppose, have something to do with the girl I had wanted to marry. He had slept with her, had a child by her. Perhaps he meant that he had saved me from marrying a girl I shouldn't have. That she would never have made me happy. I do not know. But that was the kind of man he had become. All I know for certain is that it was I, who, by saving him from bankruptcy, had saved him.'

Graham folded his hands under his chin. Bracton asked, 'Do you insist that the only reason you paid this money, year after year, month after month, was because many, many years ago Trelawney saved your life in the war? Are you telling the court that that was the only reason?'

'That and the family connection. He played on that.'

'How did he save your life? Describe it.'

Jonathan raised his hand and, involuntarily, placed it on his forehead. He began to speak, slowly, carefully. 'It was in the mountains of North Africa, towards the end of the campaign there. A few of us, including Trelawney and myself, were cut off, surrounded by the enemy. I was lying wounded on the hillside below the summit which we were defending. Another attack was coming. David Trelawney could have abandoned me, but he came for me and stood above me, firing at the attackers, driving them off. Then, despite very heavy enemy fire, he carried me to one of our fox-holes in our positions on the summit and stood guard over me all night while the enemy attacked again and again. Next day the remainder of our battalion counter-attacked from the valley below and we were relieved.' He paused. 'If he had not done what he did, I must have died. As he so often said, I owed him everything.'

'And because of what he had done for you then he later asked you for money – and you gave it to him?'

'I did.'

'And he kept demanding and you kept paying, time and time again?'

'Yes. Our connection through our families was close. He thought he had a claim on me.'

'But you hated each other?'

Jonathan was silent. Then he said, 'I have told you. We were not friends. When we were boys my father loved him and not me; my father loved his mother, not mine. Trelawney slept with the girl I grew up with and thought I loved. But he had saved my life.'

'And for the rest of his life he never let you forget?'

'No, he did not. And it was not I who ended his life.'

Bracton stood silent and very still. The pause lasted so long that Graham and the jury turned their heads from Jonathan towards Bracton. Finally Bracton said, almost wearily, 'Sir Jonathan, you are a very experienced lawyer. For many years you have either taken part in or presided over criminal trials. Some of those trials' – Bracton looked about him – 'in this very place. You, better than most, know criminal practice and police procedure. So will you please explain to the court why you never told all this to the police when they first came to question you?'

'Do you mean why did I not tell the story of my life to Detective-Inspector Johnson?'

'Yes. Why didn't you tell him what you have told us today?'

'I told him what was important. I told him that David Trelawney had killed himself.'

'He has sworn that you did not.'

Jonathan smiled faintly and shook his head. Then he said, 'He would, wouldn't he? Isn't that what they say?' Then, smiling no more and with a sudden burst of energy, he leaned forward over the edge of the witness-box. 'Detective-Inspector Johnson lied when he denied that I had told him David Trelawney had killed himself. I told him plainly that Trelawney had committed suicide. I did not tell him more, since I saw no reason why I should. By the time he came on the second occasion, the press campaign, the hinting, the suggesting, had started. And it had been started by him, the police officer who so bitterly resented what I had done in the trial of Stringer for the murder of his friend. He and that man' – and Jonathan pointed directly at Bramley seated below the jury in the press box – 'the reporter from the *Globe*, whose editor I had once fined and threatened with prison, launched a campaign suggesting that people in high legal circles were protecting some high legal figure from prosecution. They kept printing my name, saying I was the last person to have seen Trelawney alive. They put pressure on the DPP, saying he'd been my pupil and was my friend. Scandal of Establishment. Protection of the privileged. That's what they were suggesting.'

There were now two circles of red high upon Jonathan's cheeks, contrasting vividly with the parchment colour of his skin. 'Johnson,' he went on, 'found he was investigating the judge who had allowed the man he believed was the murderer of his friend to go free. It was Johnson who set the *Globe* on to me, and they were only too happy to oblige. Johnson made up his mind that Trelawney had been murdered, and by me. He was determined to bring me to trial, to disgrace me. Whatever I might have said to Johnson, it would have made no difference to him. He would have lied and denied I had said it, just as he lied in this court about what I told him.'

'If you thought that about Detective-Inspector Johnson,' Bracton interrupted, 'why didn't you speak to his superior officer?'

'To the superintendent who arranged for me to come to the station to be charged and whom Johnson defied when he arrested me shortly after dawn, after carefully arranging for the TV cameras to be present! Speak to that superior officer whom Johnson treated with such contempt? What would have been the point? When I was a judge I had differed with the Chief Constable, who complained about my attitude to sentencing. No, the police would not listen to me. I knew I could not defeat the combination of the police and the press. I knew there was only one way to bring this to an end, however painful it must be for me, and that was through the right of every Englishman of whatever station in life to have a public, open trial in front of a jury of twelve decent, fair-minded men and women who wouldn't be taken in by a corrupt, obsessed policeman, nor by a corrupt, sensation-mongering newspaper. I knew that only in front of a jury of my fellow countryman and women would the truth come out. So I prepared myself to stand trial and I was confident that, before an English jury, the conduct of the police, or rather the conduct of one policeman, Detective-Inspector Johnson, and the conduct of one newspaper, the *Globe*, would be exposed – and my name cleared by the only people I respect, in whose fairness and justice I could rely, my countrymen and countrywomen, a jury of Englishmen and Englishwomen.'

Jonathan stopped. He was breathing heavily, his eyes were flashing as he bent over the edge of the witness-box staring at Bracton. There was complete silence in the court. Suddenly, abruptly, Bracton sat down.

Immediately, heads began to turn in the jury-box; one juror in the back row bent forward to talk to the juror in front of him; soon all were turning to talk to one another. Graham struck the desk with his gavel. 'Please,' he said to the jury, 'silence, please.' He said to Bracton, 'Is that all you wish to ask the witness?'

Bracton rose. He half-turned and faced the jury, who were now talking even more loudly among themselves. They hushed when he began. 'Yes, my lord. I have nothing more to ask the witness. I have no more challenge to make to this evidence.' As he said this the jury looked at each other. The man in the blazer cried, 'Quite right.' 'We've heard enough,' said another. Bracton turned to look at Jonathan in the witness-box, then at the judge. 'I have considered the evidence which has been given,' he said, speaking very gravely, 'and, as counsel in charge of the prosecution, I have heard enough.'

'So have we,' muttered voices from among the jury. Graham struck the desk with his gavel. It was getting out of hand. I mustn't lose control, he thought. 'Please be quiet. I am speaking to counsel.' He tried to make himself sound severe but his voice was shaking. 'What do you mean, you've heard enough?' he asked Bracton.

'In view of the evidence of the nurse and the evidence of the telephone call recorded on the tape, the conduct of the police officer, helped by a section of the press, and now having heard the explanation the accused has given on oath, I have no more questions to ask him and' – he had half-turned again to the jury – 'not only have I no more questions but I have decided' – he was speaking very loudly and his voice rang out over the court – 'I have decided, as counsel in charge of this prosecution, that I shall now not address the jury asking them to convict the accused.'

'Well done,' said the juryman in the blue blazer. 'Quite right,' said another. Others nodded vigorously. Graves, seated beside the standing Bracton, had his head in both hands. At the back of the court, unseen by her husband, Joan put her hand to her throat. 'Oh my God,' she whispered to herself. 'What is he doing? He's destroying himself.' Then she thought, He's doing what he thinks is right, and he's brave. And I love him.'

'I'm not sure I understand you, Mr Bracton,' Graham said. 'Are you saying you are not proceeding with the prosecution?'

'I am, my lord.'

'But should you not' – he corrected himself – 'do you not wish to take instructions from the Director of Public Prosecutions?'

'No, my lord. I am in charge of this prosecution, the evidence for the Crown is complete and, having heard the accused on oath, I have decided I shall not address the jury and invite them to convict.'

He sat down. There was a moment of silence. It was broken by the voices of the spectators, like the sound of a wave breaking on the shore. Some of the jury gesticulated to the man in the blazer, encouraging him to speak. Graham struck the desk in front of him with his gavel, once, twice, then a third time. The usher called for silence, but the jurors ignored him. 'Silence!' the usher cried again. 'Silence!' But no one obeyed him. Bracton was sitting very still, looking straight ahead. Graves put his hand on Bracton's arm and pressed it gently. Colonel Basildon was leaning forward on the edge of his chair. In the press bench Bramley was staring up at the judge, aghast; Virginia stared at Jonathan, who stood, breathing heavily, his eyes on the wall above the judge's seat, looking up again at the painted wheel of the Round Table. Mordred, he thought, who was Mordred? What was Mordred's role in Camelot?

'Please, members of the jury,' Graham began, 'I must ask you to—' But the man in the blue blazer with the brass buttons got to his feet and interrupted him.

'My lord,' he said in a loud voice, 'we agree with prosecuting counsel. We've heard enough. We don't want to hear any more. We want to stop the case. Now.'

The problem over the children flashed into Graham's mind. If the case was over, it was resolved. He could fetch them himself and take them home. He forced himself to concentrate on what was happening in court. What ought I to do, he thought? What is the right thing to do?

'Mr Bracton,' he said at last. Bracton got to his feet. 'Did I understand you to say that you were no longer going to ask the jury to convict?'

'I did, my lord.'

'Before the case for the defence is completed?'

'Yes.'

'I must ask you again, do you not want, is it not your duty, to take instructions?'

'No, my lord, I do not need to take any instructions from anybody. I have the sole responsibility for the handling of this prosecution and' – he turned again to the jury – 'I have the impression that the jury also have heard enough.'

The jury chorused in agreement. Bracton turned back to face the judge. 'So I have decided that I shall not now ask the jury to convict.'

An experienced judge, Jonathan was thinking, would now adjourn to let them cool down. He should tell them to be patient and insist they hear his summing-up. That's what he'd have done.

'Is that your final decision, Mr Bracton?'

'It is,' Bracton replied. He stood looking up at the judge on the bench. Then he shrugged, his arms spread, his palms turned outward. 'The jury, my lord,' he said. 'The jury. They have decided.'

There's nothing I can do, thought Graham. I can't stop them now. 'Mr Foreman,' he said, addressing the juryman in the blazer, 'are you telling me that the jury, all the jury, want the trial stopped because you've heard enough?'

'I am. That is what we want. That is our right,' the man replied, 'as the jury.' He looked around at the others, who nodded. 'You see, my lord, we're all agreed,' he added.

'The evidence is not yet over,' said Graham.

'The evidence for the prosecution is,' said the juryman, 'and we've heard enough from the defence. We say the defendant is Not Guilty.'

Graham stared at the jury, looking at every one of them in turn. He could not make them go on if they were determined. Then he said, 'Are you all, every one of you, agreed?'

The foreman turned to face the rest of the jury. Several called out, 'We are all agreed.' The foreman looked again along the two rows of the jury. One after the other they nodded. He turned back to Graham. 'We're all agreed that the accused is Not Guilty, my lord,' he said, 'and we think, or some of us think, there ought to be an enquiry.'

'Hear, hear,' came from behind him. The foreman went on, 'We don't think this prosecution ought ever to have been brought, and those responsible ought to be investigated. There should be an official enquiry. It's been a disgrace, an utter disgrace.'

The court again fell silent. Graham still hesitated and Bracton, seeing his indecision, said: 'Having regard to what the jury foreman has just said, with it seems the concurrence of every member of the jury, I submit, my lord, that you should now take their verdict.'

Graham stared at him. The court had become very quiet. 'You wish the trial stopped and the prisoner found Not Guilty?' Graham asked. 'Is that the verdict of you all?'

'It is,' said the foreman. Graham tried for the last time. 'Are you all certain that you are agreed?'

'We are,' the jury chorused.

Virginia was watching Jonathan. For a second she saw the faintest impression of a smile on his lips. Then it had gone.

'Very well,' Graham said at last. 'If that is the verdict of you all.'

'Since the accused is unrepresented,' Bracton said, 'I ask that a verdict of Not Guilty be recorded and the accused be discharged.'

'Very well,' Graham repeated. 'Let the accused be discharged and a verdict of Not Guilty recorded.'

The court erupted. 'Silence,' shouted the usher, but no one took any notice. Amid the noise, and unnoticed, the judge rose and, without bowing to the jury or to counsel, turned and hurried from the court.

18

THE Legal Secretary hurried into the Attorney's General's room in Buckingham Gate in London. 'We've the result of the Playfair trial, Attorney.'

'Already?' The Attorney, surprised, looked up from the file he was reading. 'I thought Playfair was still giving evidence?'

'Apparently it ended very suddenly.'

The Attorney glared at him. 'How?'

'In an acquittal.'

'By the direction of the judge?'

'No, it was the jury. They intervened. They said they'd heard enough. The Director—'

'Put him through to me.'

Trent had telephoned from the court, so James Tyson was well briefed. 'At the end of his cross-examination of Playfair,' he told the Attorney, 'Bracton apparently announced that, having heard Playfair's evidence, he no longer intended to ask the jury to convict. When the jury heard this they stopped the case.'

'But I made it clear to Bracton last evening that we wanted the trial to run its full course and have a jury verdict.'

'There was a verdict by the jury, Attorney.'

'Yes, but, from what you're saying, only after the prosecution had thrown in its hand.'

'Well, that's what Bracton did.'

For a moment the Attorney General was silent. Then he said, 'Make a note, James, that the Crown will never again brief Richard

Bracton in any prosecution anywhere. Remove him from your list of prosecuting counsel.'

'As you wish, but I don't imagine that'll concern him greatly. I'm told he's going to fill the vacancy there on the circuit bench.'

'Is he now? We'll see about that. I'll have a word with the Lord Chancellor. I don't think we'll see Mr Bracton on the circuit bench – now, or ever.'

'The jury also had something to say about the prosecution. Playfair apparently suggested he'd been framed by the police, helped by the Crown Prosecution Service and prompted by the press, especially the *Globe*, to whom the police officer in charge of the case had been feeding information. He was the officer who arrested Playfair shortly before dawn in the presence of the TV cameras. The jury wanted an enquiry.'

The Attorney General remained silent. He was thinking hard. The dawn arrest; Playfair's claim he'd been framed; counsel for the Crown abandoning the prosecution; the jury's demand for an enquiry. Parliamentary questions, perhaps an adjournment debate.

'There'll be no enquiry,' he said flatly. 'Fortunately, in this instance an enquiry would not suit those who are usually the first to clamour for one, the media. So I fancy we won't have much trouble. It's a case of battening down the hatches, eh James?'

And batten down the hatches they did.

It's over, Graham thought as he disrobed in the hall in the Lodgings. But had he done what he should? He had got flustered. He knew that, and it had probably shown. But had he given in too soon? Should he have insisted the jury wait until he had summed-up? Had he been influenced by his own problems?

Priestly, folding away the robes, sensed his disquiet. 'You couldn't've done anything else, sir,' he said quietly. 'They'd made up their minds, even before hearing Mr Bracton. Sir Jonathan had got them. He'd got every one of them.'

Especially Bracton, Graham thought as they walked from the hall into the drawing-room.

'Isn't it unusual for a prosecutor,' he asked, 'to announce at the end of his cross-examination that he was not now going to ask the jury to convict?'

'Very. It takes guts for a prosecuting counsel to shoulder that responsibility.'

'Do you think he was right?'

'It was a very special trial, sir, so I'm not sure he was. I think he'd have done better to have let the trial run on. The DPP won't be pleased.'

Priestly opened the drawing-room door. 'If I may say so,' he said, 'I'd have a word with the Chief.'

Graham looked at his watch. First, he'd call the school, but before he could the High Sheriff entered the drawing-room. Colonel Basildon stood aside as Priestly left, then he said awkwardly, 'I know it's none of our business, judge, but my wife and I felt you may be having some difficulties over the children and their half-term.' He stopped.

'Yes,' said Graham tersely.

'Well, if it would help at all, we'd be very happy to have you all come and stay with us. We've plenty of room, and it'd be no trouble to put the three of you up. Susan would drive over and get them, and you'd all be very welcome.'

'You're very kind,' Graham said, 'and you're right, we are having some family problems, but now the case has ended I can fetch the children myself and take them home. But thank you very much for the offer. I greatly appreciate it. Please thank your wife for me.'

'Right,' said the colonel briskly, 'right.' He looked relieved, his duty done.

'The case, judge,' he said. 'Did you expect it to end like that?'

'No, I can't say that I did.'

'Was it – how shall I put it? – was it quite orthodox what happened?'

'Apparently not.'

'Well, I can only say, as an onlooker, that after we'd heard Playfair I thought the prosecutor fellow was right to say what he did.'

'Yes,' Graham replied. 'After we'd heard Playfair.'

'Anyhow, I'm damn glad it went that way. But are you finished down here now?'

'Yes, I was only sent down to do this one case.'

'Then I may not see you again. I won't be back in the morning and I must be getting home now.'

Graham walked him to the door and out into the hall. 'Thank you for looking after me,' he said, putting out his hand, 'and thank you again for your offer to put us up. If the case hadn't ended as it did, it would have been a godsend.'

They shook hands and the High Sheriff left. Graham went to the telephone. In London the Lord Chief Justice had already heard the news. 'I'll expect you back tomorrow to tell me all about it,' he said. When Graham explained about the half-term and that his wife was abroad, the Chief added tersely, 'Very well, come and see me on Tuesday.' When the Chief had replaced the receiver he turned to the Deputy. 'He got rattled. He should have made them listen to his summing-up before he took a verdict. There'll be a rumpus now,' he said.

But he was wrong. The press understood that any enquiry into the prosecution or the police conduct in the Playfair case could lead to an investigation into the role played by the press and their own links with their informants in the police. So the editors comforted themselves that the fuss was, after all, over the case of a wealthy man with a knighthood – not a very sexy subject, the tabloids decided, on which to found a campaign against persecution by the authorities. So no more was heard about the jury's comments and the matter was allowed quietly to fade away. Bramley and his editor were much relieved, while Detective-Inspector Johnson was quietly transferred from the plain-clothes branch back to uniform duties in the county traffic division.

From the hotel in the town Virginia telephoned Hugo Shelbourne's chambers. Isles told her that Mr Shelbourne had left for the country just after lunch. 'He was not feeling well, madam. He thinks he may have a bout of flu coming on,' the clerk told her.

Hugo Shelbourne would have to feature in her story. He was, after all, one of the main players. She would have to see him again.

When she arrived two hours later she told the driver to wait. Before she reached the front door it swung open. Hugo Shelbourne was in his shirt-sleeves. She could hear the news bulletin on the radio repeating what had happened in court.

'Can I come in?' she said. For answer he stood aside, then followed her and switched off the radio.

'The immediate question,' she said, smiling vivaciously, pulling off her gloves and running her hand through her hair, 'is whether I keep the hire car or send it away.'

'Had you thought of staying?' he replied.

'Not if you don't want me to.' She walked over to the fire. 'Not if you don't want to talk to me.'

'As I assume anything I say will appear in your article, I think I'd better say very little.'

'Hugo, darling,' she said, turning towards him, 'I've come because I wanted to see you.'

'You mean,' he said, 'you wanted to see how I was taking it.'

'Don't be silly. I came to see you – and to talk about your side of the story.'

'My side of the story!' He walked to the tray of drinks on the side table and poured some whisky into a tumbler. Quite a lot of whisky, she saw. 'My side of the story is short and simple. I was set up, like Playfair told the court Trelawney had set him up.'

'What do you mean?'

'Playfair kept back everything of importance. He told me nothing of what really happened. If what the reports say he told the court was true—'

'Do you think it wasn't?' she interrupted.

He waved his glass dismissively, as he took ice from the ice-bucket on the table and dropped it into the whisky. 'He allowed me to make a fool of myself, then he publicly humiliated me.'

'Why do you think he did that?'

'To put himself in a better light with the jury. Make them more sympathetic. Frail old man, forced to defend himself because of the outrageous behaviour of his advocate.'

He flung himself into a chair. Virginia was still standing, still in her coat in front of the fire.

'And once he's got rid of the lawyer, hey presto! Miracles begin to happen. Rabbits come jumping out of the hat, the blackmailer, the wicked policeman, the corrupt newspaper, the tape, the bank statements, letters from Lloyd's. Then he almost collapses in the witness-box, and a feeble prosecutor chucks in the towel.'

'And you think he planned it all?'

'He couldn't have planned the gutless prosecutor giving up. But what he said was probably all lies.'

'About him and Trelawney?' she said, interested.

'Well, it can't be proved or disproved, can it? How do you know that money went to Trelawney?'

'Some of it certainly went to his company in France. The documents showed that. And the rest, if it didn't go to Trelawney, who did it go to? And since Playfair proved he didn't need money, why should he want to kill Trelawney?'

Shelbourne shrugged. 'Because something happened between them. I don't know what, but all I do know is that if I'd been the prosecutor I'd've burrowed away until I'd dug out the real story behind all that balls. If I'd been the prosecutor it would have been Jonathan Playfair who'd've chucked in the towel, not the prosecution.' He sprawled in the armchair, already half-drunk. 'By the time I'd finished, I'd have found out a lot more about the saintly Sir Jonathan.'

'So you think he did kill Trelawney?'

'What does it matter what I think? He's been found Not Guilty, and he's done for me.'

'That's nonsense, Hugo.'

He glared at her. 'What do you know about it? You don't understand. You're only a hack. Well, let me tell you what people in the profession, other barristers or solicitors, will remember about the Playfair case. What they'll remember is that Hugo Shelbourne was briefed to defend Jonathan Playfair and Hugo Shelbourne got sacked. Then Jonathan Playfair defended himself and Jonathan Playfair was acquitted. End of story. End of Shelbourne.' He drained his glass and got up from the chair and staggered back to the decanter on the side table.

'I'm sorry—' she began.

He turned and looked at her. 'You're not sorry. It gives a good twist to your story, doesn't it? And to top it all off, you can describe how you found maudlin defence counsel blubbing into his whisky.'

She walked over to the table where she had put her gloves.

'I wasn't much of a lover was I?' he said. 'Not up to your class, was I? Not the old QC, not Hugo Shelbourne. Not the sexual athlete you need, was he? And you can put that in too. The human touch, isn't that what they like? That should help sell it.'

She turned on her heel and went out to the car, leaving his front door open behind her.

But Hugo Shelbourne wasn't the only lawyer to suffer from the trial of Regina v. Playfair. As the Attorney General had prophesied, Richard Bracton, who had taken so seriously his responsibility as an impartial officer of justice, did not become a judge. Nor did he receive any more briefs from the Director of Public Prosecutions. He stayed on at the bar, but at first solicitors feared he was under some kind of official cloud and were reluctant to brief him. But he persevered and his practice slowly revived. While he mourned the loss of the appointment to the circuit bench on which he had set his heart, he had no regrets over what he'd done. 'As the prosecutor,' he told Joan, 'I was an officer of justice, and I did what was right.' And she agreed with him.

19

IT was just after Jonathan had been driven away from the court that the woman approached Harold.

He had followed as Jonathan, accompanied by James and Mary, had been escorted from the court by the attendants and the police, who formed a cordon to push a way through the throng. Outside the Great Door of the castle they had been met with the flash of the cameras. Jonathan clambered into the car and lay back on the rear seat, his eyes closed, his face deathly pale. Mary got in beside him; James next to the chauffeur. For the last time the car swept out of the castle yard on its way to Pembroke House.

It was then that Harold felt the tug on his sleeve and, turning, he looked down and saw her at his elbow. The photographers were starting to pack away their kit and by now it was almost dark. The forecourt of the castle was lit only by the tall standard lamps and the lights above and beside the Great Door. At first he couldn't see her clearly, for the crowd was still pressing all round them and she was being forced up against him. But he could see she was very small and slight, and then, in the flash as a newsman took a final shot of the back of Jonathan Playfair's car, he saw she was a woman in her fifties, dressed in grey, with a grey, pinched face and grey hair emerging from a maroon-coloured hat with a curved brim.

'Excuse me,' she said. 'Aren't you something to do with the trial?'

He peered down at her through his steel-rimmed spectacles. 'Yes,' he said. 'What do you want?'

'I thought you were. I've seen you on television.'

'If you're the press, I've nothing to say.' He was anxious to get to the hotel where he had parked his car and he tried to shoulder his way through the crowd. But the crush was too great and for the moment neither of them could move.

She said, 'I've nothing to do with the press.' She still had her hand on his arm and as she spoke she looked about her, alarmed by the crush. 'I'm Mrs Sarah Peachey, from Radley St Philip in Somerset.' Both of them were being pushed and jostled as she went on breathlessly, 'I want to speak to someone who knows about the colonel and I've seen your face on the tele. I saw you talking to the man they've let go free.'

The way she said this nettled him. 'I was talking to Sir Jonathan Playfair,' he said 'I'm his solicitor.'

'He was the man who was tried for the murder of the colonel, wasn't he?'

'He was. Sir Jonathan has just been acquitted in a trial which should never have been held. But I'm in a hurry, madam, and you must excuse me.'

She *must* be a reporter, he thought. He turned and tried again to push his way through the mass of people, but the woman tugged at his arm once more.

'Please don't leave me here,' she said. 'I'm not used to crowds. I only came here to find someone who might be able to help me.'

The crowd was thickest where they were standing, and the police and court officials were trying to clear the forecourt. A cameraman, his kit over his shoulder, pushed past, knocking her hard against Harold.

'Please,' she said, looking up at him, pleading. 'Please, help me out of here. I get so worried in crowds.'

Harold took her by the arm and steered her through the throng. Gradually they pushed their way through, until they had crossed the forecourt to the edge of the square away from the Great Door.

'It's clearer from here,' he said. 'You'll be all right now. And I must be getting away.'

'Oh, please,' she said. 'I don't know who to talk to. I've come all this way. I want to ask someone about the colonel and you're the only one I recognised. You said you're a lawyer so you might be able to help me. Please.'

Harold looked down at the small figure beside him and heard

the distress in her voice. For some reason he thought of Margaret, although Margaret was bigger and she was always smiling. This woman wasn't smiling. Their escape from the crush had obviously frightened her. He had been able to see over most of the heads but she was so short she could not. Under the lamp at the corner of the square where they were now standing he saw her face was even greyer than it had been when she had first accosted him and she looked as though she might faint.

'You're nothing to do with the press?' he asked.

'No. I've come from Radley St Philip. This morning.'

'Well, I'll walk you to the town,' he said, 'but I'll have to leave you there. I have an appointment.'

Using his key, he opened the wicket gate and led her on to the path used by the lawyers and court officials. It was dark and neither spoke as they followed the few others using the private way. When they emerged on to the street below the castle she began again. 'He was such a good man was the Colonel.'

Harold, surprised, said, 'A good man? You knew him?'

'I'd never met him, but he did so much for us.'

'For whom?'

'For Mum, and the family.'

Colonel Trelawney a good man! They were walking now down a side passage towards the main street of the city.

'I never met him, but I've the letter he wrote after Dad was killed. That was when I was a child, in the war, towards the end of the war.'

'Your father was killed in the war?'

'Yes, with the Colonel, in Africa. The Colonel was very good to us.'

'You came here today to ask about him?'

'To ask what I ought to do. I read about the trial of the man who killed the Colonel—'

Harold interrupted her. 'Sir Jonathan did not kill the Colonel,' he said severely. 'The Colonel was very ill with cancer and took an overdose, deliberately. The jury very rightly acquitted Sir Johnathan. The prosecution should never have brought the case against him.'

She made no reply as they walked on. Then she said, 'I hoped to find someone here I could ask what I ought to do about the money the Colonel sent.'

Harold stopped. 'The money the Colonel sent?'

'Yes. I keep the shop at Radley St Philip. It's also the post office. Mum had it before me, and that's where the money came. I couldn't get away from the shop before today but I was sure there'd be someone here I could tell about it. So I came to find someone, and I'd seen you on the tele.'

'I'm not Colonel Trelawney's lawyer, and if it's about his money I won't be able to help you.'

By now they had reached the main street further down the hill. She put her hand on his arm. 'Please listen. I feel so bad about what I've done. I want to do what's right.'

'What have you done that you're so worried about?'

'It's the money, the money I kept. I want to do what's right, though I can't pay the money back.'

She spoke so agitatedly that he began to think she was becoming hysterical. There was a tearoom just ahead.

'Would you like a cup of tea?' he asked.

'I would, very much,' she said.

'Come along then. But I can't be long.'

As they walked on he asked, 'Have you been in court?'

'No, I couldn't get in. I only got here in the afternoon and I waited outside. Then I heard the noise and everyone started to come out and I was pushed to the front where the man was taken away in the car and I saw you.'

In the tearoom they found a table and he ordered tea. She was, as he had thought, a woman in her fifties, worn and grey. She still looked frightened and bewildered.

'Why do you want help?' he asked.

'Mum's dead, you see. She died just after Christmas. Not last Christmas, the one before. I'm on my own. Then I read about the trial and saw the pictures of the Colonel and the man they accused. So I thought I'd find someone here who might know what I ought to do.'

'About the money?'

'Yes, the money the Colonel was sending to Mum.'

'Colonel Trelawney was sending money to your mother? Was he

'. . .' He paused and then went on, 'Had he been – a friend of your mother?'

'Oh no. He sent the money after Dad was killed in the war. It came regularly, for years and years. Every year, up to last year.'

It couldn't have been much, Harold thought as he drank his tea. Trelawney might have been able to send money immediately after the war, but not later.

'Dad was a sergeant. He was with the Colonel, Mum said, first in France, then in Africa where he was killed. Dad was one of the Colonel's men. That's why the Colonel sent Mum the money. He was very generous to Mum and the money came ever so regular, through the post office.'

'From Colonel Trelawney?'

'Oh yes. He wrote to Mum a few months after Dad died and said he wanted to help her. I was a child then of course, but Mum kept the letter.'

'What did the letter say?'

'The Colonel said we'd be looked after. He said he'd arranged that.'

'Was it much money?'

'We thought so. It came each month but Mum died Christmas a year ago and the money kept coming until May last year. Then it stopped.' She looked up at him. 'I kept it, even though Mum was dead.'

'How much money came after your mother died?'

'Two thousand five hundred pounds.'

'Two thousand five hundred pounds!'

'Yes, five months' money. January to May. The Colonel used to send five hundred pounds, regular each month. Then it stopped.'

'Colonel Trelawney sent your mother five hundred pounds each month every year since the war?'

'Yes.'

He calculated rapidly. Six thousand pounds a year for over forty years. A quarter of a million pounds! 'What happened to the money?' he asked.

'In the fifties,' she said, 'Mum and Billy – he's my elder brother – got a garage in Bristol because the money was coming in so regular. Mum turned over the post office to me and went with him. Then Billy got into trouble.'

'What kind of trouble?'

She looked down at her hands. 'He went to prison,' she said. 'Something to do with cars, stolen cars. The garage went, and Mum came back to me. They'd borrowed a lot and the money helped to pay Mum's debts. I was on my own then. Mr Peachey had gone. Mum helped with Eve.'

'Who is Eve?'

'She's my daughter. She's not quite right. She got very difficult as she grew up. Violent. She's in a home now.'

Five hundred pounds a month. That was the same sum Jonathan had told the court had gone to Trelawney. Was Trelawney passing it on to the widow of one of his soldiers? Even when he himself had none?

'Will I get into trouble?' she asked. 'I needed it so badly, for Mum lost everything with Billy and Peachey's never paid me nothing, not for me nor for Eve. I don't know where Peachey is now. The Welfare think he's abroad. I know I shouldn't've kept it after Mum was dead.'

'Couldn't you have written to Colonel Trelawney?'

'No. We'd never heard from him after the letter, and that was back in 1943 when I was a baby. All Mum knew was that the money kept being paid to the post office for her. The last few years it came in cash.'

'Did you ever try to find the Colonel's address?'

She did not reply at first. 'No,' she said. 'Ever since I've been reading about the trial and seen it on tele I've been so worried. I thought it'd come out.'

'Can you remember what Colonel Trelawney wrote when the money first came?'

'Oh, yes,' she replied. 'Mum kept his letter. I have it here.'

She put her hand into her bag, a large cloth-covered bag, and brought out a crumpled single sheet of light blue paper and handed it to him. It was an air-letter form which folded and was stuck with gum to make an envelope. Harold put on his glasses and began to read the faded ink.

North Africa. May 1943.

Dear Mrs Willis,

By now you will have been officially notified of the tragic death in action of your husband, who was killed on Bou Arraka, Tunisia, on April 17th last.

I served with your husband three years ago in France and I was with him when he died fighting gallantly by my side here in North Africa. He was a very brave man, an outstanding non-commissioned officer whose loss all of us mourn. I considered him a friend.

From talking to your husband when he was alive I know something of your circumstances and, as your husband and I were comrades, and as a token of my esteem for him, I hope you will accept some arrangements which I am making to help you and your family.

Your husband had told me you keep the post office at Radley St Philip, so I am arranging that a monthly sum will be sent to you there to supplement the pension you will receive and to help you and your family during the difficult years which must lie ahead for you and your children.

Yours sincerely,

David Trelawney.

Harold turned, over the single sheet. He saw it was addressed to Mrs Jack Willis, The Post Office, Radley St Philip, Somerset, England. It was postmarked Field Post Office, M.E.F. and dated May 23rd 1943. On its back, where 'Sender's Name' was printed, was typed 'Major D. Trelawney, D.S.O, M.C., PO Box No. 1658, Middle East Forces'.

Harold looked up at the woman sitting on the other side of the tea-table and then handed the letter back to her.

'I've been so worried by what I did. I thought some of his family might be at the court and I came to explain what I'd done. But when I asked at the court, no-one knew. They said no-one was there. Then I saw you, and I knew you were something to do with it. That's why I talked to you.'

She paused and took out a small handkerchief. 'I needed the money,' she added, 'but I know I shouldn't've taken it. Not after Mum was dead.'

Harold looked at her worn, tired face. 'You mustn't worry about what you did,' he said. 'In his letter Colonel Trelawney said that the money was to help your mother and her family, and you're one of the family. Of course you should've tried to find the Colonel when she died, but his letter spoke of the family. You said there was only you and your elder brother?'

'Yes, Billy.'

'Did he have any of the money that came after your mother's death?' he asked.

She shook her head. 'No,' she said. 'Not after what he'd done. I needed it. He didn't.'

'Then you should forget all about it. But, tell me, when did the monthly payments cease?'

'In May last year.'

May of last year. That was when Jonathan's bank statements showed that the payments of £500 each month had ended. He looked at his watch. 'How are you getting home?' he asked.

'There's a train at seven. Then I'll get the last bus from Bath. Are you sure I should do nothing?'

'Quite sure. And you're not to worry any more.'

He called for the bill. 'My advice is, forget about the money. The Colonel is dead, and the money was for your mother and for her family, in remembrance of your father. You're a member of the family the Colonel referred to. You needed it. So you forget all about it.'

A touch of colour had come into her faded cheeks. She stretched out her hand and put it on his. Embarrassed, he pulled his away.

'Are you sure?' she asked. 'Are you sure I should do nothing?' She smiled, and Harold again thought of Margaret.

'Quite sure,' he said. 'It's all over and done with. The Colonel's dead. The money has not been missed. It was being paid, as the letter said, as a token of appreciation of your father. So a few extra months after your mother's death with you needing it for your daughter, that doesn't signify. Go home and forget about it.'

She put away her handkerchief. 'Now, come along,' he said briskly, summoning the waitress. 'We'll get my car and I'll drop you at the station. You'll be early but I have someone I must see.'

The waitress watched them leave. Such an odd couple, she thought, he so tall and angular with his wild hair over his collar, and she so small and neat.

20

'WE'LL talk about it tomorrow,' Jonathan said in the hall of Pembroke House. 'I need to rest tonight.'

'You had no lunch,' Mary said. 'You must have some supper. I'll get Mason to bring you something later.'

'No, my dear. I'm not hungry. We'll lunch together tomorrow.' Jonathan shut the door of his apartment.

'I've never understood him,' James grumbled as he followed Mary to their drawing-room. 'He puts all of us through the wringer and when it's over he's as cool as he was when it all began.'

'He's exhausted. He did very well in the court,' Mary said.

'He showed a spot of feeling – for once. I didn't know he had it in him.'

'He's always been very clever.'

'Too clever for me,' her husband replied.

Jonathan went into the bedroom and hung up his overcoat. In the bathroom, as he washed and dried his hands, he looked at himself in the looking-glass and smiled – an old man smiling at his own image.

In the drawing-room the curtains were drawn and the fire was blazing. Mason had seen to that. James had telephoned from the car, so they were in the hall to welcome him home – Mason, his wife, Tom the gardener, and Mrs Thorn the cleaner from the village. Jonathan had smiled at them, his slow, gentle smile, taking each by the hand but saying nothing.

In his chair he stared into the fire, no longer smiling. After a while he got up and went to his desk. He opened one of the small drawers, pressed the side slightly, closed it and, touching one of the ornamented wooden panels at the front, slid it to one side and drew out a large envelope. He went back to his chair and took from the envelope a sheaf of letters, then a small diary. At last, he thought, it really is over. Now is the time to be rid of this baggage of the past. It might be found after his death and it would matter to James. In the car driving home from the court James had said, 'Now we must make a real fuss. Who do you know in the House or in Whitehall we can get to take it up?'

Lying back with his eyes still closed, Jonathan had said, 'No, James. Let it be. It's over now. I'm too old. Let it be.'

So why keep these pieces of paper, and the diary? He looked at the letter on the top of the bundle in the handwriting he knew so well, and then placed the bundle carefully on the table beside him, keeping in his hand only the old, battered diary, its cover torn and stained. He didn't really need it to remember. It was all etched on his memory, those few weeks which had haunted him for fifty years, those days which were never long out of his thoughts and never out of his dreams.

His name was on the flyleaf. Captain Jonathan Playfair. And underneath, in his handwriting, 'Campaign in North Africa, 1943'. In fading pencil, scribbled on the small pages, it was all there. Except what mattered, what had happened in the battle.

He turned the pages until he came to the month of March. For a time he studied the entries for that month, then skipped forward until he came to late in May. From there on he read steadily the short, factual entries which had been written later, when he was able to write again, lying in the tents of the dressing stations as he had been moved from hospital to hospital.

'Brought down on a stretcher from the hilltop,' he read. 'Dumped on a carrier and driven to where could be transferred to an ambulance. Jolted down the track to the Field Dressing Station.' A day later: 'Main Dressing Station. First sight of a woman, a nurse in khaki shirt and slacks.'

And so it went on, the record of the dressing stations and the hospitals, from Medjez through Bone to the Base Hospital in Algiers. In the diary for one day, or rather night, there was scribbled the record of the nightmare, the dream of the body falling with the bullet-hole in the centre of the forehead. He wondered now how he had risked writing that.

Several weeks further on came the note of David's visit to the Base Hospital – David, the front of his forage cap high like that of General Alexander, the commander-in-chief, his canvas trousers smartly pressed and the new red and blue strip of the Distinguished Service Order sewed on to his freshly laundered bush-shirt next to the blue and white of his Military Cross. But there was no record of what he said, for David had come to tell what officially he had reported. Nor was there any of what they had agreed would be done once Jonathan was back in England.

A few days after that came the record of Colonel Phillip coming to say goodbye, then fuller notes about the trip home, the white hospital ship steaming through the Straits of Gibralter into the Atlantic with all its lights blazing, while those on board knew they were being watched and tracked by the periscopes of the U-boats which never attacked them. The entries ceased at the end of June.

Jonathan turned back the pages until he came again to March. Tonight, for the last time, he would start at the beginning and remember, day by day, hour by hour. Then he would burn it.

March 21st 1943. That was when it began, the night he had brought up the battalion transport to meet the infantry companies which had been ferried up by sea the night before. The rain and sleet had ceased, he remembered, as the convoy wound its way along the twisting road through the mountains. It had been bitterly cold, so cold that every hour he called a halt and ordered the drivers to run around their trucks and flap their arms to get their circulations going. On the horizon they could see the flashes in the sky from the gunfire they were unable to hear above the noise of the engines of their vehicles. That was where they were heading, to where the battalion was waiting for their heavy gear now stowed in the line of trucks moving across the mountain range towards the plain and the front line.

In the comfort of his warm room Jonathan could still remember the bitterness of the cold of that night. He saw himself as he was then, in his steel helmet, wrapped in his greatcoat with the webbing equipment buckled around it, his map spread on his knees, a torch in one hand, seated in the lead bren-gun carrier, a small, tracked vehicle with an open top. Beside him sat the driver, who was obliged to haul on the wheel to get the tracks to respond as the carrier, the first of three, led the lorries round the hairpin bends where the mountainside fell sheer from the edge of the road which was marked only roughly by stones. In the back sat the gunner, crouched behind the bren gun on its mount. Every so often the gunner and the driver changed places. Behind them, interspersed by two other groups of three carriers, stretched the line of three-ton lorries and fifteen-hundredweight trucks with only narrow slits of light coming from their shaded headlights to help them see the road.

One of the motorcyclists who all night fussed noisily up and down the line of vehicles had appeared beside the lead carrier, flagging it down. The convoy slowed and halted.

'Headquarters Company's truck at the rear of the column has gone, sir.'

Jonathan, perched on the pillion, had been taken back down the line of now stationary vehicles to where the truck, the last in the convoy before the two tracked carriers which brought up the rear, had plunged off the road. He joined the group on the edge of the road. The truck had exploded halfway down the mountainside. Jonathan ordered two men down, ropes around their waists. When they re-appeared they said there was no sign of either the driver or his companion.

They could not afford to wait. Jonathan had to get the convoy to the shelter of the forward area before the first light and the road ahead lay through what was known as Messerschmitt Alley, where the Messerschmitt 109s from Tunis machine-gunned the slow-moving convoys if they emerged in daylight from the mountains into the stretch of shelterless road. If he did not get the convoy through the Alley before dawn the battalion might see little of the gear for which they were waiting so anxiously.

'We have to get on,' he had said, and was taken back to the head of the column, leaving the remains of the truck burning on the mountainside.

Two hours later the motorcyclist was back again.

'What is it this time?' Jonathan shouted.

'Number Three Company's truck, Major Trelawney's. It's over the edge of the road, sir.'

'Gone?'

'No, sir, she's hanging on, just. The front wheels are over the edge. The column has halted. The rear carriers are trying to pull her back on to the road. Sergeant Willis is there.'

Jonathan lowered the diary to his lap. Willis. That was when the name first appeared.

When he had been taken back to the truck he saw they had hauled it back on to the road. Sergeant Willis was supervising the removal of the hawser from the truck's rear axle.

Jonathan could see him now, his blunt, pleasant features and ruddy complexion, the Somerset farmer's son with the broad forehead under the rim of the steel helmet pushed back on his head.

'What's the damage?' Jonathan had asked. 'Will it be able to move?'

'They're checking the front axle,' Sergeant Willis replied. 'The driver must have gone to sleep. Dozy idle man!'

Sergeant Willis had experience. He'd seen action in France as a corporal in David Trelawney's platoon at Dunkirk three years before, and he had been bitterly disappointed that he'd not been transferred into Major Trelawney's company when David had returned to the battalion from Special Forces just before the battalion had sailed from the Clyde. But he had been told he was too useful with the carriers under the Carrier Platoon commander, Captain Playfair, and his transfer was refused.

Now he left Jonathan and went to the front of the truck, where the driver was lying underneath the chassis, inspecting the front axle with a torch. 'What damage have you done to her?' he said.

'She's all right, Sarge,' Jonathan heard the driver reply. 'She'll go all right, now we've got her back on the road.'

'Bloody lucky for you, my lad.'

Jonathan was looking back at the head of the column, to the sky above the mountains, which was lit every now and then by the flashes from the guns. They must get going, he thought.

'Get back into the cab and start her up,' Willis ordered. When the driver had moved the truck a few yards up the road he leaned out of the cab and shouted cheerily, 'She's fine, Sarge.'

'Then stay awake and keep your eyes open,' Sergeant Willis growled. The driver grinned.

'We've got to press on,' said Jonathan. 'See that the column closes up.'

He waved up the motorcyclist. David's luck, as always, had held. David's truck had been saved.

Jonathan, too, would have liked a transfer when he had heard that David Trelawney had replaced one of the company commanders who had been struck down with polio when the battalion was entraining for Scotland to board the troopship to take them to Africa, and to battle. But Jonathan knew that at such a time he couldn't ask for a transfer just because he didn't want to serve in the same outfit with the man who had fathered a child on the girl he loved. So he had kept silent, and out of David's way. Only Rory, second-in-command of No. 1 Company, knew what he felt.

He gave the command for the convoy to move off. There was just enough time to clear Messerschmitt Alley before daylight.

The faces, even the voices, were still so vivid. Soon many would be dead. The survivors were now as old as he. For a time after the war he used to go to the reunions, when, after the years passed, as he entered the room stout, bald-headed figures greeted him – and behind the middle-aged, soon to be old, masks he saw only the confident young faces in all the splendour of youth. Then, after some years, he had given up attending.

When he had reported, the commanding officer, Colonel Philip Hartley, was in his headquarters, a farmhouse, or what remained of it, a near-ruin, heavily scarred by shell and bullet marks, nestling against the reverse side of a low ridge of hills. During the daylight hours shells from the German guns landed with a crump on the track and fields behind. They made a regular 'strafe' at 1600 hours, the English teatime, which showed, as Colonel Hartley said, the Boche sense of humour.

He was a plump, fresh-faced man in his mid-thirties with a fair, wispy moustache, a far more formidable personality and commander than he appeared. He had seen action in France in 1940 and was the only officer with battle experience, save for one other – David Trelawney, who after France had left the battalion and gone to fight with the Commandos.

For the next two weeks they lived in the holes they had dug on the reverse slopes of the hill and amid the ruins of the one remaining barn, moving up on to the crest each dawn. At night they sent out patrols of about half a dozen men under a subaltern to probe the enemy line. Not all returned. One who didn't was Timms, the Intelligence Officer, and Colonel Philip, as he was always known in the battalion, had appointed Jonathan to replace him. A subaltern from No. 1 Company took over the carriers.

A week later had come the orders for the battle they had been expecting. It began, for them, with a night march in extended order under cover of a massive barrage. They marched across flat, untilled fields comparatively unharmed by the few enemy shells which fell spasmodically among them, until they reached another ridge of hills on the flank of those they had held before. As Jonathan marched with Battalion HQ alongside the commanding officer, he looked up at the stars and back at the flashes of their own guns which were pounding the hills ahead of them. This is what all the years of training have been about, he had thought at the time. He had often wondered if when the time came he would be frightened, but now, as enemy shells landed beyond and among them, he had felt no fear. Indeed he felt as though he were an observer, as though he were watching what was happening to someone else.

That was the last of the battle Jonathan had written up in the diary. The rest was memory. Fifty years later he remembered every sound and the scent of the Tunisian fields and hills; he could remember every word that was said. As long as he lived, he could never forget. There would be no exorcism.

Soon after dawn on the next day the main attack had begun, when the guns had begun pounding the enemy position on the ridge across the valley. Clouds of dust and rock splinters rose into the sky, followed by a rolling cloud of smoke as the battalion rose from the crest and in extended order began the descent down the rocky forward slope into the valley. By his fireside, Jonathan stirred again. The diary lay on his lap, the pages blank.

Into the valley of death they had gone, he had thought at the time. In the first rays of sunlight they could see, ahead and below, the heads of the corn in the plain swaying in the faint breeze, yellow-gold, spotted with crimson – the poppies, like those in the fields over which Beau and his friends had fought more than twenty-five years before. There could be no shelter until they reached a cluster of olive groves on the far side of the valley, from which gullies led up the steep, rocky face of the hill held by the Hermann Goering Division.

By the time they'd gone a little way the sun was up and in contrast to the cold of the night, it became warm. Jonathan marched with Colonel Philip, their orderlies and signallers around them, slightly to the rear of the leading infantry companies. Ahead, he had seen the tall figure of David Trelawney prominent with his lead platoon. They marched steadily down the forward slope—as if they had been on the Horseguards in Whitehall. But long before they had reached the cornfield men began to fall as the enemy opened up with spandaus and six-barrelled mortars. To avoid the wounded being crushed by the tanks that would follow them into the valley, Colonel Philip had ordered that when a man fell his rifle should be stuck, bayonet down, into the earth and his helmet placed on the butt. Soon the cornfield became crowded with a forest of reversed rifles.

One of the first to fall was the commanding officer's orderly. For a moment Jonathan had hesitated. Then he thrust the man's rifle into the ground. 'Come along, Jonathan,' he heard Colonel Philip say quietly. 'Keep up, but not too close. Keep going.'

Jonathan never knew how they managed to reach the cornfield, or how they crossed it; all he remembered was the noise and the cries. They paused only to leave the forlorn markers as they brushed through the waist-high corn until, at last, they reached the temporary safety of the olive grove at the base of the hill they had still to attack. The forward infantry companies had regrouped here, but by the time Battalion HQ reached the grove they were already out of sight above them, clambering up the ridge in the face of the withering fire poured from above.

In the olive grove Colonel Philip tried to contact the forward infantry company commanders on his command W/T set. After a minute he pulled off his earphones. 'Jonathan,' he had said, and Jonathan could hear his voice now although he had not heard it since they said goodbye in the Base Hospital before Jonathan had left for home and Colonel Philip for his death on the plains of Sicily. 'I can't reach any of the company commanders. Take one of the signallers and go up and find out how far they've got. They should be approaching the summit by now. Try and let me know the position before I launch the reserve company. The carriers won't be able to make it up the hill, but I'll send up the Carrier Platoon dismounted, as reinforcements. If we've got the crest, it's to be held until tomorrow. Off with you.'

Jonathan scrambled up over the rocks, the signaller with his heavy W/T set on his back beside him. Through the storm of bullets and hand grenades they clambered, stumbling over the dead and wounded. Twenty-five yards below the summit Jonathan heard a cry and, turning, saw the signaller roll over and fall down the hill, his set smashing and splintering as the body bounced from crag to crag. Jonathan climbed on. In twenty minutes he was on the summit.

'Who's in command?' he shouted.

'Keep down, you bloody fool,' a voice yelled. It was Rory Connor. 'Who is that?'

'Jonathan,' he shouted back.

'David's in command of what's left of us. He's along the crest, to your right.'

There was a lull in the fighting and Jonathan made his way along the reverse slope just below the crest until he came to a complex of trenches from which the German defenders had been driven. He walked along a trench until he came to a corporal sitting on the ground, his hand bandaged with an emergency dressing.

'Where's Major Trelawney?' he asked. The corporal pointed to a tarpaulin sheet and Jonathan pushed it aside. The cave, its earth walls lined with the wood of ration boxes and the floor with straw, was lit by a solitary oil-lamp. Squatting on the ground, filling his tommy-gun with a fresh magazine, was David.

'Reinforcements, by God,' David said. 'Welcome to the recently vacated HQ of the Hermann Goering division.' He patted the straw beside him and Jonathan sat. 'It's good to see a friendly face,' David said. He looked at Jonathan. Then he added, 'Or rather a fresh face. Why have you come?'

Jonathan gave him Colonel Philip's message and reported the loss of the signaller and the W/T set. David took his flask from his breast pocket. 'There's only one other officer left, that's Rory, and about thirty men.' He handed the flask to Jonathan. Jonathan shook his head and David shrugged his shoulders. 'Suit yourself,' he said. 'I've learned never to be without it.'

He took a pull and then added, 'I've no W/T, so I've sent a runner down, telling them where we are. God knows whether he's made it.'

Corporal Lawson pushed his head through the tarpaulin. 'Message from Captain Connor, sir. Boche patrols are working their way around us. They're now on the slope Captain Playfair just came up.'

'Thanks, Lawson. Wait in the trench for me.'

Lawson's head disappeared. 'Now you'll have to stay, Jonathan. They'll be counter-attacking soon. Go to the north and take command of what's left of Number Three Company. Lawson'll show you where.'

'Brigade wants us to hold on for twenty-four hours,' Jonathan said.

'They'll be lucky if we hold out for half a dozen.'

There were about twenty men left of No. 3 Company, mostly in pairs in the German slit-trenches. Jonathan selected a fox-hole for himself which he manned alone, retrieving a bren gun from a dead gunner. A lance-sergeant was in the slit-trench furthest from him. Then the mortaring began in earnest, and a little later the first attack. Wave after wave came struggling up the hill to retake the position while the defenders blazed away at them. By noon, Jonathan learned by calling to the men in the fox-holes around him, there were only a dozen of them left. Still the attackers came on. From time to time, to his left, he had seen David standing, careless of the danger, flinging grenades, firing a bren from his hip, then leading a few in a counter-attack to drive any surviving attackers from the rocks they had managed to reach.

By mid-afternoon they were down to eight effective and unwounded, strung out along the north edge of the summit. In the intervals between the attacks Jonathan drank from his water-bottle, crouching at the bottom of the hole, his head in his hands, only standing to get back to his bren when he heard the shouting that announced another attack was coming in.

All that long hot day they clung on, until at last the darkness came. And with it the cold. A great lassitude and exhaustion had come over him but he knew that he must get out of his slit-trench and encourage the survivors. So he summoned up the energy and crawled from fox-hole to fox-hole, doing what he could to chat up the few who survived, arranging for look-outs, doling out morphine to the wounded, telling them that soon help would be coming. Then he crawled back and lay huddled at the bottom of his fox-hole, hugging himself to get some warmth. Suddenly, silhouetted against the night sky above him, he saw a tall figure. It was David.

'Jonathan,' he whispered. 'I'm concentrating everyone in the centre, around the cave. Come along.'

Jonathan hauled himself up and, with the few who had survived, he followed David along the summit, walking upright because David was. When David had posted the men in their new positions he took Jonathan along the trench to the cave. 'Are you all right?' he asked.

Jonathan nodded. David again handed him his flask, and this time Jonathan drank.

'The Boche are all around us. When Number Two Company tried to come up they were driven back to the olive grove. So we're on our own for the rest of the night. But some of your old platoon, the carriers, got up during the day.'

'How many?'

'Sergeant Willis and eight others, and they brought ammunition. But we've no food or water. Only our iron rations and what's left in our water-bottles. Sergeant Willis gave me a message from Colonel Philip. He says we're to hold on until dawn when the rest of the brigade will attack.' He got out his map. 'The Boche are regrouping. It'll be harder for us in the dark. Rory's out now, having a scout around to see where they are concentrating. I want

236

you to go to the south end of the ridge and see him in. Take charge there and send Rory to me when he's back.'

David put his head out of the cave, pushing aside the tarpaulin. 'Lawson, take Captain Playfair along to what's left of Number One Company to the south.' He turned to Jonathan and put his hand on Jonathan's arm and smiled. 'It's been a long time, Jonathan.'

Jonathan said nothing and David dropped his hand. 'Good luck, if I don't see you again.'

Jonathan took his bren and some fresh magazines and followed Lawson out of the cave and along the crest to the most southerly group of fox-holes.

'There's your place, sir. Captain Connor should come back about here. He's been gone twenty minutes. Sergeant Willis is over there, just behind you.' Then Lawson left.

Jonathan crawled to Sergeant Willis's slit-trench. 'Where are the rest of the Carriers?'

'The major's scattered them around. I'm here on my own.'

'I'm to see Captain Connor in. I'll be in the slit-trench just ahead.'

Jonathan crawled back and dropped into his fox-hole.

He heard Rory's cry before he saw him. Then an enemy flare lit up the sky and he saw the crumpled figure twenty yards from him down the hill. He climbed out of the slit-trench and on his belly worked his way down to where Rory lay. 'It's me, Jonathan,' he said, and grabbed at Rory, trying to pull him up the hill.

'Jesus Christ,' Rory had screamed. 'My legs, my bloody legs.'

The spandaus opened up again from below and when they ceased he tried again. But Rory cursed and swore at him and again the spandaus opened up. 'Get back,' Rory had said. 'The buggers'll be coming any moment. They're forming up now, right below us. Piss off, Jonathan. Get back to the trench and your bren. They're coming again.' So he had given Rory the last of his morphine and crawled back to the fox-hole above where Rory lay. For a time quiet had fallen on the hill, and it was then that Rory's songs had begun – the songs which had ended with the prayer: 'Pater nostris, qui est in coelum . . .'

Afterwards, long afterwards, when it was all over and he dreamed about that night or when he was remembering as he was now in front of the fire, Jonathan always told himself that it was Rory's singing that had done it. The songs Rory had sung as he lay there, dying, unable to move. The songs of Ireland, about the Wild Geese, and all the heroes the English had killed. How strange the Germans would have thought it if they could have understood! But it was those songs, Jonathan believed, that had caused him to do what he did. Not the mortar bombs, not the night attacks, not his wound, not the hunger nor the thirst and exhaustion. It had been the songs. He was as certain of that now as he had always been during the past fifty years.

The silence that had followed Rory's prayer had not lasted. It was only minutes before Jonathan saw the first of the dark shapes coming up the slope. Behind him a flare soared up into the sky and his and Willis's bren opened up. He heard the screams of the enemy as their leading files fell like ninepins. More flares lit the sky, this time from further in the rear by the cave, and he saw the figures turn and hurry down into the darkness. He had laid his revolver on the parapet beside him so that he should be ready for them when they got close, and he reloaded the bren with his last magazine. Then they came again, and once again the brens stopped them. When they had disappeared down the hill into the darkness the mortars opened up, not the single mortars but the six-barrelled mortars whose bombs whined and howled through the night air before they fell and burst with an ear-splitting crash in the rocky ground. At first the bombs fell short, then long. But soon they found the range. Two, one after the other, landed almost on the parapet as he crouched at the bottom of his pit. They were followed by a third, and then another and another, crumbling the earth, flinging up slivers of metal and splinters of rock. The blast of one swept over his head, and a splinter gashed his helmet, knocking it from his head. Blood poured down his face into his eyes and involuntarily he stood up. Another splinter hit his left arm, wrecking the bren, flinging him across the rock of the fox-hole, face down. Yet another landed within feet of where he lay. Then it happened. Sitting in his chair, remembering, he did what he always did when in his memories he came to this part. He put both hands to his face and rocked slowly back and forth, back and forth.

For when that last bomb had landed on the rim of his fox-hole, with a cry he grabbed his revolver with his right hand and hoisted himself out of the slit-trench. Stumbling and running, his right hand holding the revolver, pressing it against the wound in his left arm which lay limp by his side, he began to run. Falling, rising again, stumbling on, he careered back along the crest of the hill with the bombs falling around him. On he ran, past the other fox-holes, until he reached the trenches by David's cave. By then he could hardly see from the blood running from his brow as he threw himself into the trench, and crawled the last few yards to where the tarpaulin covered the entrance to the cave. He pushed it aside. The cave was empty, lit now not by the lamp but by a single candle guttering in the neck of a bottle. He flung himself face down on the straw on the rock floor.

He heard a voice behind him, calling his name – 'Jonathan. Jonathan. What are you doing here?' – and he thought of his mother calling him when he had run from the accident after the tractor had fallen from the field. He lifted his head and looked over his shoulder. The blood was running down from his forehead but he could see that it was David kneeling beside him. David pulled at him, trying to turn him on to his back, tugging at his shattered arm. He screamed, and David let him go. He still had his revolver in his right, uninjured hand. Then Jonathan heard another voice and he rolled over on to his back so that he was staring at the entrance, wiping the blood from his eyes with the back of his uninjured arm with his pistol still in his hand. David, kneeling beside him, had also turned and shone his torch on the entrance to the cave. The tarpaulin was pulled aside and a head appeared. The tarpaulin opened further and the figure of a man was framed in the entrance. He had one hand on the tarpaulin, in the other a bren gun. It was Sergeant Willis.

'He ran,' Willis shouted. 'The buggar ran!'

Jonathan, now half-sitting, could see in the beam of David's torch Willis's mouth as he shouted the words. 'The buggar ran,' Willis shouted again. 'He ran, he ran.'

A salvo of mortar bombs landed on the trench outside the cave, but not before the cave had reverberated with the sound of a single shot from within it, and Sergeant Willis fell forward. The tarpaulin split into shreds as he fell, and then the blast from yet another salvo of bombs swept into the cave. The last thing Jonathan saw before all the light was quenched was the strip of tarpaulin clutched in the hand of the dead man who lay within a foot of Jonathan with a neat, round hole from the bullet of a revolver in the centre of his forehead.

The diary had fallen from Jonathan's lap and lay half-open on the rug at his feet. His head had sunk on his breast. Then he raised his head, bent and picked it up. For a moment he held it in his hand. Then he tossed it on to the fire.

The pages burnt quickly; the flames licked at the black imitation leather of the cover. Then that too, or most of it, had gone.

He sat watching the small, black, crinkled pile of ash on the topmost log, until it fell in a small shower on to the bright red base of the fire.

21

THE room was in almost total darkness when Mason knocked for the first time. It was only when he knocked a second time and, getting no reply, opened the door, that light from the hall flooded into the room. From where he stood he could see, above the rim of the armchair, the back of Jonathan's head, resting on his right hand.

'Mr Benson is here, sir.'

Jonathan made no reply and did not stir. 'Mr Benson is here,' Mason repeated. 'He is very anxious to see you. He's in the cloakroom at the moment.'

Still there was no reply, and Mason crossed the room. 'Are you all right, sir?,' he asked, bending over the chair. Jonathan lowered his hand from his head. 'Yes,' he said. 'I was dozing.'

'The fire's got very low, sir. Shall I make it up?'

'Please do.'

Mason knelt. He could see from the mound of ash that Sir Jonathan had been burning paper. Taking the poker he stirred the ash from the embers and threw on some kindling twigs, which caught and burnt brightly; then he added fresh logs.

'I must have been dozing for quite a time,' Jonathan said.

'You've every right to be worn out,' Mason said, still on his knees, the poker in his hand. 'You must be glad it's over.'

'I am.'

'If I may say so, all of us in the house are very happy for you.'

'Thank you, Mason. You've all been very kind.'

Mason poked vigorously, shifting as he did so some small squares of the leather of the diary cover which had failed to burn.

'You should never have had to undergo it, sir. That's what we all think.'

Shouldn't I? Jonathan thought. Shouldn't I?

'Show Mr Benson in when he's ready,' he said, 'and switch on the light over the chair opposite.'

When Mason had done what he had asked, Jonathan turned off the light beside him. The large room was now lit by the light coming from the hall, the pool of light from the lamp on the table opposite Jonathan and the fire, once again burning brightly.

'It'll be quite dark when the door to the hall is closed. Will there be enough light for you and Mr Benson?' Mason enquired.

'Yes. It will do. Show him in, please.'

When he heard Harold enter Jonathan called over the back of his chair, 'Come in, Mr Benson. I wasn't expecting you tonight, but I'm always glad to see you. Come and sit opposite me.'

Harold, his grey hair wilder and more tousled that ever, put his briefcase beside him on the floor and sat. The firelight flickered, lighting Jonathan's feet and legs; the rest of him was in shadow. All Harold could see was the shape of the head with one hand resting against it.

'Your coming gives me a chance to thank you, Mr Benson. You have been a tower of strength.'

Harold made no reply.

'Would you like some whisky? I'm sure you need it and I know you deserve it.'

Harold was sitting very still and upright, both hands on his knees, his face set, his glasses glinting in the light of the lamp beside him. 'I have just come from talking to Mrs Peachey,' he began abruptly.

'Mrs Peachey?'

'Yes.'

'Do I know Mrs Peachey?' Jonathan asked.

'You may not even know of her.'

'Should I know of her?'

Harold had clenched his hands. Now two fists were resting on his knees. 'Mrs Peachey's mother,' he said, 'died last year.' He paused. 'She was called Willis, Mrs Willis.'

The silence that followed was broken only by the sound of logs crackling in the fire. Harold said at last, 'She was a widow. Her husband, Mrs Peachey's father, was killed in the war.' He paused. 'He was a sergeant, one of David Trelawney's men. He was killed in North Africa.'

Harold saw the hand on which the head had been resting fall so that it lay along the arm of the chair. He still could make out only the shape of the other's head, a white blur beneath white hair. 'You were in North Africa with David Trelawney when he saved your life. Did you know Sergeant Willis?'

Again nothing was said for what seemed to Harold a long time. Then Jonathan broke the silence. 'It is strange you should ask me about Sergeant Willis. Before you came I had been thinking of him. Now you are asking about him.' He paused. 'Yes, I knew Sergeant Willis.'

'Mrs Peachey, his daughter, came up to me outside the court, just after you had been driven away. She told me that ever since her father's death her mother had been receiving money from David Trelawney. Five hundred pounds, every month.'

Harold paused again, waiting. Then he went on. 'It was paid each month for over forty years. That is a great deal of money. You told the court that Trelawney had no money. You told the court that you paid five hundred pounds in cash each month to Trelawney, and you produced your statements from the bank in Jersey to prove it. I now believe that that money was being paid to Mrs Willis and that you knew the money was going to her and not to Trelawney.'

Again there was a long silence. 'Yes,' Jonathan said. 'I knew.'

'Then you deceived the court by pretending this money was for Trelawney. That was a lie.'

'It was, but it had nothing to do with what the court had to decide, which was whether or not I had killed David Trelawney.'

'But you made the court believe those payments were paid to Trelawney because he'd been demanding money from you. In fact it was going to Mrs Willis.'

'I told the court, Mr Benson, that over the years Trelawney had

243

been demanding money from me, a great deal of money and that, year after year, I had paid him. That was true, and that was relevant to the issue the court had to try. The money for Mrs Willis was not.'

'Then why did you pretend that money was going to Trelawney for himself? And why was the money going to Mrs Willis?'

Again Jonathan did not immediately reply. Then he said quietly, 'Do you have to know, Mr Benson? You have said that Mrs Peachey's mother, Mrs Willis, is dead. It is now all over. Is there any point in raking over the past? Why do you have to know?'

'I believed in you, Sir Jonathan. I thought you had been falsely accused by very wicked enemies. Now I learn that you did not tell the court the truth. That you lied. I want to know the truth. I deserve to be told the truth.'

Jonathan raised his hand to his brow. 'If anyone deserves the truth it must be you, Mr Benson. I owe you much for your loyalty and support. But are you so certain you need to be told?'

'Yes. I believed in you, Sir Jonathan. I want to go on believing in you. You must tell me.'

There was another long silence before Jonathan spoke. 'Very well. I shall tell you. But I shall not enjoy telling you the story, nor will you enjoy hearing it.' He paused. 'I did not pay all that money to David Trelawney because he saved my life, and that young judge, that clever but inexperienced young judge, suspected that there was more to it than that. No, I paid that money time and time again, because Trelawney threatened to expose me if I did not.'

Harold leaned forward in his chair, trying to make out the face in the shadows. 'Expose you? For what? What had you done?'

'The money paid to Mrs Willis, which I paid first through Trelawney and then, when he had his bank account removed, directly but anonymously in cash, was what in the past they called blood money.'

'What do you mean?'

'Can't you guess, Mr Benson?'

'No. What do you mean by blood money?' He saw Jonathan stir in his chair. 'I can't see you properly in this light,' he added. 'Will you not turn on the lamp beside you?'

'I'd rather not, Mr Benson. My eyes are very tired and this light soothes them. We can talk just as well as we are.'

Harold now had his elbows on his knees, peering at the figure in the chair. 'Blood money? Whose blood?'

'Don't you understand? I was responsible for Sergeant Willis's death, so David Trelawney and I arranged that money should be paid to his widow. That is why I called it blood money, money paid for the price of blood.'

Harold half-rose to his feet. 'You killed Sergeant Willis and Trelawney was blackmailing you?'

'Sit down, Mr Benson,' Jonathan said wearily. 'Sit down, and listen. You have started this and you must wait until it is finished. You came here for an explanation. You said you wanted the truth. Now you must listen.'

Harold sank back into his chair.

'Trelawney never saved my life in battle.'

'That was not true?'

'No, it was not true, although by keeping silent David Trelawney may have saved me from being shot, or hanged. In that sense, he saved my life.'

'Hanged? I don't understand. You said David Trelawney stood over you when you were wounded and saved you. Was that all lies?'

'Yes, all lies. As I lied about much else. I'm telling you everything now, Mr Benson, because you have insisted that I should. I did not tell the truth to the court about what happened on the afternoon David Trelawney died.'

Harold put both his hands to his head. 'Are you going to tell me that you did kill David Trelawney? That you murdered him?'

'I am going to tell you what happened, Mr Benson, as you have insisted I should. Then you can decide yourself whether I murdered David Trelawney. You can act, if you wish, as both judge and jury.'

'This is too serious to joke.'

'I am not joking.' Jonathan paused. 'I could never be tried now for the murder of Sergeant Willis. That is all buried in the mists of the past. But I could not have borne what Trelawney might have told about what I did in that battle. And I cannot be tried again for the murder of David Trelawney. But when you have heard me out then you can tell me whether you think I am guilty of the murder of David Trelawney.' Then he said more loudly, 'I lied to the court because I was not content to be convicted of the murder of David Trelawney.' He paused and again spoke softly. 'Are you still certain you want to hear?'

'Yes,' Harold said. 'Now I must know everything.'

'Very well, you shall hear everything. As you will remember, Trelawney urged me to come to him because he said he was very ill and wanted to give me some letters from the woman he knew I had loved all my life and who, during the war when the bombs were falling on London and life was so precarious, had borne his child, which later died. After the war she went back to America and married and once, years later, I met her again with her husband, an older man – a surprising man, I thought, for someone as beautiful as she. But I supposed he'd been kind to her. So when Trelawney said he had letters from her and they were about me, I thought they would be letters written when we were young and I wanted very much to see them. This was the inducement which led me to go and see the man who for so mány years had been taking money from me in exchange for his silence, silence about what he called my cowardice, silence about what I had done to Willis. My pride, Mr Benson, would not permit me to allow the world to know what I had done, even though it was so long ago and little could have been done had Trelawney published what he alleged. When I heard about his illness I was glad, glad that, instead of me, the trust would now be paying him. But I was not distressed for money, although I pretended I was. So another reason for going to see him was that I hoped I would find that he was dying. All that I told the court, and that was the truth. And he did explain the pain-relieving apparatus which was attached to him, and he did say that the doctor had told him that if all the contents were pumped into him in one dose it would kill him. And he did say that was what he had decided he would do, that he'd had enough, that he wanted to go. And he did speak about the past and told me he was sorry. All that was true. It was when we spoke about the letters that I did not tell the court the truth. For he did not tell me to keep the envelope and only open it when I got home, as I told the court he had. On the contrary, he told me to open the envelope there and then, and to read the letters which he so much wanted me to have. "They are about you," he said. "About what she felt about you, and you will be interested by what you will read."

'I took the envelope from the box to the chair and opened it. Inside were not blank sheets of paper, as I told the court, but a number of letters, all in her handwriting. "The letters," Trelawney said, "will show you whom she really loved." And when he said that I, in my foolishness, thought that what he meant was that the letters would show that she had always loved me. Then I began to read.'

Jonathan turned and took the letter from the top of the small bundle on the table beside him. 'They were love letters, from her to him, written over almost forty years. They showed that it was him that she loved, had always loved. Some parts of some of the letters were about me, laughing, derisive. About me. And he had tricked me into coming and reading them, while he watched.'

He stretched and turned on the lamp on the table beside him, and now Harold could see his face.

'I shall read you one. It is the last she wrote to him, for she is dead now. It was written in 1973 from her home in California, and it was addressed, as all the letters were, to him.'

He began to read:

Darling, I'll be in Paris in October, arriving on the 8th. Ted has his usual business in Lyons and Marseilles, and this year he has also to go to Zurich and Geneva. So we'll have longer together. I'm counting the days, which is pretty silly after all these years and me with my grey hairs!

Jonathan looked up and Harold could see plainly the pain on his face. Then Jonathan went on reading:

Speaking of years, you'll not believe who I ran into a few weeks ago. That dreary old Jonathan Playfair! I hadn't seen him since London in the war. He looked every inch the judge he now is – silver hair, very grand, still as pompous as ever. Looking at him, I could not believe this was the man who you told me had run away in the battle and shot his own sergeant before your eyes! But there he was, so dignified and respectable. In the old days he was in love with me. Grandma doted on him. She would! I think she wanted me to marry him. She made me go to Cambridge just before the war, and I only went because I hoped I'd see you. It was the weekend before you took me to Bray. Our first time together. Remember? Anyway, he still has no idea about you and me because he flinched when he said something about your mother, as tho' the name Trelawney must be painful to me! I had to turn away to stop myself from smiling. When I had last seen him during the blitz in London and I was pregnant, and very blue, I remember he asked me why you didn't marry me. I think I said you hadn't asked me! I didn't say you always said you couldn't afford me!!! You'd have been impossible as a husband. You've been far better as my constant and, I hope, faithful? lover. He'd be terribly shocked if he knew that Ted knew all about us, and always had. But talking to him took me back to my childhood in Sussex when I first saw you.

Darling David, we have lasted a long time, haven't we? Middle-aged and grey as I am, I can't wait to see you soon – in Paris.

All my love, darling,

Nicola

Jonathan lowered the letter to his lap. For a full minute he remained silent. Then he said, his face turned to the fire, 'That was the last of the letters he tricked me into reading. The earlier ones were written before the war, in the war and after the war. In some of those she sometimes referred to me. In the same way, making clear what she thought of me. And I sat there in his room while he watched me read them. That's what Trelawney wanted me to do. He wanted me to know. He had got me there to learn what she thought of me.'

'It was abominable,' Harold whispered.

Jonathan turned his head and looked at him. 'Their love affair had lasted all her life, up to and throughout her marriage to her American.' Again he was silent. Then he went on, 'With the letters was a typewritten statement, headed "An Eye-witness Account of the Shooting of Sergeant Willis." It was the story he had told her, of how I had broken during the battle, of what he called my cowardice, of what I did to Willis.'

He put the letter back on the table. 'The letters,' he said, 'were to taunt, to provoke; the statement to threaten. And they did. It was what he wanted, what he had planned. He was going to die, to kill himself, and he would implicate me. He hated me so much, for what I was and what he had become.'

He bent forward in his chair. 'Do you understand, Mr Benson? Do you understand?'

'Yes,' said Harold quietly. 'I understand.'

'When I had read the last of the letters, the one I have just read to you, I looked up and saw he was smiling, grinning. "I wanted you to know what she thought about you," he said. "I wanted to prove it to you. You believed, didn't you," he said, "that she loved you, that secretly she was sorry she hadn't married you? That's what you wanted to hear, didn't you? Well, now you know. You! You, at whom we used to laugh. You, whom she despised."'

Jonathan was not looking now at Harold. He had turned his head and was again staring into the fire. 'I got to my feet, the letters in my hand and I went across to his bed. I wanted to hurt him as he had hurt me. I wanted to strike that grinning face, to beat it to pulp. I wanted to kill him. And that was what he wanted. He looked up at me, his eyes full of derision. "You wouldn't dare," he said. "You haven't the guts. You'll run away, as you always have." Then he opened his pyjama jacket so that I could see the tube taped to his chest, he pointed to the syringe lying along the top of its case on the table beside him. "Go on," he said. "Press the syringe." He was grinning up at me. "Press it," he repeated. "You wouldn't dare, would you? Press it." And I did.'

Jonathan stopped. He was looking down now at his hands as he had done so often during the trial. In his chair Harold sat very still.

'My hand was shaking as I started to press the head of the syringe. He said, "You haven't emptied it. Press it further." When I made no move, he himself with his right hand stretched over and pressed the head of the syringe and held it down for several seconds. "There," he said, "now you can watch how a brave man dies. You, who were always so frightened of death. I knew I could make you, once you'd read the letters. You've done what I intended you should." He pulled his pyjama jacket across his chest and turned on his side. "For killing Willis," he said, his face on the pillow turned from me, "you had to pay in money. For this, you'll have to pay with more than money." And he did not speak again.'

Jonathan stopped and sat very still. Then he picked up the letters from the table beside him. 'I did not then understand how much he had already prepared in his plan to implicate me, to have me suspected of killing him. And by leaving that house as I did, I helped his plan succeed. That, and Trelawney's statement about the death of Willis. I kept the letters because they were from her, even though they were addressed to him and showed what she really thought of me. Even though every time I read them they pained me more, I read and re-read them. I couldn't bring myself to destroy them. You see, Mr Benson, I had loved her all my life.'

Again he paused, looking at Harold. 'An hour or so ago I started to burn my past. Now that I have told you everything these too can go.'

He leaned forward. Slowly, one by one, sheet by sheet, he fed the letters into the flames. When the last had flared and lay in ashes on the topmost log, Jonathan leaned back in his chair. '*Consumatum est*,' he said. 'It is all over.' He shut his eyes, and when he spoke again they remained closed. 'I have lived with the shooting of Willis all my life. I know I deserved to stand trial for murder. When I did, I never felt that it was wholly unjust.' He opened his eyes. 'I lied to the court at my trial, Mr Benson, but, as I said, I was not content to be convicted of the murder of David Trelawney.'

The last of the ash of the last letter fell into the embers and he said, almost in a whisper, 'Well, was what I did murder? I intended to kill him. But it was Trelawney himself who completed what I had started. So was it murder?'

He had his head lowered as he said this. Now he raised it and looked directly at Harold. 'Am I guilty, Mr Benson, of the murder of David Trelawney?'

For a long time neither spoke nor moved. Then Harold said, almost in a whisper, 'No, Sir Jonathan. No.' He rose from his chair and stood looking down at the white head of the old man staring into the fire. He bent to pick up his briefcase, and as he did so he heard Jonathan say, 'Don't abandon me, Mr Benson.'

'I won't,' Harold said. He walked across the room to the door, opened it and stood for a second in the light that poured in from the hall, looking back. He could see Jonathan's head, turned towards the fire. Then he went out into the empty hall, and out of the house.

For a while he sat in the car. How lonely we both are, he thought. But it cannot be long for him. For me, it will be longer. Then he drove home. No, he would never abandon Sir Jonathan Playfair.

In his chair, Jonathan heard again Beau's voice. They were standing under the cedar tree which David and he had been climbing after the accident with the tractor seventy years ago. His father was holding his hand.

'It doesn't do to run away,' Beau said, as they walked back to the house. 'It never does.'

And David had come running towards them.

All Orion/Phoenix titles are available at your local bookshop or from the following address:

> Littlehampton Book Services
> Cash Sales Department L
> 14 Eldon Way, Lineside Industrial Estate
> Littlehampton
> West Sussex BN17 7HE
> *telephone* 01903 721596, *facsimile* 01903 730914

Payment can either be made by credit card (Visa and Mastercard accepted) or by sending a cheque or postal order made payable to *Littlehampton Book Services.*
  DO NOT SEND CASH OR CURRENCY.

Please add the following to cover postage and packing

UK and BFPO:
£1.50 for the first book, and 50P for each additional book to a maximum of £3.50

Overseas and Eire:
£2.50 for the first book plus £1.00 for the second book and 50p for each additional book ordered

---

BLOCK CAPITALS PLEASE

name of cardholder ....

....

address of cardholder ....

....

....

....

postcode ....

delivery address
(if different from cardholder)

....

....

....

postcode ....

☐ I enclose my remittance for £...............................

☐ please debit my Mastercard/Visa (delete as appropriate)

card number ⬜⬜⬜⬜⬜⬜⬜⬜⬜⬜⬜⬜⬜⬜⬜⬜

expiry date ⬜⬜⬜⬜

signature ....

prices and availability are subject to change without notice